Praise for Sandy Blair's
The King's Mistress

"*The King's Mistress* is a wonderful story of mistaken identity, chivalry, and the power of attraction. Blair uses a classic history plot and throws in twists and turns that are unexpected. The power of the leading man takes your breath away and leaves you craving another scene. I would suggest this story to any historical fiction lover."

~ *Fresh Fiction*

"Sandy Blair shows once again that she is the queen of Scottish romance. *The King's Mistress* is an entertaining tapestry of intrigue, humor, and heart-rending emotion that will stay with the reader long after she turns the final page. Unforgettable!"

~ *Lorraine Heath, New York Times bestselling author of* Waking Up With the Duke.

"Heartwarming historical romance at its best. Blair captures you on page one and doesn't let go until happily-ever-after!"

~ *Janet Chapman, New York Times bestselling author*

"In her first effort for Samhain, Blair uses historical events from 13th century Scotland as the backdrop for a solid, if not stellar, effort."

~ *Library Journal*

"This is a wonderfully written
~ *The Good, Bad, and Unread*

Look for these titles by
Sandy Blair

Now Available:

The King's Mistress

The King's Mistress

Sandy Blair

Samhain Publishing, Ltd.
11821 Mason Montgomery Road, 4B
Cincinnati, OH 45249
www.samhainpublishing.com

The King's Mistress
Copyright © 2011 by Sandy Blair
Print ISBN: 978-1-60928-609-5
Digital ISBN: 978-1-60928-583-8

Editing by Linda Ingmanson
Cover by Kim Killion

First Samhain Publishing, Ltd. electronic publication: July 2011
First Samhain Publishing, Ltd. print publication: June 2012

Dedication

In memory of John Alkire, a hero to his beautiful wife, his charming children and to the community of Hampton Falls.

Acknowledgements

I would like to thank:

Editor Linda Ingmanson and the staff at Samhain for turning this manuscript into a reality bound between two beautiful covers;

Paige Wheeler, Agent extraordinaire, for her invaluable advice and enthusiasm for this work;

Scott Blair, Husband and lover, who encouraged me to take the premier office space in our new home so I might write faster;

Alex Blair, Son and computer wizard, for keeping a straight face every time I misplace a manuscript in my computer;

dearest friends and critique partners Suzanne Welsh and Julie Benson (again, I couldn't do this without you),

my fabulous Foxes, whose enthusiastic support and goading even at a distance keeps me going;

DARA for teaching me how to write,

The Wet Noodle Posse, aka Golden Heart Class of 2004, and the terrific authors of Romance Unleashed for providing insight and humor whenever it's most needed;

Billie Jo Case, the brilliant mind behind the Fan Club, and to all the wonderful members who go there each morning to visit with me, in particular avid romance readers Joy Brown, Danny Bruggeman, Sandy Marlow (my fabulous video trailer artist), Pam Pellini, Julia Pham, Dawna Richard, Michelle Siudut, Lynn Rettig, Marie Sherman, Jennifer Yates, and Ivka Vuletic;

and lastly my heartfelt thanks to all of you who took the time to once again suspend your disbelief and travel back with me into the past.

Most sincerely,

Sandy

"Where there is a cow, there will be a woman and where there is a woman will be temptation."
~ Old Scottish proverb

Chapter One

"Counsel can be given but not conduct." ~ Old Scottish Proverb

Edinburgh Castle, Scotland
March, 1285

"His Majesty requests the pleasure of your company in the solar, my friend."

Britt MacKinnon looked up from his breakfast of cold venison and porridge to find the king's chief advisor, Lyle Ross, standing at his elbow. More likely their liege had said something to the effect of *"get that bastard's sorry arse in here"*, but then Lyle was naught if not tactful.

Britt grunted and went back to eating his meal. Around a mouthful of oats, he asked, "Pray tell, what does Randy Sandy want now?"

Lyle, his tall, thin frame wrapped in fox fur and plaid from chin to shins, settled on the empty bench across from Britt, drew his *sgian duhb* from his sleeve and stabbed a piece of prime venison on Britt's trencher. "Now what would be the fun in my telling you that?"

"Ross, I'm not in the mood." Not after spending the night sitting outside the royal solar keeping the likes of Widow MacMichael at bay. Thankfully, just her catching sight of him on the landing had been enough to send the silly cow, her cheeks flushed with embarrassment, scurrying in the opposite direction.

Lyle hailed a passing serving lass for a tankard of ale, then turned his attention back to Britt's trencher. "He didn't say, but be warned. He's in a foul mood. Apparently he spent a cold and lonely night."

"Damn right he did." And Alexander would continue to do so until such time as His Majesty got Her Highness Yolande de Dreux, formerly of France and now Queen of Scotland, with child, if Britt had any say in the matter.

Lyle grinned, and Britt's spoon stopped halfway to his mouth. "Please tell me you've received word from one of your lovely spies that our queen consort is with child."

The pair had been married almost five months now. Certainly long enough for a man of only two score and four who'd fathered three bairns on his first wife—all of whom had sadly passed—to produce at least one with his skinny twenty-year-old bride.

His friend shook his head. "If only I could. Lady Campbell suspects—but cannot confirm—that the queen's courses started before she left for Kinghorn. Her Highness is apparently keeping such information along with her French ladies-in-waiting close to that sparrow's breast of hers, while doing her utmost to keep *our* ladies at arm's length."

"Damn." His appetite ruined, Britt pushed his trencher toward Lyle. "I'm coming to loathe this place, my friend, and my role in it."

Lyle's ice blue gaze raked Edinburgh's crowded hall. "Aren't we all."

"Unfortunately, nay." If those lounging about felt as Britt did, then they'd be home tending to their own affairs instead of depleting the castle larder and gossiping about whether or not their king was man enough to beget an heir on his new queen. And then speculating on who among them would rise like cream should he fail.

As things stood now, should something happen to Alexander, his infant granddaughter, Princess Margaret of Norway, would inherit the throne, a child betrothed to young

Prince Edward of England, son of that bastard Longshanks, Edward I.

Most about Scotland had approved the peacekeeping measure at the time. After all, they had young Alexander IV and David, should anything happen to their father. But now their princes were gone, which meant Longshanks could become regent until his son came of age and could assume the thrones of both England *and* Scotland.

A monumental disaster in the making, if ever there was one.

Lyle slapped his shoulder, pulling Britt out of his depressing reverie. "You need a rest, my friend. Have you thought to go home? Just for short while?"

"Does the bitch still breathe?"

"Aye."

"Then you know better than to even suggest it."

He and Lyle, hailing from differing Highland Isle clans, had been seven and spoke only Gael and a smattering of French when they found themselves fostered to the same liege lord, the powerful Earl of Blair Atholl in the Scot-speaking Lowlands. Frightened out of their minds, they'd bonded quickly and had remained friends since. So Lyle knew Britt couldn't trust himself *not* to kill Cassandra on sight.

Lyle heaved what sounded like an exasperated sigh. "You're doubtless the most stubborn bastard alive, but that's why I've faith you can keep our king on the straight and narrow 'til we've a pudding in the oven."

Britt snorted, not the least sure he could. Alexander, married for the first time at age ten and faithful, was now a widower in his prime. He was not only obsessed with the fair administration of the law, but a man obsessed with beautiful women. He had several lovers and was now prone to slipping past his guards and sneaking out of the castle at night to meet with one or another whenever an opportunity to tup presented itself. Which was why Britt, Captain of the King's Guard, had assumed the night watch.

But more damning of their king, in Britt's opinion, was Alexander's squandering of royal juices. Even a dolt knew that if you wanted a grain harvest, you did not cast seed upon salted ground.

Britt came to his feet. "I suppose I've delayed the inevitable long enough. I'd best get up there."

"Chin up, friend. It cannot be much longer."

Feeling as if he carried the weight of the country's future on his back, Britt mounted the winding wooden staircase leading to the third floor royal apartments.

Too soon for Britt's comfort, he stood in his king's solar, where a roaring fire was losing its battle against the frigid winds seeping in around the heavy tapestries that hung over the chamber's shuttered apertures. He bowed. "Good morn', sire."

Alexander, dressed for hunting in a rich sable cloak, quilted jerkin and braies, looked up from the papers he was studying at his desk. As his gaze raked Britt, his hooked nose wrinkled in oblivious displeasure above thin lips and a trim red beard. "You look like shit, MacKinnon. Where have you been? Out whoring?"

Humph! Coal had bollocks calling the skillet black. Britt hadn't had time to bed a woman in... Hell, he couldn't remember when, thanks to his liege lord's antics. "Nay, sire. Something I ate had me up all night."

"Ah. 'Twas likely the oysters. Stay away from them. I need you healthy."

"Aye, sire." An easy pledge, since Britt never touched them.

"I need you to go to the border."

Britt scowled. "The border, sire?"

Last he'd heard, the border lords were enjoying a truce of sorts. And had there been another English incursion into Scotch territory, surely he'd have learned of it before now.

His king flopped onto the tall, heavily draped canopied bed dominating the left hand corner of the room and stretched out, crossing his arms behind his head. Grinning at the red-and-green-decorated ceiling, he said, "Aye, I want you to go to

Buddle and fetch Lady Armstrong back to court. Whatever family crisis took her away must surely be resolved by now."

Christ's blood on the cross.

Having thought himself well rid of Alexander's favorite paramour a month past, Britt struggled to mask his anger. They'd never get their heir with that woman about.

Worse, the queen had thought herself well rid of her lady-in-waiting, as well. Yolande finding the vivacious Greer Armstrong back under foot would be tantamount to setting fire bombs off beneath Her Highness's skirts.

"Sire, I really don't think it wise—"

"MacKinnon, after ten years of service you should know by now that when I desire council, I ask for it."

"Aye, sire, but—"

"If you value your head, MacKinnon..."

Britt did indeed value his head, was in fact quite fond of it. Teeth clenched, he bowed. "As you lust, Your Majesty."

"I knew you'd see it my way. See that you take a gentle mount for her. I don't want Lady Greer exhausted upon arrival."

Heaven forbid.

An hour later, having put the fear of death into the men who would guard Alexander in his absence, Britt stood in the shadow of Edinburgh's curtain wall with his arms crossed as grooms raced about trying to ready his black, eighteen-hand destrier and the gray, doe-eyed palfrey he'd selected for Lady Greer. In no hurry to be off, he merely watched as two fair-headed grooms—brothers, by the look of them—struggled to secure his stallion's massive saddle while his horse did his utmost to sniff the heart-shaped haunches of the pretty palfrey tied next to him. After the lads' fifth failed attempt, Britt pushed off the wall to assist. Before he could take a step, his mount shook like a wet dog, and Britt's prized saddle fell to the ground with a mighty thump, raising a cloud of choking dust.

Both lads gasped, their gazes shooting from the mound of expensive leather and silver lying facedown in the dirt, to Britt, then back to the saddle as if not believing their eyes. The elder lad stuttered, "I...I'm so sorry, my lord. I...I..."

Britt sighed. He had no one to blame but himself. "No need to worry, lads."

He eased them aside, scooped up the heavy saddle, gave it a good shake, then tossed it onto his destrier's broad back.

"I'll fetch a cloth," the youngest murmured as he swept tears off his dirty cheeks. "Won't be but a wink, I promise."

As the lads dashed toward the storeroom, Britt shouted, "Take your time." They could take all day for all he cared.

He had no choice but to fetch Lady Greer Armstrong, but he did have a choice in how they'd return, and he'd decided on taking a very long road, traveling northwest toward Glasgow, then north over the Western Grampians. With any luck at all, it would rain like hell, and they'd have to slog through knee-deep mud, which could add another week, mayhap even two, to their travel. Surely by then Randy Sandy would have grown weary of waiting and, anxious to sink his cock into something warm and wet, would have visited his wife. And gotten her with child.

Please, God.

Britt glanced around and, not seeing either of the grooms, plucked his stallion's bridle from a nearby hook.

Mayhap the king's pretty paramour would enjoy a visit to the Isle of Mull. He hadn't been there in ages. 'Twas a lovely place dotted with isolated fishing villages, a deserted abbey, windswept murrains and lovely stone hieroglyphs. And cliffs.

Chapter Two

"He will make of you a tool, and of me a liar."
~ Old Scottish Proverb

Buddle, Scotland

Genny Armstrong wanted to throttle her twin as she held a bucket beneath Greer's chin. While Greer retched and struggled to keep her waist-length hair out of the way, Genny wondered, not for the first time, how her beautiful and talented sister could have allowed herself to be bedded by a married man— much less the king.

That Greer was now obviously with child only made matters all the worse.

Greer finally stopped retching and reached for the cloth Genny held out to her. "'Tis over."

"No more eggs for you. Leastwise not until after the babe comes."

Greer looked up with huge blue eyes so like Genny's own. "How long can I expect this hellish sickness to last, Gen? I cannot take much more."

Genny wrapped an arm about her sister's thickening waist and helped her to her feet. "Since you've not had your courses since Hogmanay, it should pass soon. If you're one of the less fortunate, the illness will last until the babe comes."

The king's babe. God help them.

Her sister placed a protective hand over her belly as Genny guided her into their cottage. "I shan't let them take him from me. I won't."

"No one knows about the bairn save you and me, not even the king." And thank God not the queen, for if she did, Greer's life wouldn't be worth a farthing.

And to ensure Her Highness did not learn of the impending birth, Genny had dismissed their few servants with a pence and a bag of flour—all she could spare—saying she regretted their having to leave. And she had. Her workload had trebled without her shepherd, gillie and maid.

In the kitchen, she settled Greer on a stool before the hearth, then washed her hands and resumed kneading the dough she'd left resting on the table when her sister had bolted out the back door.

From behind her, Greer said, "We're in love, you know."

Genny's hands stilled. Love?

Their handsome, impoverished knight of a father had pledged his undying *love* to their mother prior to them marrying. Too late, her mother realized he was naught but a charming sot intent on his own destruction. 'Twas only their mother's blood relationship to the Earl of Kerr that made their father trackman of this wee village, that they even had a roof over their heads. Worse, their father's penchant for drink had left their mother with the task of collecting the taxes and tithes—which did naught to endear any of them to their neighbors.

And *love* was to blame for Greer going to court in the first place. Had their mother not *loved* them so much, wanted brilliant matches for them, she never would have written to her childhood friend, Queen Margaret, God rest her soul, asking that they be considered for ladies-in-waiting. A year later, she received a missive from the queen congratulating their mother on having a daughter and requesting her presence at court, although her court was at capacity. Their mother had been crushed. She'd written that she had two daughters, but since there was barely room for one, she decided Greer, being the eldest and most accomplished, should go. Genny, for her part, hadn't been the least disappointed. Having no patience for pomp or frippery and no talent for song or dance, she was actually most grateful the queen had misunderstood her mother's missive. Grateful, that was, until Greer came home in her current state.

Had she also gone to court, she might have prevented this nightmare.

Genny slammed a fist into the dough. "Were I king, *love* would be outlawed. People would only be allowed to breed by strict husbandry. Good solid stock"—she thumped the dough—"would only be bred"—she thumped it again—"to good solid stock. The rest would be gelded or left barren."

Greer made a derisive sound at the back of her throat, then muttered, "You only say that because you've never been in love."

"True, and I diligently pray that I may return to my Maker many years hence still ignorant of it."

Love. What a sorry excuse for Greer spreading her legs for a man she knew could not commit to her, much less for her stealing the affections rightly belonging to another woman.

Which of the two was the greater sin, Genny dared not ponder.

But she was certain of one thing—she, Mary Geneen Elliot Armstrong, would never lie with a man who was not free to marry her, to proudly call her wife before one and all. To protect her and any bairns they might have together.

Her sister huffed. "You truly are most cynical."

"Nay, not cynical, but sensible."

"Are you still collecting the taxes and tithes?"

Genny nodded as she flipped the dough into a greased bowl to let it rise. "And will until such time as our new earl discovers Father died, which, pray God, will not be for a very long time."

By all rights and heaven, she should have written to the earl last spring informing him of their parents passing, but having no place to go, Genny had quietly slipped into her mother's shoes assuming the role of trackman. The new Earl of

Kerr—now unfortunately only a very distant blood relation—apparently cared little about what happened on his estates so long as his tenants kept the peace and sent in their rent tithes in timely fashion. Which she took great pains to do, lest they be left homeless and impoverished.

Her sister pulled the steaming kettle from the hook above the fire and poured hot water into the bowl of dried sliced apples at Genny's side. "I've had my fill of bannocks and dried fruit. I can barely wait for fall, for fresh apples and pears."

"And the babe."

Greer set the kettle on the hearth. "And the babe." After a moment, she murmured, "Should I decide to remain here, are you absolutely certain you can handle the birthing?"

Genny dusted flour from her hands. "I've assisted the birthing of all manner of beasts, from cattle to kittens. They're all much alike."

"But a howdie—"

"We've already discussed this, Greer. Asking Old Maude to assist your delivery is out of the question. She's the worst of gossips. Without a husband pacing seven times sunwise around this cottage or standing before the door shooting arrows east to west 'til he empties his quiver to ease your pain..."

"Aye, aye. Everyone for a hundred miles around will be speculating on who the father is."

"Precisely. 'Tis why you need to seek shelter with Lady Macintyre. She has the room. More importantly, I've often heard Irish howdie-wives are far more skilled than ours." A lie to be sure, but she had to convince Greer that going to Ireland was her safest course. If push came to shove, Genny could act as howdie-wife—she'd been discreetly questioning mothers since learning of Greer's predicament—but she'd much prefer not to attempt it. The babe could be breech or too big. Or Greer could bleed beyond what was expected...

"But this is the king's—"

"Nay!" Genny spun and glared at her sister. "This is *your* babe, yours alone. And you'd best not forget it, or one day you'll say the wrong thing and find the bairn taken from you."

Greer blanched. "Never. This babe will never go through the hell his father went through."

Genny had no idea what hell her sister referred to and truthfully didn't care. All she cared about was her sister's safety and that of her unborn babe. Softening her tone in hopes of making her sister see reason, she said, "You ken Auntie loves you."

"Aye, but Ireland is so far away. I'd never see you."

"I'll miss you as well, dearest, but the farther away you are, the safer it is for the babe." Their great aunt, Lady Macintyre, would surely take Greer under her wing if she believed Greer to be recently widowed, heartbroken and in need of a change. "And it's not as if you'll be traveling alone. I'll be with you until you settle in."

Greer pouted in pretty fashion, something Genny had never managed, and settled on her stool. "I still don't see why I can't remain here. What difference does it make if I pretend to be a widow here or there?"

Lord have mercy, her sister could be so bullheaded at times. "What if the babe has his ginger hair and brown eyes?"

Greer, looking mutinous, crossed her arms over her swelling breasts. "He could just as easily have our blonde hair and blue eyes."

"Aye, but by all accounts, all of the king's previous bairns bore his stamp. And unless you are known to have slept with another ginger-headed, brown-eyed man at court—"

"*Oh!* How can you even think that, much less say it?"

"You've just made my point. Everyone at court can count to nine and kens that you were sleeping with *him.*"

Greer, her expression crumbling, leaned forward, cradling her head in her hands. "I hate you sometimes. I truly do."

Heaving a sigh, Genny knelt and wrapped her arms about her distraught sister. "I understand, dautie. At times I hate myself." But her sister had to face the hard cold truth: so long as their new queen remained barren, Greer and her babe were in mortal danger. No amount of wishful thinking or well-practiced wheedling or pouting on Greer's part could change that. Or the fact that her bairn could still be in danger even if the queen did give birth. Heirs to thrones—legitimate and otherwise—too often had very short lives.

She slipped a finger beneath Greer's trembling chin so she could look into her eyes. "Dearest, you showed great courage when you realized you were with bairn and came home without anyone suspecting why. I have no doubt you can be courageous again."

Salty rivers coursed over Greer's blotchy cheeks. "Oh, Gen, I'm so terribly frightened."

"I know, dautie, believe me, I know."

As her sister wept in inconsolable fashion, the cold knot of fear that had settled in Genny's middle upon learning of her sister's dilemma bloomed into pure black terror.

If Greer chose to remain here or died in childbirth...

From the moment Genny had taken her first breath, her sister had been there, waiting. Not a moment in childhood had passed that she hadn't shared it with Greer. Then Greer had left for Edinburgh, taking the laughter and music with her. Finding joy in the mundane had proved difficult enough with Greer living so far away. Life without Greer in it was beyond comprehension, would be impossible. Greer was their light, the balance to Genny's own darker, more plodding nature and practical sensibilities. She'd lose the very best half of herself if she ever lost Greer and would thus lose her mind, but there wasn't a damn thing she could do. The decisions were Greer's alone.

"Genny, someone's at the door."

Startled by the panicked note in her sister's voice, Genny dashed tears from her own cheeks and looked about. "What's wrong?"

"Listen. Someone is beating on the door."

Someone was, and with a hammer, by the sound of it. Heaving a sigh, Genny rose and pulled off her apron. "Stay here. 'Tis likely the smithy. I asked him to make a new latch for the front door months ago, and he's probably just gotten around to it."

In the parlor, Genny sniffed back the last of her tears—wouldn't do to have a tenant see she'd been crying—smoothed her bodice and opened the door, only to gasp, finding the largest man she'd ever laid eyes upon standing on her granite stoop.

"Good morn', Lady Armstrong," the armor-clad mountain barked. "His Majesty requests the pleasure of your company back in Edinburgh."

Chapter Three

"The wise man is deceived but once." ~ Old Scottish Proverb

Britt had never seen a lass turn so white in his life. Humph! Mayhap the lady wasn't as enamored with Randy Sandy as His Majesty presumed. 'Twould serve him right.

The king's paramour wavered in the doorway, and Britt grabbed her arm, fearing she might topple. "Lady Greer, are you all right?"

She swallowed in gulping fashion and jerked her arm away. "Fine. I'm quite fine, thank you."

"Excellent." She didn't look the least fine to him. In fact, she looked totally distraught, not to mention dowdy in her plain tunic of gray homespun and with her pale, waist-length tresses caught in a simple braid, but then she hadn't been expecting him. "May I come in?"

Her right hand flew to the long white column of her throat. "In?"

"Aye, *inside.*"

"Oh. Aye, please come in."

"Thank you." He stepped over the threshold as Lady Greer scurried backward, her cornflower-blue eyes growing as huge as tankard tops, her gaze raking him from boots to hair roots as if she'd never set eyes on him before. Knowing that not to be the case, he tensed and immediately scanned the whitewashed room and the open sleeping loft above for an intruder. Hand on the hilt of his sword, he murmured for her ears alone, "Is something amiss, my lady?"

"No!" She cleared her throat. "I'm sorry. I'm simply surprised to be summoned...so soon."

"Ah." He relaxed his stance. "His Majesty trusts that whatever crisis took you from his side is now resolved?" The queen had not deemed it necessary to tell anyone why Lady Greer had gone home.

"They died."

He scowled at her. "I beg your pardon? Who died?"

"Father and Mother. Both of them."

"Oh. My deepest condolences, my lady. May I be so bold as to ask how?" The last thing he wanted to do—orders or no—was to escort a contagious Lady Armstrong back to Edinburgh.

She wrung her hands. "A carriage accident."

He nodded. Good. Well, not good for her parents, of course.

He looked about the modestly furnished room, this time taking note of the basket filled with skeins of green and yellow wool, the odd chair, the bench and small bowl overflowing with dandelions sitting on the stone hearth, of the oil lamp, a handful of well-worn texts and a few candlesticks. There was little enough of a personal nature. One trunk at best, which his destrier could easily carry. "Your father was trackman in service to the earl, I believe."

"He was."

"So, with a new man coming and nothing left to hold you here, am I correct in assuming we can pack up and be on our way before gloaming?"

"Umm, umm..." Lady Greer looked about in panicked fashion. "But I've yet to say good-bye to the animals, sir!" She blushed to a pretty rose, something he couldn't recall her ever doing in the past, then waved in dismissive fashion. "I meant to the tenants, of course."

"Of course." Grief could make idiots of us all, he supposed. And likely explained why her voice sounded deeper then he recalled it being. Aye, she was likely hoarse from weeping, although weeping didn't explain why she spoke in such stilted fashion.

"Sir, I've yet given thought to what I should take or leave behind." She took a deep breath and straightened her shoulders. "I need a full day to pack and set my affairs in order."

Since he was in no hurry to return her to their king, he said, "Why not take two? You have many a woolly beast in yon pasture you doubtless wish to kiss good-bye."

Her cornflower blue eyes narrowed. "Doubtless."

"But please be mindful of my horse as you pack. He'll also be carrying me."

"Does that mean my taking the rocking chair is out of the question?"

"Absolutely!" He huffed, then realized she was only taunting him, that she was trying not to grin, then lost the battle, which brought light into the low-ceilinged room and an odd sensation to his belly. My God, he'd always found Lady Greer pretty but had never thought of her as truly beautiful... Until now. That smile. Absolutely captivating. Why hadn't he noticed it or the dimple in her right cheek before? No wonder his liege had become so enamored.

His gaze drifted down the long column of her neck to the gentle swell of her breasts. Feeling heat rise in his loins, he gave himself a hard mental shake and cleared his throat.

Christ's blood. Lusting after his king's prime flesh could prove a fast route to the gallows. He blew through his teeth.

He'd need a place to bed down for two days. Randy as he felt and without her having a chaperone, his staying here—even in the barn—was definitely out of the question. "Whilst you settle your affairs, I shall be at the small lodging I passed in the village."

Her lovely eyes went wide again. "Oh no! Not there. No, no. The place is crawling with fleas. Loads and loads of fleas. Bucketsful."

"Bucketsful?"

"Oh, aye." She made a delicate shudder, setting the golden wisps framing her face to fluttering. "You'll be far more comfortable staying at the abbey in Morehead. Simple but clean. Much nicer, truly. And you'll not be getting weevils with your porridge...as you could expect at Mr. Bailey's."

He arched an eyebrow. "Mr. Bailey has fleas *and* weevils?"

"Aye, 'tis a terrible place. Truly."

He couldn't help but grin. She looked so earnest, but he suspected her defaming poor Mr. Bailey was more likely due to a female aversion to anything crawly rather than to the actual number of crawlies Mr. Bailey might have. Britt had stopped at the establishment to quench his thirst, and the hostel hadn't appeared any worse than most. But to be assured he wouldn't be munching weevils when he broke his fast, he said, "As you lust, my lady. Please direct me to the abbey."

The moment she closed the door on their unexpected visitor, Genny collapsed against it, tears springing to her eyes.

Why on earth had she blurted that her parents were dead? Now the earl would learn the truth; she'd be evicted, and with nowhere to go...

Saint Bride and Columba preserve us.

"Oh dear God, Gen!" Her sister rushed to her side. "I thought I'd faint when I heard his voice."

"*You?* I nearly expired on the threshold. Who, pray tell, is that man?" She'd never seen anyone so tall, so broad of shoulder or so muscled of limb in all her days. And the way he studied her with those pitch-black eyes! A dozen times she'd readied to scream, certain he was about to snatch her up by the hair and declare her an imposter. Certain, that was, until he began teasing her. As if she'd kiss her sheep good-bye. Well, mayhap Ol' Duffy. She did cherish her old ram, stiff-legged and grumpy as he'd grown.

Greer wrung her hands. "'Twas Sir Britt MacKinnon, Captain of the King's Guard. I can't believe he's here. What are we going to do, Genny?"

"I've yet had time to think. Have yet to get over our good fortune that he did not think to question who I was." Or over her shock that she'd actually taunted so obviously lethal a man.

Greer cocked her head in question. "Why would he? We look alike."

"But knowing that we do, wouldn't he have asked to whom he spoke?" In response, Greer twisted the wide silver band she wore on her right index finger to cover a scar—a sure sign she'd done something wrong or was about to lie—then turned away. As she began rearranging the dandelions in the bowl, a painful realization finally dawned. "You never told them about me."

"Well..."

Her throat growing tight, Genny examined her work-worn hands. Her nails were ragged. Firm calluses crossed her palms. She looked down. Her simple tunic was stained at the knees, and her boots water-marked from her morning chores. All was as it always had been and would likely always be. "You're ashamed of me."

Her sister gasped. "Oh *no*, never think that. 'Tis just that when I arrived in Edinburgh, I was introduced simply as Greer Armstrong. For the first time in my life, I was no longer *the other* Armstrong lass, no longer one half of a matched pair. People didn't say, 'Which one are you?' as they greeted me. They simply accepted me...for me." Greer had the decency to duck her chin, then murmured, "'Tis all."

'Tis all?

Having spent the last year and a half talking of little else but Greer to anyone who would listen, Genny could only stare at her mirror image.

"Gen, I cannot go with him."

"*Hush!* I need to think." Think about MacKinnon and the fact that her sister, whom she cherished beyond all else, had kept her very existence a secret from her new and influential friends.

"I'm sorry. So sorry."

Seeing fresh tears coursing down Greer's cheeks, Genny cursed under her breath. Now was *not* the time for either of them to be wallowing in self-pity like sows in mud.

She opened her arms, and Greer, sobbing, fell into them. "Hush, now. I'm the one who should be sorry. I shouldn't have shouted at you."

At least she'd garnered them time by pleading for another day and then sending MacKinnon off to the distant abbey, in the opposite direction from which they'd be running. They could get to Annan in two days' time, but what if there wasn't an Ireland-bound ship waiting? They might have days to wait, and MacKinnon didn't strike her as a man easily thwarted. Better mounted, he could easily catch up with them, at which time all hell would rain down on their heads.

Her sister needed more time. Aye, and her admission might well have provided it.

She took her sister by the shoulders and gently pushed her toward the ladder leading to the sleeping loft. "Greer, pack as quickly as you can for both of us. I'll saddle the horses."

In the kitchen, Genny removed a loose brick above their domed ingleneuk. She slipped her hand into her secret kist and pulled out the leather pouch containing all the coins she had in the world, the majority of which were only coppers and brass.

Dear Lord, what she wouldn't give for another day so she might barter the wool and grain she'd been hoarding. She counted the coins. There was barely enough for a single passage to Ireland and mayhap a year's bed and board, should their aunt have fallen on hard times. Or be dead.

"Gen?"

She turned to find Greer standing in the doorway, two satchels at her feet. "What's wrong?"

Spinning her ring, Greer looked at the floor. "I want to go to England. We've not seen Auntie since we were bairns. She could be dead now, for all we ken."

"She's *not* dead. The family would have sent word." At least she hoped they would have.

"But what if a missive has yet to reach us? We'll be adrift in a land we know naught about."

"Greer, we know naught of England, either, and if MacKinnon is the man I suspect him to be, he'd cross the border without hesitation, then leave no stone unturned until he lays hands on what he came for. Namely, you."

Tired of the arguing, still upset that her sister obviously hadn't missed her as much as she'd missed Greer, Genny grasped her twin by the arms. "Are you certain you told no one about me?"

Shrinking back, Greer nodded like a woodpecker. "Aye, I'm certain."

"Very well, then." She released her sister and blew out a puff of air. "We can make Langford by gloaming. From there, 'tis an easy road to Annan, from which you can take a ship to Dublin."

Genny marched toward the back door. Behind her, Greer shouted, "Wait! You said you'd come with me. You promised!"

She'd always thought of Greer, who could memorize dances and mile-long ballads with ease, to be the brighter of the two of them but was now really beginning to wonder. "Aye, but that was before I learned we no longer had months to prepare but only *hours*."

"But what of you?"

"I'm taking your place, Greer. I'm going with MacKinnon to Edinburgh."

"*What?* But you can't. You know nothing of court. You sound like a crow when you sing. You can't dance." She waved a frantic hand that took in Genny from head to foot. "And just look at you, Gen. You can don one of my gowns, but you'll not be making a silk purse out of a sow's—"

"Ouch! Look here, mistress! I'm not the one who spread my legs like some common slut for a man I knew could never marry me, but I *am* the only one who can get you out of this appalling situation."

Her sister, blanching, staggered back as if slapped. "You call me a *slut* knowing we love each other?"

"You love him? Prove it! Cease fighting me at every turn, and protect his babe by teaching me on the way to Annan all that I need to know to pass for you."

So I might survive long enough to bleed my courses before queen, God and country and prove beyond any doubt that you, dear sister, are not with child before running like a terrified hare for home.

God help me.

Chapter Four

Kinghorn Castle

"Scotland has to be the most miserable place on earth."

Yolande tugged her embroidered mantle close about her shuddering shoulders. Beyond her solar windows, an ashen sea churned beneath an equally dark and brooding sky.

Why anyone fought over this godforsaken country, much less chose to live here, was beyond her understanding. Not when there were glorious, sun-drenched places like Nice and Marseille in which to live. Even Paris, with its raw, drizzling winters, was preferable to this desolate country, with no decent roadways, no palatable wine and too few glazed windows.

She sighed. At least Kinghorn, the smallest of her husband's twenty-six barbaric keeps, was easily heated, unlike drafty Edinburgh Castle in which she'd shivered continuously. Here, at least, she could cry in comfort.

Her courses had come yet again.

Alexander, who had proved himself fertile with his first wife, had done his husbandly duty by her on a weekly basis, so there could be no shifting of blame. The fault was hers and hers alone. And all would soon know it.

At her back, her ladies-in-waiting were doubtless casting worried glances in her direction as they spoke in hushed tones and continued to embroider delicate fluer-de-lis and petals on swaddling clothes for the infant that only she knew was yet to be. A child all expected to distance the Scottish throne from that of the English and permanently bind Scotland to her beloved France, a country impoverished by constant war and in sore need of allies.

"Your Highness?"

Yolande turned to find Evette Franchot, her cousin and dear friend, at her side. "*Oui?*"

As Evette leaned closer, the cauls holding her sable hair brushed Yolande's cheek, and she caught the scent of lavender. "Mademoiselle Duval begs a word with you in private. She has news regarding Lady Armstrong."

At the mention of her husband's favorite paramour, the fine hairs stood on Yolande's arms. Lord forgive her, but she'd hated that woman from first sight.

Tall, golden-headed Greer Armstrong, confident in her knowledge that she was the king's favorite, had moved—nay, *glided*—about Edinburgh Castle as if the stronghold was hers but for the asking. As if she'd been born a Saxon princess instead of being the spawn of some landless knight. Adding insult, Yolande had been forced while in Edinburgh to sit night after night in the great hall at Alexander's right hand while the whore sang one sanguine ballad after another like some gilded songbird...and her love-struck husband all but drooled in his lap.

"Please tell Mademoiselle Duval to meet me in the herb garden."

There the ladies Campbell and Fraser, the Scot ladies-in-waiting who had been thrust upon her, would be hard-pressed to overhear anything Helene had to say.

She loathed spies but acknowledged their necessity. At court, information was often more valuable than gold.

Yolande faced her ladies-in-waiting and found all ten sitting with idle hands staring at her. She forced a smile. "Ladies, I have need for a breath of fresh air." As they began to rise as one, she waved them back to their chairs. "Please stay and continue your work. I shall return in a short while."

Outside, Yolande found the youngest of her ladies-in-waiting pacing in tight circles in the pathetic patch of walled ground their Scot cook had the audacity to call a garden. "What is it, Helene?"

Helene jerked in surprise, then dropped into a deep curtsy. "Your Highness, the wash maid we left behind in Edinburgh sent word that Lady Armstrong was seen retching near the stables before she left."

"So?" The woman had imbibed too much wine. Served the whore right.

"In the morning, Your Highness, several days in a row."

Yolande shook her head. Dear merciful God, no. The whore could not possibly be with child.

This could not be happening.

"Why am I just now learning of this? Lady Armstrong left Edinburgh a month ago."

"Yes, but our maid wasn't the one to spy Lady Armstrong retching. Another did."

"Who?" How many knew, for heaven's sake?

"A scullery maid spied her but said naught until early last morn when our wash maid offered to help her clean the great hall. They'd drunk the last of the night's wine and were telling tales, as staff often do. The scullery maid, who'd witness Lady Armstrong's many discomforts, apparently found it humorous that a highborn lady should find herself being unwed but with child as she herself once had."

Merciful mother of God, why was it that every female in the realm could breed like a hare—save for herself, the queen upon whom so much depended? "How many know?"

"Only four, including yourself, Your Majesty."

Only four? Dreading the answer, she asked, "Did either maid speculate on who the sire might be?"

Helene shook her head. "Not according to our wash woman."

One blessing, at least.

Helene wrung her hands. "There's more, Your Highness."

"*More?*" What other horrendous news could there possibly be?

"Our wash woman formed a romantic liaison with one of the king's guards. Last night he was unable to meet with her because he had to stand guard at the king's solar in place of Sir Brett, whom the king has sent to the border"—she swallowed—"to fetch Lady Armstrong back to court."

Yolande's hands fisted as fury rose hot within her chest. Helene, apparently sensing her distress, scurried backward.

Yolande took a deep breath. "Fear not, Helene. I'll not kill the messenger." She wanted to kill someone else entirely.

As her mother had counseled, Yolande slipped off one of the many strands of pearls she always wore about her neck for moments like this, took the girl's shaking hand in hers and spilled the lustrous gems into her frightened lady-in-waiting's palm. "Thank you."

"Oh no! Your Highness, I cannot possibly take—"

"You must, for you've done me a great service. And of course, you'll not speak of this to anyone."

Helene had the good sense to look aghast. "Never, Your Highness. My loyalty is to you and you alone."

"Thank you. Now please join the other ladies while I ponder all you've told me."

When Helene, pearls clutched in her fist, disappeared into the keep, Yolande gave in to the pain blooming in her chest and, folding at the waist, groaned aloud.

This cannot *be happening.*

Alexander had made her, his second cousin and a mere countess, into a queen for the sole purpose of garnering an heir. What was to stop him from dispensing with her now that another woman was in the process of providing him with what he desired most? Queens were well known for dying most unexpectedly from unknown causes when thrones were involved. What need had he now for her, Yolande?

None.

"Your Highness, are you all right?"

Yolande jerked upright. "Evette, you startled me. You must tread harder when approaching me."

Her cousin grinned. "My apologies, Your Highness. Henceforth, I shall only stomp. Here. I worried you might catch your death and brought your cape."

Yolande, chilled to the bone as much from the mention of death as the brisk wind coming off the sea, murmured her thanks as her cousin slipped the heavy fox pelt about her shoulders. "Evette, I need speak with Monsieur Montre. Please summon him to me here."

Evette's brow furrowed. "But you're shaking with cold. Would you not be more comfortable meeting him inside?"

Yolande glanced over her shoulder at the sentries walking along the tall tower at her back. "Out here, the walls have fewer ears."

Knowing better than to argue, her cousin heaved a sigh and headed for the keep.

Before Yolande could master the fear welling within her breast, she found her longtime confidant and guard striding toward her.

Dear Anton, whatever would she do without him?

Their bond had been forged on the day of her birth, when he'd been ordered to stand guard at her mother's birthing-room door. But instead of hearing the lusty cries of a newborn which he was to report to her father, he'd heard a woman screaming, "*Nooo!*"

Alarmed, he'd charged into the room and found his countess weeping hysterically and the midwife holding her, a lifeless infant.

He'd snatched her from the midwife's hands and, placing his mouth over hers, breathed life into her. And Yolande had cried for the first time.

Anton's brown eyes and hatchet nose had been the first features she'd ever beheld. Not her mother's, not the midwife's, but his. And he'd had been at her side ever since.

While her mother taught her to pray, embroider and manage an estate, Anton had taught her to ride, curse and to know when a man lied or cheated at cards.

At thirteen years of age, when she'd developed tender feelings for a visiting diplomat's son, she'd gone not to her mother but to Anton for advice. A man of few words, he told her, "My sweet lamb, a stiff cock has no conscience." He then asked if she recalled why they'd placed a ring in the bull's nose. When she nodded, he told her, "A ring is the key to controlling a man as well." Laughing, he'd held up his right hand. "No ring."

Today, at two score and nine, Anton was still as muscular and fit as he had been then, as any man half his age, and he still wore no ring. And here she was once again, in sore need of his advice on men.

"Countess—" He grinned at his lapse. "*Your Highness*, how may I be of service?"

"I've had some disturbing news...about Lady Greer Armstrong."

"Ah. You've learned MacKinnon has been ordered to the border to fetch her back to Edinburgh."

Not the least surprised he had his own spies at Edinburgh, Yolande nodded as she fought the tears burning at the back of her throat.

You're a woman grown, for heaven's sake. Not some frightened child. Act it!

He lifted her chin with a finger and looked deep into her eyes. "Oh, now, what have we here, lamb?"

Undone by the childhood endearment, she threw herself into his arms and began sobbing, her tears streaking his leather breast armor. When she finally managed to catch her breath, she stuttered, "That...that slut is with child, Anton. His. And...and I am not."

There, she'd said it aloud. Yet the ache and fear remained.

"I see." He held her, stroking her back in fatherly fashion while she cried out her pain in gasping, slobbering sobs.

"I wish... I wish..."

"She would disappear."

She nodded while his massive chest rose and fell beneath her cheek. Yes. She wanted that woman gone.

"How many know?" he asked.

"That I'm not with child?"

"Yes."

"Only you...and me." She took a shuddering breath, relieved she no longer carried the shameful burden alone. Dashing the tears from her cheeks, she stepped out of his arms. "Evette may suspect, but I've been most careful to hide the evidence of my monumental failure in the fires I keep burning in the solar."

His gaze shifted to the distant hills that footed the treacherous Grampian Mountains beyond. "Does His Majesty know his whore may be with child?"

"He never would have permitted her to leave Edinburgh if he had."

"True."

Yolande began pacing the frozen earth, which crunched and poked like brittle rushes beneath her doeskin slippers. "If he learns of it, I fear I'm a dead woman. Widowed, he would be free to marry her and have his legitimate heir."

Montre grabbed her hand, bringing her to an abrupt halt. "Have no fear, lamb. This...inconvenience will be dispatched forthwith."

"My dearest Anton." Her lifelong friend and teacher would dispose of this threat. "But what of my husband? Won't he grow suspicious when the wench and MacKinnon fail to return? I've done naught to mask my hatred for the woman."

Anton remained silent for several minutes, then whispered, "He'll have no reason to be suspicious of you if you send him a missive stating you believe yourself to be with child. Overjoyed with the prospect of a legitimate heir, he won't spare a moment's thought on the whore but will race here to be at your side, whereupon you must use every womanly wile at your disposal to keep him in bed until such time as you *are* with child. By the time he does give Armstrong a thought, he'll be too content to care what happened to her."

The wind shifted, bringing the sound of distant feminine laughter into the garden. Frowning, Anton studied the windows and battlements above them. Apparently satisfied they held no threat, he turned his attention back to her. "But bear in mind, MacKinnon knows this land and I do not. I'll need time to track him. But most importantly, your husband has spies here and is doubtless aware of your current state of discontent. Before you can send your missive saying you think yourself to be with child, you must convince your court that you believe yourself to be so. You must appear happy and perhaps thoughtful—as if harboring a delightful secret—mayhap even act queasy in the morning, if you are to be believed and to remain blameless in Armstrong and MacKinnon's disappearances."

Yes, she could do this. What a wondrous plan.

Her nemesis would be dealt with in quiet fashion, while she remained safe and had time and opportunity to fulfill her destiny as Queen Consort of Scotland.

With her heart lighter than it had been in months, Yolande rose on tiptoes and kissed Anton's scruffy cheek. "Bless you and God's speed, my dear, dear friend."

Chapter Five

"A cottie stool cannot stand on two legs." ~ Old Scottish Proverb

Annan, Scotland

"No, no, no. Lady Campbell is Sir Lyle Ross sister's sister-by-marriage, not his brother's, and Lady Fraser is his cousin." Greer huffed, then tugged on the woven girdle at Genny's waist. "And you wear this lower...thus."

Genny frowned at the ornate silver-and-black rope riding low on her hips. "But now the girdle will fall as I walk."

Rolling her eyes, her sister took a step back. "You shan't be tromping through fields in Edinburgh, Gen, but gliding across wooden floors. The girdle will stay put. And stop fiddling with that necklace. You'll break it."

"'Tis heavy." Genny pushed up the cold jet crucifix suspended on large silver beads—doubtless a gift from the king—to relieve the pressure on the back of her neck. A weighty price, even for her deception.

"Aye, and most valuable, so do take care," Greer growled and held out the delicate leather slippers she'd pulled from her satchel. "Now put these on, and we're done."

Genny snatched the foolish-looking pointy-toed shoes from her sister's hands and settled on a three-legged cottie stool, the only seating in the stable's storeroom. Seeking a night's shelter for Greer in the nearby Bruce stronghold had been out of the question. Several within would have recognized her.

The air in the stable might hang heavy with the scents of moldering hay and dung, but no one would see them, and for two pence the smithy's mistress had provided a coarse but clean blanket to place upon the rush pallet nestled in the corner, a pitcher of fresh water, a few slivers of mutton and a loaf of brown bread.

Greer, looking about, muttered under her breath, "How far we have fallen."

"It could be worse." Genny wiggled her cramped toes, surprised to learn her sister's feet were apparently a tad smaller than her own.

Her sister snorted in derisive fashion and turned to stare out the chest-high window carved into the barn's plastered wall. After a moment she murmured, "You'll find no friends at court."

Genny frowned. "But what of the ladies Campbell and Fraser?" The French ladies at court likely kept to themselves, but surely the Scotswomen—

"They were welcoming when I first arrived, before Alexander took notice of me. Then they grew distant and more so with each passing month."

"I see." Apparently her sister's life at court hadn't been a bed of flower petals any more than her life in Buddle had been. At least none at court would expect her to share confidences with them.

No one, that was, save the king. How she, an imposter, would deal with the philanderer she had yet to fathom, but deal with him she would. Aye, this deplorable situation her sister found herself in had more than one author.

Noticing the shadows had lengthened, Genny reluctantly rose. "I fear I must take my leave for Buddle. MacKinnon may decide to return early to check on you."

"He shan't. He never approved of my relationship with Alexander. I suspect he came under duress."

"Be that as it may, we dare not risk that he won't return early."

Her twin, obviously still smarting from the cruel but truthful accusations Genny had hurled at her the day before,

Sandy Blair

lifted her chin in haughty fashion. "Very well, then. Thank you for the coins."

"I wish there were more."

"'Twill do."

God's teeth. "I hate leaving you with all this anger festering betwixt us. 'Tis not right."

When her sister just shrugged in response—her twin was naught if not stubborn—Genny picked up the satchel containing Greer's finer kirtles, mantle and frippery and, heart heavy, crossed the threshold.

Behind her, Greer murmured, "You do look lovely."

Genny stopped and, finding her sister now watching her, raised a tentative hand to her hair, dressed for the first time in elaborate braids and decorated with a delicate silver coronet. "Thank you. I shall take great care with your possessions."

Greer nodded as if never doubting that Genny would. "Should I write when the bairn comes?"

You are breaking my heart, sister. "Of course you must write. But do so most cautiously for both your sakes."

When Greer only nodded, Genny, tears welling, let the satchel containing her new identity slip from her hand and stepped forward with arms outstretched, intent on a last farewell embrace. But Greer, her face still vacant, put her back to her and again stared out the window.

Britt slammed a fist against Lady Armstrong's cottage door. Not only had his morning porridge come with weevils *and* his abbey bed been naught but a slab of granite mounted into a stark chamber wall, but he'd had to suffer the annoyingly persistent Brother John, the hound-eyed monk determined to oversee his salvation.

Every damn time he'd turned around, there was Brother John whispering, "You must repent your sins, my lord." Or "Killing, even in the name of the king, still breaks the Lord's commandment." And it mattered naught to Brother John the number of times Britt, with his teeth bared, glared, reminding the pest, "Some men deserve killing."

42

He pounded on Lady Armstrong's cottage door a second time and looked about her modest husbandland. To his left stood a stone dovecote, a pole barn and shearing shed. To the right of the cottage lay a fallow, walled kale yard tilled and ready for spring. Every farming implement and stone had its place. Someone—and he doubted it was Lady Greer—took great pride in the holding.

Next to the kale yard, in a forty-acre pasture, foraged a flock of about two hundred fat ewes alongside a shaggy cow and ox. Beyond the grazing cattle he could see a dozen small cotholdings, their chimney pots already puffing wispy gray columns into the cold dawn.

A handsome holding all in all, and the likes of which he wouldn't mind having himself.

Deciding enough time had passed for a legless man to respond to his knocking, he pressed the latch and opened the door. "Hello! Lady Armstrong, 'tis MacKinnon."

Receiving no response, he stepped into the parlor. "What on earth...?"

The interior reeked, reminded him of the abbot's ale house where he'd spent the better part of yesterday hiding from Brother John.

He found the culprit in the kitchen—fermenting dough, apparently left to rise and now overflowing its bowl.

Now why would a woman go to the trouble of making bread, then forget to bake it? She wouldn't. Something had taken her from her task. She'd either fallen ill or been injured.

Within a heartbeat, he, fearing what he might find, was up the parlor ladder and peering into the sleeping loft, but the large pallet was empty, as were a line of clothes pegs.

So she'd packed.

A moment later, he jerked open the back door, scanned the yard, then headed for the stable.

But the stable stood empty, save for four scratching chickens and a large gray-and-white cat that studied him through narrowed yellow eyes.

Distinctly recalling a horse neighing when he'd ridden up two days ago and his destrier nickering in response, he looked into both stalls and crumbled the few droppings he found in his fist. "Two horses." Neither of which had been in the barn for at least two days. So where were they?

Dusting the manure from his hands, he again studied the distant pasture. Lady Armstrong would not have run off. She had no cause. Nor would she attempt to make the trip to Edinburgh alone, leastwise not with all her worldly possessions strapped to a pack horse which brigands could easily snatch. Which left only one possibility.

She—the king's mistress—had been kidnapped.

Jaw clenched, he strode to the front of the cottage where he'd left his mount, his eyes sorting through hoof prints on the hard packed earth. Heads would roll when Alexander learned of this, and Britt's would be the first. Unless he found her.

Genny jerked upright in her saddle and looked about in confusion, surprised to find the sun high and the crumbled ruins of Ballilock tower standing at her right. Good heavens, she'd fallen asleep in the saddle.

"Good lad, Toby, we're almost home." Praise God for the auld destrier's barn sense, else God only knew where they'd have ended up.

Squinting into the sun, she picked up the reins and patted his neck. "Greer should be well on her way to Ireland by now."

And she'd soon be home. Only five more miles and she'd pass the wee stone kirk in which she and Greer had been baptized and its surrounding collection of mottled headstones, two of which belonged to her parents. The path would then turn and she'd be able to see her cottage. Aye, just another few miles and she and Toby could head for their beds and—

"*Lady Armstrong!*"

Oh my God, 'twas MacKinnon.

Heart thudding, Genny twisted in the saddle, looking for him. Toby, ears alert, spotted him first on the tree-lined ridge above her. Hoping to appear guiltless, she waved as if happy to see him.

He barreled down the sloping pasture toward her. As he jumped his powerful stallion over a chest-high hedge, her breath caught. Had she attempted such a feat, she'd have broken her neck, and still he came, straight and proud in the saddle, the ground vibrating beneath his destrier's huge hooves.

Obviously incensed, MacKinnon pulled up before her, his stallion snorting. "Where have you been? I've been scouring the width and breadth of yon hillock, scaring crofters and bairns out of their minds for miles about, thinking you'd been kidnapped."

Oh dear. How long had he been hunting? Well, she couldn't very well ask, and the best defense was often offense, or so her sot of a father had often bragged.

She lifted her chin and squared her shoulders, hoping she'd mastered Greer's haughty air. "And a pleasant good morn' to you too, my lord."

MacKinnon, apparently not the least impressed, glared at her. "*Well?*"

Genny rolled her eyes. "If you must know, I was bringing a babe into the world, one too big of head and shoulders for his poor mother's—"

"Enough." MacKinnon shuddered, then stroked his agitated destrier's neck. "You should have left a missive."

"I'll be sure to do so should the situation ever arise again."

Black eyes glinting, he growled, "Do so." He then guided his stallion around Toby, his gaze raking her and her father's swaybacked destrier. Spying her satchel, bow and full quiver secured to Toby's saddle as he came up on her right side, he arched an eyebrow. "At least you're armed and packed. You need to change mounts—per His Majesty's orders—then we shall go."

"Go?" The very thought of remaining in the saddle another minute made her chafed thighs throb. "Nay, I need settle the cattle on my nearest tenant, else the poor beasts starve in my absence." Seeing the muscles in his jaw flex, she ran a quick mental inventory of her winter-depleted larder. "And surely you must be as hungry as I. We shall dine on chicken with chestnut dressing and apple tarts if only we delay just a wee bit."

Please, please, I beg you, say aye.

MacKinnon blew through his teeth. "Very well. Then we leave."

"Thank you." Her relief knew no bounds until they arrived at her cottage, she waddled into the kitchen and found it reeking of soured dough. "Auch!"

By midday, the stuffed pullet she'd promised was ready to eat, and her livestock had been turned over to the herder's family, all while under the ever-watchful eye of MacKinnon.

More disconcerting than his constant observation was his ability to take up most of the air in whatever room they happened to occupy, most markedly here in her wee kitchen.

Seated across from him, she poked at her meal while he devoured his with obvious pleasure and abandon, his large hands pulling bread and joints apart without effort. He sucked meat from bones rather than using his blade, and then licked his fingers while his gaze drifted slowly from her mouth to her décolletage. His eyes took on a predatory glint. Feeling heat bloom in her cheeks, she turned and tugged up her gown's embarrassingly low neckline.

What on earth was wrong with her? True, a man had never looked at her in such fashion, but really!

When the last of the meat and gravy disappeared, MacKinnon leaned back. "Lady Greer, you are a splendid cook. Better, in fact, than any in Edinburgh."

Unaccustomed to receiving compliments, Genny ducked her chin and rose before he could see her blush yet again. Her back to him, she murmured, "You exaggerate, but I thank you."

"I must confess I find you having such talent surprising."

Oh no. Her mind scrambled over all Greer had told her about court and finally recalled her sister's warning that she would find no friends there. "Had any at Edinburgh bothered to learn much about me, you wouldn't have been surprised."

"True. Few have bothered, save the king."

Not daring to comment on that observation, she placed what few meat scraps could be found into a small bowl, then threw the bones on the fire.

When she set the bowl on the back step for her mewling cat, he asked, "Why not just toss him the carcass?"

Happy he'd shifted his attention from her to the cat, she murmured, "Had I, the greedy beast would have no reason to hunt, and we'd be overrun with mice by the morrow."

"Where is the ale-swilling dog?"

Huh? She frowned in confusion, then, realizing Greer had apparently made up some tale, she mustered what she hoped was a sad but resigned expression. "Shep died, and I've yet to find a pup to replace him."

"Shep?"

Oh Lord, had she blundered again? Before she could come up with a reply, he shrugged and rose, towering over her. "We must take our leave now."

"But—"

"Nay. Your cattle are in good hands, and your possessions secured. 'Tis time."

"As you lust." She squared her shoulders and, with head held high, glided as best she could ahead of him.

In the parlor, she stroked the back of the rocking chair her grandfather had crafted and again mentally cursed her stupidity for saying her parents had died. The chair, made with more love than craft, would now either be commandeered or chopped to kindling, depending on her cottage's next occupant's wealth. Reluctant to leave all she'd ever known, she murmured, "I really should check the loft one more—"

"My lady, you've checked this holding from chimney pots to floorboards no less than a dozen times. Enough."

He snatched her sister's fur-trimmed cloak from the peg by the door. Standing so close his boot tips disappeared beneath her skirts, he draped the weighty garment about her shoulders. Heat washed over her as he secured the brass clasp at her throat with calloused fingers twice the length of her own. He smelled of horse, leather and the wine they'd shared, and of something quite pleasant she couldn't identify.

How much time passed before she realized his hands had stilled and he was staring down at her, she could not say. Was he already suspicious? Before she could venture a guess, he cleared his throat, placed a palm at the small of her back and firmly ushered her out the door.

Hearing a cock crow, Britt opened his eyes and found Lady Greer just as he'd spied her most of the night, sitting upright on her pallet with her legs pulled close to her chest, her arms wrapped tightly about them, her chin on her knees as she stared at the dying embers. Had he not known better, he'd think her a woman on route to her doom.

"Good morn'."

At the sound of his voice, she jerked upright and hastily rearranged herself, then glanced at the sleeping crofters who'd offered them a place before their hearth for the night. In a whisper, she said, "You sleep like the dead."

Grinning, he stretched and rolled to his feet, taking care not to crown himself on the low-slung ceiling beams. "One sleeps when and how one can, m'lady."

And last night—like any night whilst on the road, his sleep had amounted to only a few quick catnaps.

He held out a hand. Ignoring it, she rose on her own.

As she dusted bits of straw from her gown, he pulled two bodles from his sporran and placed the coins on the hearth where the crofter's wife would find them when she awoke. He bent and whispered in Genny's ear, "I'll ready the horses whilst you seek what privacy there is to be had."

Outside, he found fog blanketing pasture and knoll, the sun gilding the distant mountains. Their ride would prove comfortable, unlike his charge. Lady Greer, normally a chattering and laughing wench, had been uncharacteristically reticent since leaving her cottage.

Although he'd kept an eye on her in Edinburgh, he'd made no effort to form more than her passing acquaintance. Mayhap if he engaged her in conversation, she'd stop looking at him as if he were taking her to the gallows.

He caught a flash of bright blue. Glancing left, he found the king's normally gliding mistress charging with long, determined strides through reeds toward the babbling burn behind the croft like a ship plowing through high seas. How odd. He shook his head and turned his attention back to securing their possessions. The woman was a conundrum.

The next time he looked up, she was again gliding as she normally did, this time with their breakfast in hand. "Here," she said, holding out a square slice of oat cake and a cup.

He looked in the cup. "Milk?"

She nodded, biting into her oat cake. "There's a lovely cow in yon paddock."

"'Tis warm."

She looked at him blankly as if not understanding his meaning, then blanched white as the cup's contents. "I...I found a bucket half full of milk by her side. A tenant must have begun milking her but been startled away by me. I took only a wee bit but... Oh dear, I've no coins..."

"I left enough coins."

Nay, she could not have milked the cow. The queen's ladies-in-waiting were just that: ladies, the pampered daughters and sisters of landed men. He very much doubted any knew which end of a cow to approach for milk. He couldn't imagine any knowing how to hobble a cow, much less stooping beneath one and pulling on teats. Aye, she must have found the milk as she said.

His qualms settled, Britt tried to suppress his bone-breaking shudder as he drained the cup. Never let it be said that he lacked chivalry.

He dropped the cup on the croft stoop. "If you're ready, we should leave."

She looked up at him, her bonnie blue eyes shimmering as if on the verge of tearing. "Aye, I'm quite ready."

Nay, she was not, not in the least.

He placed his hands above the silver girdle she wore, marveling once again at how small her waist was. When her hands settled on his shoulder armor, he lifted her negligible weight, bringing them face-to-face. What was she thinking as she stared into his eyes so solemnly? Was she simply wary, or did she feel the same charge he felt when he held her so close? How easy it would be to capture her mouth with his, to taste the forbidden fruit he'd been thinking about since she'd cocked her head and smiled at him in her parlor.

Too easy and too dangerous for both of them.

He settled her on the gray, then leapt onto his patient destrier. Determined to put her at her ease, he said, "What new songs have you to entertain the court?"

"Uhmm...none. I've had no opportunity to learn any."

He nodded. Of course she hadn't had time, what with her having to arrange her parents' funerals, then notifying the earl and her extended family of their passing.

They rode on in silence as the day grew warmer, he alert to danger and Lady Armstrong yawning in the saddle. When the sun reached its zenith, he stopped by a burn, and Lady Armstrong jerked upright, asking, "Why are we stopping?"

"Because I'm hungry, as are the horses."

Helping her dismount, he again caught the scent of lavender and roses, his blood heated, and he quickly set her down and turned his attention to their mounts. He pulled free their wine skin and his saddle bag and handed them to her. "I'll water the horses if you would be so kind as to set out something for us to eat."

She mustered a smile, her first since leaving the croft.

With their mounts tended, he settled on a sun-warmed boulder next to her and accepted the oatcake and dried fruit she'd packed. "How many years have you been in the king's service?" she asked.

Mesmerized by the halo of sunlight bouncing off her silver coronet and glossy braids, he murmured, "Near a decade."

"Ah, you must enjoy it, then."

He straightened and looked about. His remaining at the king's side had naught to do with enjoyment. "Duty and honor before pleasure, my lady."

They finished their repast in silence. Dusting the crumbs from her kirtle, she said, "We should be going."

In no hurry, he suggested, "Why not rest a bit. You must be tired."

She rose. "Nay, we need be on our way."

They rode on. And as he could have predicted by gloaming, Lady Armstrong was head down and eyes closed, weaving in her saddle. They were but a few hours' ride from the stronghold of Meade Mont, but fearing she'd topple and crown her lovely noggin, Britt steered his destrier to a grassy wee glen and dismounted. The gray followed without any assistance from their king's sleeping mistress.

Shaking his head at the woman's stubbornness, Britt secured his mount, gathered deadwood, then cleared a spot in the grass to lay a fire, all while Lady Armstrong slept. Accustomed to sleeping in the elements, he needed no fire, but from what he'd observed, Lady Armstrong enjoyed her creature comforts. And God forbid she should grow ill.

When the fire caught, he spread his *breachen feile* on the ground at a safe distance from it, then lifted Lady Armstrong from the gray. As she settled on his plaid, she mumbled something incoherent about love and castration—a decidedly unsettling thought—then, sighing, curled like an exhausted kitten before the fire.

He pulled his whetstone from his sporran, then freed his blades from their sheaths. As he ran a finger over his broadsword's edges, testing the sharpness, he watched her by the glow of the fire. Aye, his king was a lucky man but had no clue to what extent. His Majesty had been blessed first with a fertile and sensible wife, then been granted a second wife, one half his age, and still his eye wandered.

51

Shaking his head at the sad waste of blessings, he sheathed his broadsword and began honing his more oft used *sgian duhb*.

And what on earth was this woman, now tossing in restless sleep, thinking? She'd been gifted with incredible beauty and a voice that could make songbirds weep with shame, yet she too squandered her gifts. Was she such a rustic, such an innocent, that she did not know she'd ruined all hope of her ever making a good match by acquiescing to Alexander?

She could just as easily have said, "Thank you, but no." His Majesty was lusty—no denying that—but he was also chivalrous. Oh, he would have sulked and made everyone's life miserable for a day or so, but then he'd have shrugged it off and sought out one of his other paramours...or the queen.

Women. Be they fair or foul, royal or not, he would never understand them.

Lady Armstrong, brow furrowed, flipped onto her stomach and cocked a leg. Looking at her well-turned ankle and calf, at the lovely swell of her rump, he sighed. At least he well understood what his liege was thinking.

Chapter Six

"No lie lives long." ~ Old Scottish Proverb

Midway through their second day, MacKinnon asked, "What think you of the new rooms in the Constable's Tower?"

St. Bride preserve her! How many more questions did this man have, and how much more could Greer have neglected to mention?

First MacKinnon had asked her about her new songs, then fables, and then what she thought of their new queen's habits, cooks, ladies-in-waiting and confidant, and now he wanted her opinion on some ominously named tower? She had no notion of its construction, much less whether this tower was large or small. Greer had never mentioned it. And why should she care about its rooms? Having no means by which to even imagine it, Genny kept her gaze on the rushing burn to their right and murmured, "Most lovely."

MacKinnon made a thick, decidedly masculine sound at the back of his throat. "The coins would have been better spent on cannon."

She'd heard Smithy's tales of cannon but had never seen one. She wanted to ask this handsome hulk if they truly were as fierce and thunderous as she feared, if there were many at Edinburgh, but didn't dare. Greer would likely already know.

Hoping to distract MacKinnon from his questions, she asked, "How often have you been in battle?"

Her father had never tired of recounting his bloody encounters, all of which grew more gruesome and grandiose with each telling.

"My lady, war, like bread and sleep, is a necessity of life. One's exploits are not something one denigrates or brags upon."

Hmmm, MacKinnon was not only modest but held convictions. Interesting.

"Are you in discomfort, m'lady? Need we stop?"

Had she been frowning? "Nay, I'm quite comfortable, thank you."

She truly was, riding for the first time on a horse that suited her, not astride but with her legs draped properly to the side as they should be instead of sticking out like a scarecrow's arms. Her hips and thighs no longer ached as they had on her long ride to and from Annan.

She patted her mount's smooth withers. "Who owns this palfrey, and does he have a name?"

"He's just one of many in the Edinburgh stable."

Ah. 'Twould be lovely if she could have use of him while in Edinburgh. If so, then she would have the privilege of naming him. She studied MacKinnon's glossy black destrier prancing beside her. "And your stallion? What do you call him?"

"Horse."

"He's a new acquisition, then?"

MacKinnon's wide brow furrowed. "Nay, I've had him more than a decade, since earning my spurs."

Genny gaped at him. "And you've yet to name him? No wonder he's always prancing and tossing his head."

"He prances and tosses because I'm making him keep pace with your palfrey."

"Oh." She warily eyed the stallion. He did look impatient, slobbering on the bit. "Well, you should still give him a name."

MacKinnon looked at her as if she were daft. "You name all your cattle?"

"Of course. How else will they know to come when I call?" She started ticking off names on her fingertips. "Toby, our

father's destrier, is now my mount and plow horse. Then there's
Bess our cow and Sam the ox. Mittens is the cat whom you've
met, and MacDuff is my lovely auld ram."

"And your sumpter?" When she frowned, he said, "The
second horse you had in the barn."

Oh merciful saints! He meant Greer's mount. How could he
know there were two? "Ah, you mean Mother's mare, Maisey.
She's with the smithy now."

"Odd, I would never have thought you so sentimental...that
you'd name beasts."

Genny arched an eyebrow. "Well, I would never have
thought you so unsentimental that you would *not* name them."

MacKinnon's laughing bark, deep and rich, echoed through
the canopy, startling not only her but a pair of mourning doves
from their perch. "*Touché*, m'lady."

The forest abruptly ended, and they entered a glen awash
in sunshine, every frost-coated blade and branch gleaming as if
coated in glass. Enchanted by the sight, Genny murmured,
"How lovely."

"Aye. Reminds me of a glen at home."

Not knowing if she should already know of his home, she
said, "Do tell me more."

He eyed her in speculative fashion for a moment, then took
off his helm and ran a hand through his black mane. "I was
born on Skye, a lovelier place you're unlikely to find. I was the
youngest of four sons but am now the only one. My eldest
brother was called..."

As he spoke, he often gestured and occasionally laughed.
She suspected his tale was of a time and place he rarely spoke
of, and felt privileged that he'd chosen to share his memories
with her. When he spoke of his lost siblings, her thoughts
turned to Greer and their awkward parting. How often they'd
hugged and laughed in play, and now her twin was gone,
mayhap forever. The thought brought burning to the back of
her eyes.

Hoping to distract herself, she again focused her attention
on MacKinnon and the threat he posed.

His hair, now flowing free in thick waves across his armor-clad shoulders, flashed blue like raven feathers with the simple turn of his head. And his eyes, framed by thick black lashes, weren't black as she'd first thought in the shadows of her home but were, in truth, a dark sable brown. She smiled, wondering if MacKinnon knew that he and his stallion had the same coloring.

His features, which she'd first thought too sharp and found menacing, appeared somehow softer in sunlight, or mayhap it was only the faint stubble that now lined his square jaw. Nay, 'twas the fact that he was no longer scowling but appeared relaxed. And look at that... His nose had been broken. She decided the slight crook only added character to his handsome countenance.

"A bodle for your thoughts, m'lady."

"I find you—" Genny coughed to cover her near blunder. The saint's preserve her! Cursed with frank speech since infancy, she'd nearly blurted that she thought him most handsome. Bad enough she spoke her mind too often at home. To do so now would mean her death.

She really had to pay more heed.

Genny cleared her throat and tried again. "I was thinking you'd make a fine bard."

The armor plates on his shoulders clinked with his chuckle. "You're the first to think such."

Praying she remembered Greer's information correctly, she said, "Sir Lyle likely thinks so as well."

"Ah, mayhap, since he instigated most of our mayhem."

She grinned. Another hurdle crossed.

At the end of the glen, they entered a copse of thick pine where the land dropped off sharply and the path they'd been travelling split into two. MacKinnon took the lead and turned left. Frowning, Genny brought her palfrey to a halt and studied the short shadows cast betwixt trees and the rolling hills in the distance. Shielding her eyes, she then glanced at the sun. "MacKinnon?"

Riding a several yards ahead, he pulled up and turned in his saddle to look back at her. "Aye?"

"You've turned the wrong way, m'lord. The sun moves to the west, so we must take that path"—she pointed to her right—"in order to reach Edinburgh."

"I've matters to attend in Glasgow, so we must go there first."

Panic bloomed in her chest. "Nay, I fear that will not do, sir."

"I fear it must."

"Then you must go on without me." Traveling alone, she would have to push her mount in order to limit her nights on the road, to minimize the possibility of her being set upon by thieves, but there was no hope for it. Her courses were due on the full moon. She had to be in Edinburgh before they started if her plan to protect her sister's child—and herself from the king—were to succeed.

"M'lady, I am not leaving you to your own devices. Come." With that he turned in his saddle and kicked his horse into a trot going in the wrong direction.

Well, of all the bollocks!

Fine. He could go to Glasgow if he was so inclined, but he'd be going without her.

As MacKinnon disappeared behind a huge boulder and began clattering down the ravine, Genny reined right. Her gelding, reluctant to leave the stallion, pranced sideways, fighting the bit. Having manhandled lazy auld Toby for years, she heaved a sigh and kept the gray's head turned. The palfrey finally gave up the battle and trotted with his ears pinned back down the path to Edinburgh.

Only yards down the slippery shale, Britt realized the only sounds he heard were those made by his mount. No shale clattered down the mountainside behind him. He reined in, looked over his shoulder and found the path behind him empty. Where the hell was she? Knowing the dangers, surely she wouldn't have been so foolhardy as to go off on her own? But she obviously had.

"Damn the woman!"

The path was too narrow to turn the stallion. They'd fall to their deaths if he tried. Worse, the wall of granite on his left continued for as far as the eye could see, while the sheer drop to his right continued for twice the distance. He had no choice but to continue on at a snail's pace until the path widened.

Cursing, he nudged his destrier forward.

He never should have let his guard down. Had Lady Armstrong been a man, he would have ridden behind, not ahead. This was what he got for being chivalrous, for ruminating over her direct gaze, the way she cocked her head as if she truly cared about what he thought or said. Asinine, truly. She must think him an idiot. Aye, and when he caught up with her, she'd rue this day.

A torturous half mile later, he found a hollow where a tree had lost its hold on the cliff, and turned his mount about.

A mile down the trail leading to Edinburgh, he finally spied her riding along at a brisk trot as if she hadn't a care in the world. "Lady Armstrong! Halt!"

To his surprise, she glanced over her shoulder, waved, and then, ignoring his order, continued trotting north.

"Bloody hell!"

He kicked the destrier into a full gallop, not caring that his thundering steed would startle her mount and thus toss Lady Armstrong's fine hurdies into the air. He'd had enough of her foolishness.

As expected, her palfrey shied, then spun as he came up behind it. That she managed to keep her seat when he grabbed her reins and pulled the panicked gelding to a stop he found remarkable...and annoying.

"What, pray tell," he shouted, "were you thinking riding off like that?"

Rather than wither beneath his fury, Lady Armstrong blinked like an owl. "Why, I was thinking to keep you safe from the king's wrath, m'lord."

"*What?*"

"His Majesty must be most anxious to see me, else he wouldn't have sent you to fetch me. Our going to Glasgow would have added a week or more onto our trip, and I'm sure His Majesty would have been most angry with you." She then took a deep breath and looked about. "Lovely day, don't you think?"

Jaw muscles working with pent-up fury, Britt could only stare at Greer Armstrong in disbelief.

She'd issued a threat as artful as it was insidious.

She'd not defied him. Oh no. She'd just taken it upon herself to keep him out of trouble. And if he thought to insist upon them going to Glasgow, she'd taken pains to remind him that she too had the king's ear. The conniving wench. And she'd done it all while cloaking the threat beneath a flighty woman's *illogical* logic. Aye, that's what she'd done, and it wouldn't work.

"Lady Armstrong, you risked life and limb by running—"

"Please address me as Greer." She smiled up at him, and the elusive dimple he'd spied in her parlor again made its appearance. "Lady Armstrong sounds silly out here in the middle of nowhere, don't you think?"

Britt ground his teeth. "Greer, you risked life—"

"You truly are most accommodating. And I shall address you as Britt if you've no objection...so long as we are alone. To do so at court would appear most unseemly. I provide the gossips with fodder enough as it is."

"Since when has gossip ever concerned *you?*"

She blinked, and then with hurt obvious in her eyes, she heaved a weary-sounding sigh and looked away. "You're quite right, of course." She tugged on her reins. Reluctantly, he let them slip from his control. As she adjusted the leathers in her hands, she murmured, "Now that we have all that settled, shall we go? Our king awaits."

Seething, he waved her ahead. "After you."

Riding in her wake, he took what pleasure he could in staring daggers into her lithe back. Which woman was the real Lady Greer Armstrong? This determined conundrum, who would not be denied...or the flirtatious and thoughtless songbird he better knew from Edinburgh?

He had no idea but *would* find out.

Scotland's security could well rest on him doing so.

An hour later, Lady Greer twisted in her saddle to look back at him. "Britt?"

"Aye?"

"Why do you ride so far behind? The trail is wide enough for two now."

Why indeed. He'd learn nothing more about her by glaring at her bonnie arse. Coming abreast of her, he asked, "Content?"

She slid a sidelong glance at him from beneath thick lowered lashes. "Aye, and I wish to apologize."

"Oh?" This was likely the first time she'd ever done such.

Turning her attention to the forest surrounding them, she murmured, "I understand that you're in an untenable position. You're obviously an honorable man, and I suspect my...words have made your task all the more unpleasant for you. If it helps ease your mind, please know that the mistress loves her king as he loves her."

Humph! He hadn't expected her to hold out so large an olive branch. "Lady Armstrong, my liking for a king's order is never a consideration. I do my duty, like it or not. As for your relationship with the king, I do not challenge that you love him. He can be most charming when he's of a mind."

But the lady was very much mistaken if she thought her feelings were reciprocated. She might be the king's favorite—not only was she most lovely on the eye but could prove most disarming—but she was also one of six women the king regularly bedded, including the consort.

She cocked her head and studied him in that earnest way she had. "Do you wish to say something else?"

Aye, he wanted to say he found her confession and demeanor to be at odds with the self-serving female he knew but then thought better of it and shook his head.

She heaved a resigned sigh. "As you lust. I just wanted to be sure you understood that I hold no ill will toward you, that there are simply times when—like it or not—we have to do and say what we must."

"If that be so, then why bother to issue a threat?" The woman was driving him mad.

"Mayhap someday you'll come to understand."

The path split before them, and without a word, he pointed to the right, and she obediently eased her palfrey down the deep boulder-strewn glack cut into the land by the rushing burn before them, dividing glen from forest. Reaching the far embankment, her palfrey stumbled, then limped to a stop. Suspecting the gray had picked up a stone, Britt charged through the water and up the embankment. Before he could dismount, however, Lady Greer sprang from the palfrey, tucked the gray's injured hoof neatly betwixt her skirted knees and, with blade in hand, expertly extricated a stone.

Shocked a lady-in-waiting would think to do such, much less know how, he waited until she dropped the hoof to grab her wrist. Her wee smile of satisfaction at a job well done instantly dissolved when he tightened his hold. Her fingers unfurled, and the short-bladed *sgian duhb* she'd secreted in her pocket fell to the ground.

"What have we here?" He ran his thumb over a surprising number of calluses crossing her right palm and fingers. "Been hard at work, have we?"

"Nay, just a few tasks, country life you know…" Blushing, she laughed in dismissive fashion, and the hairs on the back of his neck stood on end.

Gone were the charming peals he'd so often heard at court. In their place were rich husky tones he would never forget. His grip tightened further. Her voice, her faulty memory, the cow's milk, the blushing, her lack of flirtation, her stomping about rather than gliding, the frankness of speech and now this. A chill danced down his spine. All the discrepancies now made sense.

He had the wrong woman.

61

Chapter Seven

"Better caution than danger." ~ Old Scottish Proverb

Genny yelped when MacKinnon jerked her up against his massive chest and hissed, "Who are you?"

"You're hurting me!"

His eyes turned coal black as he loomed over her. "You'll have more than bruised arms if you don't tell me your name this instant."

Oh dear merciful God! "You know who I am. I'm the king's mistress."

He shook her. "Stop lying!"

Fearing she might faint, she insisted, "I'm *not.*"

He huffed in disgust and pushed her toward the palfrey. Before she could catch her breath or her thudding heart could steady, he grabbed her by the waist, his thick, long fingers squeezing the breath out of her, and tossed her onto her saddle, then bound her hands to the saddle horn with one of the reins. "Aye, you are lying. There have to be two of you. *Twins.*"

Oh Lord, he knows. What will he do now?

Using the free rein, Britt pulled her palfrey after him. As it danced in agitation, he, cursing under his breath, vaulted onto his stallion, then turned south, heading back from whence they'd come.

Nay! The moon was already three quarters full! "MacKinnon...Britt, please listen. We have to head north to Edinburgh."

He glared over his shoulder at her. "Why? Do you fear if we return to your cottage I'll find your sister hiding beneath the hay? Or mayhap in the loft you were so anxious to check again before we left?"

The saints preserve her. Could Greer have returned to the cottage? Nay, she wouldn't be so foolish, wouldn't dare put her bairn in such peril. But then she'd been so frightened. Oh God...

Genny's tears spilled unchecked as she mentally ran through the myriad of troubles her sister could have encountered. Greer might not have found a ship to take her to Ireland. She might have found a ship but then spied someone she knew onboard and then fled home. Someone might have accosted her and stolen what coins she had, and thus her means to garner passage. Or she might have just taken it into her pretty stubborn head to go home.

"Please, MacKinnon, please turn about."

"Tell me your name."

"I've told you."

With a look of pure disgust, he tugged on the palfrey.

Hour upon hour, only the clacking of hooves and creaking of leather broke the silence. When she could stand it no longer, needing to pace, to do something other than be hauled about, she said, "I have need for privacy."

Glancing at her over his shoulder, he curled his lip in derisive fashion. "Hold it."

"I can't."

"Then you'll have a wet—"

Something whizzed past Genny's cheek—so close it burned her skin—before hitting a nearby tree with a loud *thwangggg*. Her gray shied as she stared in horror at a vibrating arrow imbedded in the dense bark not a yard before her.

Sandy Blair

MacKinnon, cursing, jerked around, his gaze raking the path and woods. Before she could ask why someone would shoot at them, he kicked his destrier into a full gallop and she, terrified and nearly unseated, found herself being hauled pell-mell into the wood. Shouting broke out behind them and to their right as pine boughs slapped her face. MacKinnon hauled her mount up shale and through a burn before reining in behind a huge boulder outcrop and vaulting from his saddle.

Heart thudding, she cried, "What's happening? Why would someone—"

"Later." The rein binding her wrists fell away, and he hauled her off her palfrey. His arm came about her waist, and he started running. "Hie now! Into the hole."

Breathless, her mouth suddenly parched by fear, Genny stumbled over her skirts and into the boulders' shadows. He pressed on her shoulders, and she fell to her knees within a nest of winter-dead leaves and needles, a spider's web brushing the cheek the arrow so nearly penetrated. Shivering, she batted the gauzy threads away.

He grabbed her chin to get her attention. "Do not move if you want to live. I'll be back."

"But—"

His mouth closed over hers, firm, warm and moist. Instinctively, she closed her eyes and yielded. His tongue swept past her lips, startling her, caressing hers, causing inexplicable heat to flare deep within her chest and middle.

He pulled away and whispered, "I had to know."

Swamped by sensations she had yet to sort out, it took her a moment to realize he meant to leave her alone. Horrified he'd even think to do such, she gasped as her eyes flew open.

He was gone.

"Your Highness appears most pleased this morn'," Lady Campbell murmured.

For the third day in a row, Yolande smiled in shy fashion just as Anton suggested, which was no easy task, given her worry. He'd been gone four days. "The day is most pleasant."

Her court turned toward the window, and in unison, frowned at the dark sky looming overhead.

"Most pleasant," Lady Fraser murmured, glancing surreptitiously at Lady Campbell.

Yolande held the little bed gown she'd been working on to the lamplight to admire the tiny leaves she'd embroidered and allowed her smile to broaden. "I'm famished, Evette."

Her cousin looked up from her work. "But you just ate but an hour past."

"*Oui.* Would you be so kind as to ask Cook for a basket of her wonderful buns, a bit of cheese and a few olives? No, I should like a dozen olives."

"Of course, Your Highness."

Yolande waited until her cousin crossed the threshold to call after her. "And sardines! And..."

Evette poked her head back in the solar and, grinning, asked, "Perhaps something to drink?"

Yolande beamed at her cousin. "*Oui!* A chalice of milk."

All in the room gaped at her, obviously aghast at the thought. Only Mademoiselle Dupree dared mutter what all were thinking. "Milk, Your Highness?"

Yolande picked up her embroidery needle and, smiling, murmured, "*Oui.*"

By mid morn', Yolande's middle heaved in fiery revolt. She fought for composure for as long as she dared, then bolted, a hand over her mouth, toward the garderobe.

As she flew past her commiserating court, she heard Lady Campbell murmur in their crude tongue to Lady Fraser, "Tell Ross."

Britt, broadsword in hand, ran on silent feet as far as he dared from Lady Armstrong before deliberately stepping on a felled branch. The resounding crack echoed through the forest. A pursuer somewhere to his right shouted, *"La-bas!"*

Down there. God's teeth! Their attackers weren't hapless thieves but French. The queen's men.

More branches fractured as their assailants rushed forward, one running directly toward him, the other moving fast at right angles to the depression in which Britt had sought cover, doubtless trying to outflank him.

More worrisome than not knowing their number was the bastards' lack of stealth. Their orders apparently weren't to capture the king's mistress but to kill her.

Britt heaved a hefty rock into the undergrowth to his right. The man closest to him bolted toward the sound. When he drew within striking distance, Britt rose from behind the bramble masking him, his broadsword gripped in both hands.

Tempered steel sliced through flesh and muscle as if through fresh bread, then vibrated, hitting bone. The man gaped in surprise. Before he could topple, Britt was off on silent feet after the next would-be assassin.

Entering a stand of dense wood, he sheathed his broadsword and palmed his short *sgian duhb*. Rocks clattered and leaves crunched to his immediate left. Britt lunged and landed on the man, who, lighter than he by a good five stones, fell flat on his face, air whooshing from his chest, a blade falling from his outstretched hand. A flick of Britt's wrist and the man was dead. Britt stood. Two down. He looked about, then cocked his head, listening. Nothing. Mayhap he'd taken down the last—

Searing pain took his breath away. He looked down in surprise as his knees buckled. His hands instinctively closed around the thick shaft protruding from beneath his chest armor. Damn. Why hadn't he heard the telltale ratcheting of the bastard's crossbow? Black spots danced before his eyes, and he toppled onto his side, jarring pain exploding in his middle.

Lady Armstrong. He had to get back to her.

The mossy ground beneath his cheek began to vibrate with the weight of rushing footfalls. He let his body go limp and held his breath. A boot slammed into his ribs mere inches above the arrow, and he had all he could do to keep from screaming, writhing in agony.

Deep in the boulder's shadow, Genny pressed shaking fingers to her lips. Why would thieves try to kill them? They'd had the element of surprise. They could have simply taken what valuables she and Britt had and then been on their way. But then again, they had no way of knowing that Britt would fight to the death rather than run the risk of her being captured. He still had no certain proof that she *wasn't* the king's mistress.

And why had Britt kissed her? She'd deceived him at every turn. And why had her body and heart responded? She'd felt naught when the butcher had accosted her, had slammed his wet mouth against hers that May Day and summarily suffered the consequences. Deciding this was all too complicated to fathom in her current agitated state, she focused on what she could do—stay alive.

She strained to hear something, anything, beyond her damp hidey-hole. Surely Britt had dispatched the villains by now. But what if they'd—

Nay, she'd not even think it. He stood head and shoulders taller than any, would prove stronger than any. He would return. But what if they found her before he returned? Britt had her blade. Her bow and quiver were still hooked over the gray's saddle horn. She had no means by which to defend herself should the knaves find her before Britt returned.

She couldn't just sit here hoping for the best.

She crawled forward into mottled sunshine, where the unearthly silence continued—not a bird twittered, not a leaf moved.

Palms sweating, she came to her feet, pressed her back to the cold stone, her gaze scouring the forest for signs of friend or foe. Seeing neither, she slowly edged around the boulders and found Britt's destrier amazingly still in his absence, whilst her mount, its ears pinned back, upon spying her began prancing in agitation at the destrier's side. She darted to the destrier, taking what comfort she could from his massive size and armor-curtained sides. Praying her palfrey's antics wouldn't draw unwanted attention, she eased beneath the destrier's neck and stroked her pretty mount's side. The gray immediately settled, and she lifted the bow and quiver from the saddle horn.

Within a heartbeat, she had her quiver on her back and had nocked an arrow. Feeling immeasurably better, she heaved a sigh, only to startle when a heavily accented voice said, "Good day, Mademoiselle Armstrong."

Terror surging within her breast, Genny spun, bow rising. From long habit, her arm pulled back, and the bow went taut. Heart hammering, she stared at the stranger dressed in chain mail from crown to boots, a steel helm masking all but his eyes.

"Drop the bow, mademoiselle."

"Where's Britt?"

He snorted in derisive fashion. "So now 'tis Britt, huh?"

Heart hammering, fearing the answer but needing to know, she screamed, "Answer me! Where's Britt?"

His head jerked to the left. "If you must know, MacKinnon is dead, an arrow in his gut. Now put the bow down."

She shook her head. "You lie." Britt couldn't be dead, but then the man did have a huge crossbow hanging on his back. Waving a thin rapier slowly before him, he took a step forward.

"*Halt* or I'll shoot!"

He stopped but laughed. "You forget, mademoiselle, I've seen you at games. You couldn't hit a curtain wall if it fell on you."

Who is *this man?* Why had he killed Britt, and why was he now threatening her...or rather her sister? "What do you want?"

"You've ceased being a mere embarrassment to our queen and are now a serious inconvenience."

Oh dear God above, did he know Greer carried the king's bairn? Did the queen? Aye, they must, and they fully intended to see her dead.

She had only one clear target, thanks to his helm and armor. If she missed, he'd be upon her before she could nock a second arrow.

He sprang; she gasped and released.

The arrow hit its mark. The man screamed and fell on his side, his hands reaching for his face.

As the man went deathly still, the bow slipped from Genny's hand. Sobbing, her stomach roiling at the sight of her arrow protruding from his helm, she edged closer to see if his chest still rose and fell. It did, while blood pumped from what remained of his right eye. She hadn't killed him outright as she had so many hares and quail, thank God. To kill an animal for the table was one thing. To kill a man, another entirely.

But her relief was short-lived with the realization he could regain consciousness, and then she wouldn't stand a chance. He *would* kill her. She paced before his inert form, wringing her hands. "What to do, what to do?"

She couldn't kill him with a second arrow as he lay there defenseless, she just couldn't. But then she couldn't allow him to get up, either. And she had to find Britt. He could well be alive, just as the man lying before her was. She looked about. A length of rope hung from the destrier's saddle. Mayhap she could truss the man as she would a hog going to market. Nay. The very thought of touching him made her ill.

Legs quaking, she ran to the destrier and grabbed his reins. She would decide what to do with the bastard later. First she had to find Britt.

Branches snapped several yards to Britt's left. Careful not to jar the arrow imbedded in his right side, he pressed his back to the nearest tree and held his breath. Someone was moving fast, mindless of the racket they created. Most likely the queen's confidant Montre, the bastard who'd left him for dead. Had he found the Armstrong lass? Or did she remain safe in her hidey-hole?

"MacKinnon!"

God's teeth, 'tis Lady Armstrong! She was alive, praise the saints, but she'd get them both killed if she didn't stop shouting.

Having no idea where Montre might be lurking, Britt wrapped his fingers around what remained of the arrow after snapping off the shaft and silently jogged toward her. A flash of blue, then the black and gold of his destrier's livery peeked through the dense underbrush.

"MacKinnon! Oh God, please answer me!"

Please, woman. Please stop shouting.

He whistled as loud as he dared. His mount nickered, and Lady Armstrong yelped. A heartbeat later, the pair crashed through the undergrowth, his snorting destrier in the lead, the gray behind them.

Lady Armstrong, tear-streaked and dirty, tangled braids falling about her shoulders, spying him, dropped the reins. He was nearly knocked off his feet as she slammed into him. Throwing her arms about his neck, she cried, "Thank God, you're alive! He said that he'd killed you."

"*Shhh,* m'lady." He pulled her back into the protection of the ancient tree. "I told you to stay hidden. Do you ever mind?"

"On occasion, but you were gone so long—"

"Who said I was dead?"

She stroked his cheek and studied him, as if not believing her eyes. "I've no idea. He's large but not so tall as you. He came up behind me with sword in hand and said you were dead. He said I'd become a serious inconvenience to the queen and then tried to kill me!"

Wondering how she managed to escape, he asked, "Where is he now?"

She blanched and pointed behind her. "Back there. I shot him...in the eye. Heaven help me, I only meant..."

"Is he dead?"

"Nay, but badly wounded and—Merciful God, you're bleeding!" She was staring at his blood-drenched side and the broken shaft protruding from it.

"Aye, but we'll tend to it after I deal with the blackguard." Men like Montre could take an arrow to the heart and still keep fighting. Britt pushed off the tree and took her hand. "Come."

At the outcrop of rock where he'd left Lady Armstrong, he found Montre helmless and covered in blood, an arrow lying at his side. At the grisly sight, Lady Armstrong keened and staggered away, a hand over her mouth. Britt leaned over Montre and discovered the man still lived.

Hmm. Should he put the bastard out of his misery now or haul him back to Edinburgh where he could answer to a furious Alexander? The first option held the most appeal, given the bastard's arrow was still imbedded in his side. But His Majesty needed to know of what level of duplicity—of what lengths—his new queen was capable.

Teeth grit, Britt reached up and pulled the rope from his saddle, then bound Montre hand and foot. Once satisfied Montre would be most uncomfortable but secured should he awake, he took his wound kit from his saddlebag. "M'lady, a moment of your time, please."

Lady Armstrong, her coronet and braids askew, dashed the tears from her bonnie blue but now red-rimmed eyes. Taking pains not to look at Montre, she asked, "Aye?"

"I need your help removing this arrow."

Her brows tented as she looked at his bloodied side. "What would you have me do?"

He held out his *sgian duhb*. "Hit the shaft firmly with the blade's hilt so I might remove this damn arrow."

"Uhmm...of course."

Britt handed her the blade, then, wincing, pulled his right arm free of both chain mail and shirt.

Nodding like a sandpiper, she wiped her palms on her skirts, bent and explored his side with tentative fingers. "Dear God above, MacKinnon. The tip has another two inches to travel."

"Aye, just give it a hard whack and drive the point through. I'd do it myself, but as you can see, the shaft is at an angle I can't readily hit." When she made no move to do his bidding, he glanced over his shoulder and found her gnawing her lower lip. Hoping to distract her from the task at hand, he murmured,

"And I thought we agreed to call each other by our Christian names."

A single tear spilled over her thick lashes as she took a shuddering breath. "My name is Geneen. Greer is my twin."

Ah ha! As he suspected. "How do you do?"

She dashed the wetness from her cheek. "Not at all well at the moment, if you must ken."

He grinned. "Nor I, but let's be done with this, shall we?"

Britt faced forward so as not to make her anymore anxious than she already appeared and grit his teeth. And a good thing he did. Geneen Armstrong held naught of her eight stones back when she finally struck the shaft. Muscle and flesh tore with searing intensity. When he could finally breathe again, he gripped the fully exposed steel tip with his right hand and pointed with his left to the leather pouch at his feet. "In there you'll find what you'll need to bind the wound."

As Lady Geneen hauled whisky and bandages from the pouch, Britt again gritted his teeth and jerked the arrow free. Before his heartbeat could steady, his best whisky was burning its way through his flesh. "God's teeth, woman, enough!"

"Hush! 'Lest you end up doing this yourself."

He huffed, then glanced at Montre. Seeing he was still out cold, Britt murmured, "You're quite the iron maiden, Geneen Armstrong."

"Iron to the core, MacKinnon." She tied off his dressing and then, heaving a sigh, took a step back. He twisted a wee bit to test the dressing. Satisfied it would stanch the bleeding, he murmured, "My thanks."

"'Twill hold?"

"Aye."

"Good." Her lovely blues eyes then rolled back in her head, and to his utter astonishment, she fainted dead away at his feet.

"Ouch!" Merciful heavens, her head hurt.

"My apologies, my lady, but the compress is needed to stem the bleeding."

MacKinnon! Her eyes flew open. The day came rushing back in one awful flash when she found Britt staring down at her. Their argument, the attack, her shooting Montre, her driving an arrow through Britt's side, then...nothing. "What happened?"

And why was she prostrate on Britt MacKinnon's lap? She struggled to sit, but his arm tightened about her waist.

"Nay, be still. You fainted. Right now we need talk...before Montre awakens."

Oh Lord, not now. She looked away. "Talk of what?"

"Are you daft?" He grabbed her chin, forcing her to look into his handsome face. "Why did the two of you not just hie off? Why go to all this trouble masquerading as your sister? From what I've seen of you, 'twill be most obvious to the king that you are not Greer the moment he tries to bed you." He huffed, then nodded toward Montre. "And you do realize he's *not* Her Highness's only henchmen, aye? You need tell me what you're about before you get us all killed, your sister included."

He's right, damn him. She did need his protection and therefore had no choice but to confide in him...to a point. Genny took a shuddering breath and whispered, "Greer's with child."

"Are you certain?"

"Aye, most certain. The babe will arrive by Samhain."

"Where is she?"

Oh no! That she wouldn't tell him. "I'm taking Greer's place at court for only a short while." She cleared her throat. "For only as long as it takes to prove I am *not* with child, and then I'll take my leave."

Britt looked incredulous. "And what makes you think you'll be allowed to leave at will? If the king says you're to remain at court, you remain. And doubtless in his bed."

"None will wish me to remain." She reached into her pocket and pulled out the packet she'd carefully wrapped in a scrap of oiled cloth. "This will make everyone most happy to see me gone."

Watching her open the packet, he asked, "What is it?"

"A poison nettle. When the time comes, I need only rub its sap on my skin to make large painful boils rise within hours. I'll look like I have pox."

After a moment, he nodded. "They are most protective of their well-being, so 'twill work."

Relieved he thought her plan would work, Genny pocketed the nettle.

Britt rose, then helped her to stand. "And in the meantime? Can you sing, dance? Play the lute or play the whor—"—he cleared his throat—"courtesan?"

Heat infused her cheeks at the very notion of him thinking her *that* kind of woman. "Nay. To *all*."

"Humph." He looked about. "We need go."

Happy he'd ended his inquisition, she pointed to the queen's assassin. "What of him?"

"We're taking him with us."

She shuddered at the thought. "But..."

Before she could give voice to her fears, Britt tossed the bleeding Montre onto her pretty palfrey, then grabbed her by the waist and set her onto his destrier. She shifted sideways. Before she could hook her right leg around the wide pommel, his fingers closed about her ankle.

"Nay, Geneen." His thumb stroked her instep, sending a shiver skittering up her leg. "You need ride astride so we ride as one."

"But—"

"Trust me. Should we be set upon again and I have to spur this horse, you'll thank me."

Reluctantly, she swung her right leg over the destrier's neck, mindful that her skirt rode up and that both her legs were now exposed to God and country up to her knees.

Praise the saints her mother wasn't alive to see it.

Britt slipped into the saddle behind her and picked up the reins.

Within minutes—and despite both trying to keep a modest few inches betwixt them, his groin pressed against her hurdies thanks to his well-worn saddle. Good Lord! Was that long firmness what she thought it was? Aye! 'Twas.

She glared over her shoulder at him.

"My apologies, my lady, but I am a man."

She huffed and faced forward. "So I noticed."

Please, merciful God, keep dear Anton safe.

Seven agonizing days had passed since he'd taken leave to deal with the whore.

Having done all that her mentor and guardian suggested, the time had come for Yolande to carefully pen the lie that would save her life. She dipped her quill in ink, then took a deep, settling breath to steady her shaking hand.

My beloved and honorable husband,

I have a most important and joyful secret to share. I pray for your quick and safe arrival and that my tidings will bring you as much joy as they do your devoted servant and loving wife.

Yolande, Queen of Scots

She dusted and carefully folded the parchment, then lit her sealing-wax candle. When a sizable puddle took shape along the fold, she pressed her signet ring into the red wax. "Evette, I've a task for you."

In the nearby window alcove, her cousin looked up from her reading. "*Oui?*"

Yolande held out her sealed missive. "Please see that this is delivered to His Majesty—and only to him—as soon as possible."

Evette, grinning, came to her side. "I've been wondering how long you could keep your secret to yourself."

Yolande blinked in owl fashion as if caught off guard. "And what secret might that be?"

Evette rolled her eyes. "That you're with child, dearest. Your entire court has suspected such for a while." She slid a sidelong glance to the ladies Campbell and Fraser, who were embroidering before the roaring fire. "In fact, I wouldn't be the least surprised to learn the news has already reached Sir Lyle's ears."

Yolande, suspecting as much, still stiffened. "And to the king's?"

Surely he would have come to her by now had he heard. His doing so was imperative to her truly begetting a child.

Evette shook her head. "Ross is no fool. He knows the king would be affronted learning others in Edinburgh knew of the upcoming blessed event before he did."

Relaxing, Yolande wrapped an arm about her cousin's waist and gave her an affectionate squeezing. "Thank you for reminding me that I'd be foolish to think I could ever keep anything secret here."

Chapter Eight

"Fighting is better than fear." ~ Old Scottish Proverb

The vivid hues of gloaming had been swallowed by the deep soot of night when Britt murmured, "See yon light?"

Gen looked in the direction he pointed and saw a faint yellow flicker against the black mountains. "Aye?"

"'Tis the watch fire on Edinburgh's southern wall."

"Oh." Now that they were within sight of their destination, she wanted nothing more than to turn and run. Around a tight dry throat, she asked, "When will we get there?"

"Depends. If you're tired, we can spend the night at a friend's croft and arrive by afternoon. Or we can keep going and be there by midmorn'."

Middle beginning to quake, she weighed her options. Edinburgh was but a few hours away, and she'd yet to pose her most pressing questions to Britt for fear of the answers. She looked at the waxing three-quarter moon. Her courses were due any day. Saddle sore, she would have welcomed the reprieve of a night on a pallet, but she hadn't the luxury of time. "We should continue on." She then looked behind. Montre, his hands and feet bound and head covered by a feed bag, had slumped forward in the saddle in sleep. Or was he simply feigning? Not knowing but needing answers to her questions, she whispered, "Why have you agreed to help me?"

"I have my reasons."

"I don't doubt that you do, but how can I trust that you won't name me an imposter the moment we pass through Edinburgh's gates? Have me thrown into the dungeon?" The very thought made her blood run cold.

He made a thick sound at the back of his throat, then murmured, "Scotland needs a legitimate heir born of Yolande if we're to keep the peace and keep England at bay. You proving yourself not to be with child, then going away will squelch any rumor that there could be a contender—any other heir but hers."

His response made sense, but dare she risk her life on it? She sighed. Given her circumstances, she really had no choice but to do so.

Now to the question that had been keeping her awake these past two nights. "Are you in love with my sister?" She couldn't blame him if he was. Greer was most accomplished, could charm the birds from the trees when she set her mind to it.

He laughed, a quiet but deep rumble that caused her heart to inexplicably trip. "Nay, my lady. Your sister—and Alexander's obsession with her—have been the bane of my existence for nigh on to a year now."

How curious. "Then why did you kiss me?"

He said naught for a long moment, then said, "Why do you ask?"

Dare she tell him? Aye, she'd best, or she'd never get any sleep. "Because you kissed me as if...well, 'twas not a peck, some meaningless kiss good-bye." There, she'd said it, and the devil take her. His kiss had seared her, had felt as if he'd hated parting from her. That he cared. Not for her, of course. He hadn't known who she—Genny—was at the time.

"If you must know, I kissed *you*, a woman for whom I had no name but whom I've very reluctantly come to admire." Surprised, she twisted in the saddle to better judge if he spoke the truth, and he shrugged. "Truth to tell, I had to know what you tasted like...in the event I never returned."

Oh my. "I would have sworn you wanted nothing more than to strangle me."

He grinned. "That has crossed my mind as well."

She grimaced and faced forward. "I can well imagine it has."

Saddle leather squeaked as he leaned forward, his warmth and decidedly masculine scent washing over her. "So why did you kiss me back?"

She snorted. "I did not."

His breath caressed her ear, setting sparks dancing down her spine. "You most certainly did so."

'Twas true. She had kissed him back. Had melted into his warmth and strength like a wanton, but rather than admit such, she muttered, "You took me by surprise."

Britt pulled the destrier to a sudden halt. "Listen. Someone's coming."

She glanced back at Montre, who now sat upright, alert in the saddle. "He's awake."

Britt nodded. "Likely has been for some time." He untied the rein securing the palfrey to his destrier and handed it to her, whispering, "Quick, lead the gray and Montre into yon trees whilst I see to the rider."

She nodded, not sure what was happening. The moment her feet hit the ground, Britt kicked his destrier forward. She'd barely gotten the growling Montre and her reluctant palfrey into the wood when she heard someone shout, "MacKinnon?"

Grinning, Britt slapped Lyle's back in greeting. "What in God's name are you doing about at this hour?"

Lyle grimaced. "Randy Sandy is on the loose again."

"Heads are going to roll for this."

Lyle waved a dismissive fashion. "You should know better than any that you can't get a man to do his job when his job depends on him not doing it."

Britt made a derisive sound at the back of his throat. 'Twas true. His Majesty did not take being thwarted kindly. Heads tended to roll. Literally. "So what happened this time?"

"One of Her Majesty's ladies arrived with a missive. Not long after, he raced to the stables. Your men were fast on his heels, but his mount was already saddled and waiting whilst theirs were not. When Angus came to me with the news, I went to the solar and discovered the missive on the desk." Lyle grinned. "'Twas from the queen and vague, but I do suspect we may have a loaf in the oven, my friend."

Britt blew through his teeth. "'Bout friggin' time." This would make Geneen's mission and escape all the easier. "So he's off to Kinghorn, then?"

"I suspect so and sent men after him." He looked about and frowned. "I thought you were supposed to be fetching Lady Armstrong back to court."

"Oh shit." How could he have left her alone with Montre for so long? Britt immediately turned his destrier around. "Come."

Rounding the granite outcrop, he shouted, "'Tis safe, my lady. You can come out now."

When Geneen came into view, Lyle murmured, "Good Lord, what happened to her, and who's that tied on the gray?"

"Montre."

Lyle scowled. "Care to explain?"

"As soon as I find out why the bastard is falling off the palfrey."

As Britt dismounted, Lyle murmured, "My lady."

Geneen shoved hair out of her eyes and executed an awkward curtsy. "Good eve—or rather night, my lord."

While Lyle took in her disheveled appearance, Britt pulled Montre upright in the saddle. When his hands came away slick with fresh blood, he jerked the hood from Montre's head. Seeing a broken nose and battered mouth, he looked at Geneen. "What happened to him?" Surely she hadn't taken a club to him?

Geneen, obviously vexed, threw out her arms. "He started to shout for help. I had to do something. So I swatted the gray's rump...and a low-slung branch did the rest."

Britt shook his head. "Remind me never to cross you."

After replacing the hood and checking the ropes binding the again slumbering Montre, he told Lyle, "Yestermornin', he and two of his men attacked us."

"On orders from Yolande?"

"How else? When Montre confronted Lady Armstrong at sword point, he told her she'd become an *inconvenience.*"

"Yolande will not be pleased to find her favorite in our dungeon."

To his left, Geneen muttered, "She should have thought of that before she set him on this mission. He shot Britt!"

Lyle's right eyebrow arched in question. Not knowing if his friend's surprise was due to Gen's use of his Christian name or from the fact that he'd let the bastard get the better of him, Britt, ignoring Lyle, glared at Geneen. "'Tis only a flesh wound."

To his annoyance, she thrust her hands on her hips and glared back. "Do *not* take that tone with me, Britt MacKinnon. 'Tis more, and well you ken it." She then pointed an accusing finger at his bound middle. "There, Sir Lyle, see? The arrow was still imbedded in his side when I found him."

Lyle, his countenance an expressionless mask, looked from him to Geneen, then back again. "Why do I sense there's more here than meets the eye?"

Geneen, huffing and muttering, stomped off toward his destrier, and Britt growled low in his throat. With his gaze locked on his annoying charge, he asked Lyle, "If you think Alexander is headed to Kinghorn, why are you riding south?"

Lyle's gaze returned to Geneen. "On the chance I'm wrong and Alexander is on his way to meet Lady Margaret."

Ah. A prearranged tryst would explain Randy Sandy's horse being saddled. "Very well. Take care. We'll talk at length when you return."

Lyle picked up his reins. "Count on it."

When Lyle disappeared, Geneen slumped against his destrier. "Oh Lord, I thought he'd never leave."

"You did well. But henceforth, could you please refrain from pointing out my shortcomings to my friends?"

"I never pointed out—oh, you mean my telling him you were wounded?" When he continued to glare at her, she heaved a sigh. "Henceforth I shall try to restrain myself."

"Thank you."

"You're most welcome."

Teeth clenched—not believing for a moment she'd be able to keep her pledge—Britt hoisted her up and into the saddle. As he settled in behind her, she asked, "Why did Ross stare so at me? Do you think him suspicious?"

God grant me patience. Of course he's suspicious! Her sister would never have been so outspoken. But there was no point in telling Gen that. She'd only grow agitated and fearful. "He stared because he's accustomed to seeing a perfectly turned out Lady Armstrong...and you are anything but, at the moment."

"I pray you have the right of it."

"I do."

"So who is Lady Margaret? I don't recall Greer mentioning her."

Should he tell her? Aye, better Gen learned the truth now rather than discover it on her own later. God only knew what she'd say. "She's one of the king's mistresses."

"*What?*" She twisted in the saddle to look up at him. "Nay, that cannot be. He's told Greer he loves her."

Ack, poor woman. "I imagine he tells all his mistresses such." Thinking to ease the blow, he added, "But he does hold your sister in the highest regard." Much to Britt and Her Highness's annoyance.

Looking aghast, she asked, "How many mistresses are there?"

"Six, to my knowledge."

"Six." She stared at him for a moment, then faced forward. "I suppose you of all people should know."

Suspecting she'd have gladly killed the messenger had she the wherewithal, he whispered, "I'm truly sorry, Gen." When she remained mute, he tilted her chin so he might better see her face and found her magnificent blue eyes glassy with unshed tears. "Ack, why do you cry?"

"Greer is an even greater fool than I ever imagined."

He brushed a tear from her cheek. "Love can make fools of us all, Gen." It certainly had made a fool of him.

"But he lies...just as our father did. And she couldn't—or wouldn't—see it!"

"Aye, he lies, but you can use that knowledge to your advantage."

Why he felt compelled to comfort her or, for that matter, knew to his bones that he'd do all in his power to keep her from His Majesty's clutches, he couldn't say. She regularly annoyed him beyond speech.

After silently brooding for what felt like hours, she asked, "Do all men lie when they tell a woman they love her?"

"Nay."

"Have *you* ever been in love?"

"Once...a long time ago."

She looked up at him, her brow furrowing. "What happened?"

"She lied."

Then tore my heart out.

They'd been traveling a week and a day. With Edinburg Castle now looming large, Genny tried to focus on her upcoming trials but instead kept ruminating over Britt's admission of having loved and lost ages ago, although why this should be the case, she couldn't for the life of her imagine. She hadn't kenned him at the time. Nor did she ken the woman in question. But still her questions persisted.

How could a woman not return Britt MacKinnon's love? He was exceedingly handsome and stronger than any man Gen had ever beheld. He was intelligent and had proven himself an able warrior. And thank God for that, or she'd be dead. As Captain of the King's Guard, he also had status and the wherewithal to provide for a family. Aye, and he laughed. Something she'd rarely seen men do.

Better yet, even when furious, he kept a civil tongue—and God kenned she tested him often enough to know. Oh, he glared and threatened, but he'd done her no serious harm...although he could have, and had, by his own admission, given serious thought to it.

And he smelled wonderful. And his kiss...

She sighed. Just recalling the feel of his lips on hers made her middle waver and her heart thud erratically. Aye, there had to be something terribly wrong with that woman.

Unable to stand not kenning a moment longer, she asked, "What was her name?"

"Who?"

"The woman who lied to you."

"Why do you ask?"

She decided to be honest. "So I might kick her in the shins should our paths cross...on your behalf, of course."

He brushed a loose strand from her forehead and kissed her temple, sending warmth coursing through her limbs. "I thank you for the thought, Gen, but you shan't have chance to meet."

"Then what harm is there in you telling me her name?" She'd have no peace until she kenned at least that much.

He was quiet for a long moment, then muttered, "Cassandra."

Hmm, a witch named Cassandra. "Thank you."

"Enough about her. Tell me again how you proceed to the queen's apartments."

They'd entered Edinburgh, were now trotting toward the steep roadway which led to the formidable castle. To her right and left stood dozens upon dozens of stone and plaster and wattle cottages. Ahead, some structures were an amazing three stories high, just as Greer had described. Underfoot scampered stray pullets and tatter-eared dogs with tails tucked betwixt their legs. To her right, a caged goose honked in alarm at their quick passing. A black-as-night cat eyed them from atop a stack of ale casks. Cows lowed in plaintive fashion, and doors slammed. Metal screeched, and an unseen woman keened, "God preserve us!" Cattle dung made the going slick, and she wished Britt would slow before his destrier ran over someone or lost its footing, but then the stench of so much life and death in one place was overwhelming, so she said naught.

"Gen, have you forgotten already?"

"Forgive me. 'Tis just so much here to take in all at once." Ahead, a door opened, and three giggling bairns spilled into the roadway. "I enter the great hall, walk its length, then climb the stairs I'll find behind a hunt tapestry. On the third level, I go through the doorway to my left. Then through that chamber and into the next, and I'm there. But won't you be accompanying me?"

"Nay, I've been long gone and must tend to my duties."

"And the king? When can I expect to be summoned?"

"I've no way of kenning how long he'll remain at Kinghorn with the queen, but the moment he returns, I'll bring Montre's treachery to his attention. Only after he's dealt with that problem will he think to summon you."

The saints preserve her. Their battle of wits was about to begin. But then she had months of pent-up fury and new insight into Alexander's true character as weapons. No man in his right mind would dare try to bed an irate mistress who kenned all that she now did. Not if he had hopes of keeping his poke of sweetmeats intact.

"We're here."

Genny looked about. Sometime during her ruminations, Britt had veered off what he called the high road, and they'd entered a short mews which ended at a large stone-faced building and stable. The place was a shambles, yard unkempt, shutters listing. "Where are we?"

"'Tis the hostel of a discreet friend."

"And why are we here?" Good heavens, even this place's cat had a broken tail.

"The castle walls have ears." He dismounted, reached for her waist and set her on her feet. "Here the king can tend to Montre in privacy, should he choose, and none will be any the wiser."

He unleashed their captive and hefted him onto his shoulder. Montre, apparently awake and listening, suddenly kicked, driving a knee into Britt's injured side.

"God's teeth!"

As Genny gasped, Britt dug his fingers into Montre's thighs, then heaved, whereupon their captive fell, headfirst, onto hard-packed earth and went limp.

Genny stared at Britt's side, praying she'd not find fresh blood. "Are you all right?"

"I'm fine." Britt grabbed Montre by the ankles. "Knock on the door and roust Angus MacLean whilst I haul this bastard into the stable."

Still not sure what on earth Britt was about, Genny knocked on the weathered hostel door. Were it up to her, Montre would be hanging from a tree, and that would be the end of that.

Before she could raise her hand to knock again, the door whipped opened and a mop-headed woman with bright red cheeks stuck her head out. Squinting against the sunshine, she asked, "Aye, what do you want?"

"Good morn', mistress. Sir Britt MacKinnon wishes to speak with Sir Angus."

"Now 'tis *Sir* Angus, is it?" She laughed in deep, throaty fashion before pulling back into the cottage and shouting, "Wake you, Angus! MacKinnon needs you." A gravelly voice grumbled in response, and the woman, grinning, stepped out into the sunshine, wearing naught but a scant gauze tunic of red, which did naught to mask her ample breasts and thighs to any who cared to look. Which Genny certainly did not, thank you very much. Dear God above. The woman was a whore.

"So where's that handsome devil?" The woman looked about. "Britt? Yoo-hoo, Britt!"

She calls him by his Christian name? How so? What was this...this...sloth to him—a knight of girth and sword? Shocked speechless, Genny reluctantly pointed to the stable. The woman, grinning, hastily fluffed her hair *and* her breasts, then, hips swaying, headed for the stable. Outraged for reasons she cared not to think about, to depths she dared not plunge, Genny stomped after her.

Inside the stable, she came to an abrupt halt, finding only a half dozen horses. As her eyes adjusted to the mottled light streaming through the wall slats, she listened. Hearing Britt's unmistakable laugh and then a feminine giggle, she strode the length of the barn and found naught but a back wall lined with casks.

Now where could they have gone? Hands on her hips, she surveyed the stalls. This didn't make sense.

Behind her, a man said, "And who might you be?"

Genny, a hand at her throat, spun and blinked at the barrel-chested man. "Lady Armstrong, friend of Sir Britt MacKinnon."

"*Humph.* I've heard tell of you."

Not kenning if that was good or bad but suspecting the latter from the man's narrow-eyed countenance, Genny murmured, "Sir Britt came in here, as did your lady, but I can't find either of them."

The man's gaze shifted to Genny's breasts as he shouted, "MacKinnon, the lady wants you!"

Before she could reprimand him for leering, two rows of casks piled shoulder-high at her back moved as one. Startled, she jumped back. Seeing Britt emerge, she blew through her teeth. As the whore followed, Genny muttered, "A secret room. How clever."

But why would a hosteller need such? And what had these two been *doing* in the room that had both of them laughing in such fashion? Naught good, of that she was sure, given the woman's dress and Britt's red-tinged ears.

Humph!

Not sure what she expected but fearing she'd find a pallet, she peered through the opening and saw several sets of shackles and yards of chain hanging from thick timbers. In the middle, she spied Montre, his battered face now uncovered, his arms secured behind a center post. Her annoyance vanished at the sight, and she shuddered. There was no need to ask if the room had been used as a prison on other occasions. Dark splatters mottled the walls and posts.

Britt placed a hand at her waist. "Lady Armstrong, you've met Hildy. May I introduce Angus MacLean, a trusted acquaintance of many years and owner of this fine establishment."

She pulled her gaze from the chamber of horrors and managed to muster a smile and quick curtsy for the hosteller. "'Tis a pleasure." Lord, lies were all but tripping off her tongue of late.

"My lady." The hosteller tugged his forelock, then turned his attention to Britt. "How long will his nibs be with us?"

Britt shrugged. "Depends on the king. A week at most."

Frowning, MacLean shoved the secret door closed and then kicked hay before it, masking the drag marks. "You've not heard, then?"

Britt scowled in turn. "Heard what?"

"I'm sorry to be the one to tell you, but the king is dead, MacKinnon. Went over the cliff near Kinghorn, they say."

"Nay!" Genny gasped for air as her knees buckled.

Chapter Nine

"Three that come unbidden—love, jealousy and fear."
~ Old Scottish Proverb

Nay, his king could not be dead. Alexander was only four and forty and an excellent horseman.

Realizing Genny was sliding to her knees, Britt wrapped a tight arm about her shoulders and hauled her upright. Why did she keen? She felt no love for the man. If she felt anything, 'twas most likely loathing.

Unable to think with his canny friend eyeing him, Britt signaled to MacLean to leave. Without a word, his friend grabbed Hildy by the arm and led her into the hostel.

The moment the door closed, Genny sobbed, "Oh dear Lord, Britt. What are we going to do? Greer's babe is now an heir. An heir! Dear God above and the saints preserve him. He'll never be safe now."

Britt pulled Genny into his arms. Brushing the tears from her cheeks, he whispered, "Nay, you're here to prove there is *no* bairn for others to fear."

"But...but how? Without the king's protection, how can I escape the queen's vengeance until such time as I do prove it? She's already tried to kill me—Greer—once and did so knowing she risked Alexander's wrath. What's to stop her now?"

A problem to be sure. "I vowed to keep you safe, and I shall."

She pushed off his chest and, wringing her hands, began to pace. "You'll have no choice but to do her bidding, and if she bids me imprisoned—"

"Genny, stop." When she did, he forced a smile. "Do you trust me?"

"Aye, I suppose."

"You *suppose?*" He cursed in vivid French, his native tongue being most lacking at moments like these.

Here he'd lost control of his life sometime during the night when his careless king had charged over a precipice and all because of her, and she supposed she trusted him? "Christ's blood, woman! If it weren't for me, you'd be under the sod of truth as we speak! Two men are dead, Genny, at *my* hand. Not yours. *Mine.*"

"Augh, 'tis true. I'm sorry, so, so sorry... I didn't mean—" A wretched sob shook her.

Oh God, he was acting a wretched ass taking his anger out on her. He pulled her into his arms. Aye, he'd lost his king and would ready for war, but she'd lost not only her king but now feared the loss of her sister and the babe. "Nay, Genny, I'm the one who should be sorry. Hush now."

In hopes of reassuring her, of needing comfort himself, he hooked a finger beneath her chin. Her lovely face, now mottled red, lifted, and he kissed her as he'd wanted to do since kissing her behind the boulders but out of necessity had sworn never to do again. He hadn't the right.

He wasn't free.

As his tongue swept past her full, sweet lips and into the warm confines of her mouth, she groaned. His heart soared. *Aye, lass, you ken that I need reassurance as well, don't you? To know that all is not lost. That the sun shall rise on the morrow. That men and women will eventually cease their weeping and new lives will again be born. That my beloved Scotland will endure this tragedy.*

With his arms about her, he staggered back a step and hit a wall. His hands swept down her lithe back, settling on fine hurdies. He pressed her hips so she might feel his bone-deep need for her through her layers of skirt. As if in answer, she groaned in that soft purr that was hers alone.

Dear God, why hadn't I met you years ago? Had he, his life would have been ever so different.

Reluctantly, he ended the kiss and whispered, "Your sister and her bairn will be safe. We have Alexander's granddaughter, the infant Margaret, Princess of Norway."

She sniffled as she traced his lips with a shaking finger. "Aye, but the infant is betrothed to England's Prince Edward. Our people would rather Greer's bastard than let Scotland fall into English hands—some will kill her to get him—and well we both ken it."

Aye, civil unrest could be but a heartbeat away, but then her sister's babe wasn't the only possible bastard. Alexander had been of an age where there could well be fully grown adult males crawling out of the woodpile anxious to lay claim. He heaved a sigh, reluctant to let his arms fall from her, but did and straightened. "We need go."

Finding the castle gate open but the portcullis down, Britt cursed, then yelled up to the sentry, "'Tis MacKinnon! Raise the gate and be quick about it!"

"Oh, aye, my lord."

Immediately, shouted orders were issued, gears ground, and the huge spikes began to rise. Britt kicked his mount forward, and Genny, on her gray, stiffened at his side as they entered the bailey and were surrounded by dozens of heavily armed men. He could only imagine her distress as the gate ground down, trapping her within Edinburgh's massive walls.

He quickly dismounted and reached for her waist. "'Twill be all right. Just hie to the queen's apartment and stay there until I come to you."

He waited until Genny made it safely into the keep before turning his attention to his squire, whose hands already gripped Britt's mount's reins. "How go you, Ian?"

"They brought in the king this morning." Tears filled the lad's eyes. "He's dead, sire."

Britt, still not able to believe it himself, patted Ian's bony shoulder as he scoured the bailey for his second in command. "We've weathered worse, lad, and will do so again. Now, can you tell me where I might find Tall Angus?"

Ian pointed toward the armory. "Yon."

Above him, a guard shouted to those manning the gate, "Ross coming!"

A moment later, Lyle rode in, he and his mount looking worse for wear. He dismounted, asked his squire a question, then, scowling, strode toward Britt. "Glad you're back."

"What the hell happened?" Britt's hands itched to throttle someone.

"I have no notion beyond what I told you earlier. He received the queen's missive, then rode hell-bent for Kinghorn. When his guards reached the queen and learned His Majesty never arrived, they rode back, and that's when one of the guards spotted His Majesty's mount floating in the surf. The rest you know."

Thundering hooves drew their attention to the gate once again. Spying the Campbell and Douglas chiefs riding in with their entourage, Britt blew through his teeth. "Bad news travels fast."

"I had no choice but to send word out immediately. The rest of the Privy Council should arrive fast enough."

God help them all. "And the queen?"

Lyle motioned for Britt to follow him into the keep. "She's been notified."

"How did she take the news?"

"She fainted dead away, according to the messenger. God only knows when she'll be well enough to travel."

They took the keep's winding stairs two at a time. Entering the great hall and finding it unearthly quiet, Britt whispered, "Where is His Majesty now?"

"In the royal solar. The women are tending to the body."

The body.

Britt shuddered as he looked around the hall, finding men whispering together in corners while couples held each other, many weeping.

This cannot be happening!

Ross tapped his arm to get his attention. "The Privy Council will go into session as soon as the rest of the representatives arrive. To ensure none take it into their heads to take control, I need be here, so I need ask that you go over the route His Majesty took. If 'twas murder, we need know so we can prosecute the bastard."

"I shall, as soon as I pay my respects." And as soon as he checked on Genny.

Britt raced to the king's solar, then hesitated in the open doorway. His king, a white shroud drawn up to his naked waist, gold sovereigns on his eyes, a silver salver overflowing with salt at his feet, lay in unnatural stillness on the massive bed. Britt took a deep breath, anguish roiling in his belly. The small hope he'd been secretly harboring, that his king's death was all just a dreadful mistake, died. He approached the bed on shaking legs, tears burning at the back of his throat. Lord have mercy. Had he not spent a decade in Alexander's constant company, Britt would not have recognized the man to whom he'd sworn fealty. His king's handsome countenance had been all but destroyed by rock and pounding surf, his once muscular body was now bloated and fish-belly white.

He placed his hand over Alexander's, something he would never have dared do in life. Head bowed, tears flowing, he choked out, "Why, sire? Why did you not wait for your guards? Why?"

Yolande, flanked by a dozen guards bearing royal standards snapping in the wind above and around her, shuddered passing through the gates of Edinburgh Castle. She would now be tested as never before. Within lay her dead husband and king.

And the fault was hers.

Had she not been so impatient to get him in her bed, had she just waited, sent the missive in the morning when Alexander would have had ample light as he traveled the road to Kinghorn to be with her...

But no, she'd been so anxious to set her and Anton's plan in motion, she'd sent it after midday.

Only adding to her fear was not knowing whether or not Alexander had left her missive where others might find it or if he'd had it on him when he fell over the cliff. If the former was the case, then the Privy Council would be well within their rights to blame her for Alexander's demise. If the latter be the case, then her missive was likely destroyed by the sea, and she'd be safe...at least for a while.

She could maintain her lie—of being with child—for only so long before others noted she was not enlarging as she ought. She'd be discovered.

Please, dear God, please let me find Anton within these formidable walls.

She needed his advice on what to do next, else she find herself cast out without so much as a coin or place to go.

"Your Highness?"

She looked down to find a guard waiting to help her dismount. Another was already at her mount's head, his hand fisted about the bridle. All around her, somber men stirred, most looking in her direction and bowing.

How long would that last?

"The queen!" echoed about the bailey. Doors were thrown wide before her, and she strode into Edinburgh's great hall, where eerie quiet engulfed her.

"Your Highness." Her husband's trusted advisor Ross bowed before her, then murmured, "My condolences, Your Highness. How may I be of assistance?"

"Where is Monsieur Montre?" Surely he'd heard her entourage arrive.

"He has yet to return, Your Majesty."

"I see." She looked about, at a total loss as to what to do next. What was expected of her? What would keep her safe among these heathens?

Holding out his arm, Ross asked, "May I escort you to the king, Your Highness?"

"Yes, thank you." Of course a grieving widow and mother-to-be would wish to see her husband. What on earth was the matter with her?

She placed a shaking hand on Ross's thick-boned wrist. On the second landing, her steps faltered. "Sir Lyle, what happens next?" When he frowned in confusion, she clarified, "Within Scotland."

"Ah." He took a deep breath. "The Privy Council will convene."

Fearing the answer but having to know, she said, "To what end?"

"They must make arrangements for the funeral." He paused, cleared his throat, then said, "They shall then summon the Princess of Norway, our new ruler, home."

Upon which time Edward of England would get his fondest wish. She, proven barren and having failed her king—and France—would then be sent packing with no hope of her ever again making an advantageous marriage.

She clenched her skirts in a sweaty fist and resumed her climb up the winding staircase. Had Alexander not shown her missive to anyone? Or had he been waiting to speak with her first? She was certain Ross's spies within her court had passed the rumor that she thought herself with child. Should she confirm it and declare herself with child right now, before they could send her away?

Dear God, please send Anton to me. I should not be making these decisions alone.

And what if Anton failed in his mission? What if MacKinnon, sensing danger, took a circuitous route and arrived with a bulging Lady Armstrong, months grown with child? All within these walls knew without doubt that the whore had occupied Alexander's bed and his alone for months prior to his demise. And worse, they all knew he'd summoned the bitch back. She shuddered, her decision made.

Doing her best to appear confused, she asked, "But why would they so inconvenience Princess Margaret when I will deliver them a king...or mayhap a queen...in six moons' time?"

"Your Highness is confirming she is with child?"

"I am."

Looking both pleased and greatly relieved, Ross bowed. "God's blessings upon you and the babe, Your Highness."

She smiled her thanks, not daring to say more. The lie would guarantee her shelter and privilege for a small time, at least. How she would appear to be growing or squelch rumors she was barren once the truth was known, she dared not ponder. Her father would want naught to do with her—

"Your Highness?"

She started and looked about, surprised to find herself in the royal solar, and before her, her dead husband, still as stone, dressed in his finest regalia and surrounded by wavering candles. To the right of his massive bed knelt the archbishop; to the left knelt three weeping women she presumed had prepared her husband for burial. She took a steadying breath. "I wish privacy with my husband."

"Of course, Your Highness." Ross, doubtless anxious to inform the Privy Council of the impending birth, immediately cleared the room and closed the door behind him, leaving her alone with the man who only five months earlier had pledge his troth and fidelity to her only to break his word within days.

Throat tight with pent-up fury and fear, she crossed to the bed. Staring at his battered features, she whispered, "Bad enough that you humiliated me with your dalliances, left me with barely a kind word to ponder after your passing, but you left your people with naught but a babe for protection. But what I find most egregious of all is that your seed now grows not in me, your rightful wife and queen, but in *her*. For this alone, I hope you, Alexander, rot in hell."

Tears streaming, she took a deep, shuddering breath, then, shoulders back, strode from the room.

As she crossed the threshold into her apartment, Evette, cheeks pale and eyes scarlet, rushed to greet her. "Your Highness, the Armstrong woman awaits within."

The floor moved beneath Yolande as bile rose in her throat. "But how—"

Evette, alarmed, grabbed her elbow, steadying her. "MacKinnon apparently brought her in before midday."

"And Anton?"

"He has yet to arrive, Highness."

Of course not. Hadn't Ross just said so, and had Anton arrived, Armstrong most certainly would not have. "Where is MacKinnon now?"

"He went to the site from which...where...His Majesty fell."

At least the fates had been kind in one aspect. She could banish the woman to the bowels of the keep, where she would hopefully die of starvation in short order without interference. "Summon LeBlanc and Duval to me." Anton's wiliest guards would do her bidding without question.

Evette bit her lower lip. "But LeBlanc went with Monsieur Montre, my queen."

"Then summon Duval, and with him, his most trusted guard."

"Yes, Your Highness." Evette all but threw Yolande's hooded cloak and gloves at a brittle-looking maid hovering in the corner and rushed out.

Yolande, pulse thudding in her ears, strode into her solar and found the room frigid despite a blazing fire. Her ladies-in-waiting were scattered about, the Scots red-eyed, the rest pale and obviously anxious. As they dropped into deep curtsies before her, Yolande's gaze settled on Greer Armstrong, curtsying in isolation by the window.

"You may rise."

Her French ladies straightened, murmuring their condolences yet again. Yolande paid little heed, instead casting a surreptitious glance at Armstrong's middle. Seeing no sign of a babe, she thanked God. When at last her ladies fell silent, she thanked them and murmured, "I am quite exhausted. Please take your leave so I might rest alone for a while." As they hurried to the door, she said, "Lady Armstrong."

The whore stopped in midstride. "Yes, Your Highness?"

"Remain. We wish a word with you."

Armstrong paled but remained rooted in place. When the door thudded closed, Yolande settled before the fire to contemplate her rival and the heir that should rightfully be hers.

Why not in me, Lord? Why? I grant you Armstrong is sturdier of build and some might say handsomer than I, but 'tis I, Yolande de Dreux, who prayed, begged for his child. Armstrong is naught but an ill-educated whore. She was naught to him but one more mare within his herd, of no more interest to him than any broodmare—

Oh my word. Why could this whore not act as *her* broodmare?

Could she not spirit Armstrong away from Edinburgh, then keep her in hiding until such time as the infant came, and whereupon she could then claim to have birthed the babe herself? She'd told Ross she would give birth in September, but babes were notorious for coming both early and late.

What harm could there be? The babe *was* Alexander's, after all. Would carry his lineage. And by claiming the whore's babe as her own, she would not only be doing the infant a service—provide it with legitimacy—but she would secure her own future by doing what no whore ever could. She could instill within him faith and a moral compass, would provide him with political insight and guidance, and in the process give Scotland what it most desperately needed. A rightful heir.

As for the two within these walls who suspected Armstrong was with child, she had no doubt Anton would deal with them swiftly upon his return. And then with Armstrong after the infant's birth.

A perfect plan but for the one thing that pricked her conscience. She believed in love. Had hoped to love her husband as her mother did her father, but they'd not had time to form a true attachment before his passing. Needing to know if this woman had bonded, had felt for Alexander that which she had so longed for when she'd learned she was to wed, she asked, "Why do we see no grief about your countenance, Lady Armstrong? Did you not love Alexander at all?"

Armstrong opened her mouth as if to speak, then, turning scarlet, clamped it shut. Yolande sighed. She had her answer. The whore had not only played her but Alexander for a fool. Too bad. She might have forgiven her the affair—instructed Anton to make Armstrong's death a swift and painless one—had she loved him, but obviously, such was not the case.

Her guards entered. She acknowledged them with a nod and then grinned at Armstrong. "Do you not find it ironic that you shall disappear by the very means by which you deceived me and my husband?" Without waiting for an answer, she said to her guards, "Seize her. When you have her secured below, bring me the key."

Chapter Ten

"Between denial and want." ~ Old Scottish Proverb

Fingers pressed to her swollen lips where Duval had clamped his calloused hand as he hauled her kicking and screaming down a dark staircase, Genny tried in vain to suppress her rising panic. Standing in the middle of her eight-by-eight foot cell, all she could see were damp stone walls, her only light coming through the barred, deep-set aperture many feet above her.

Oh dear God!

Something scurried in the corner to her right. Yelping, she edged away from the sound only to trip on a rank mound of straw in the corner. Imagining all manner of filth and vermin within the pallet, bile rising in her throat, she lifted her skirts and stumbled back.

Did they mean to let her die here? Or did her queen intend to hang her? *Dear Lord, send Britt to me.*

But what if they told Britt she left of her own accord? Would he believe them? Please, dear Lord, no. He alone kenned the truth.

Light suddenly pierced the gloom from a window no bigger than a man's palm imbedded in the door. As quickly as the blessed lamplight arrived, it disappeared, blocked by a man peering in. "Stand back!"

Terrified she was about to be shackled, Genny thrust her hands behind her and reluctantly backed up. Was he alone? Could she dart past him?

The moment she touched the rear wall, the door opened and a dark figure filled the doorway. "Here."

The satchel containing Greer's possessions landed at her feet. When he started to close the door, Genny darted forward. "Wait! You can't leave me here!"

The door slammed in her face, and the guard again peered in through the window. "Behave and you'll see the light of day. Make trouble and you die here."

"But I did nothing wrong. Please, I must see—"

The little window shut. Thrown again into darkness, she slammed her fists against the door. "Britt... You must tell Britt where I am."

He'd promised to keep her safe and had sealed the promise with a kiss just before leaving. Surely he meant to keep his word. Panting, she looked about her cell as receding footsteps echoed in the outside hall. Aye, she must think only of Britt, of his lips so sure on her own, of the feel of his hand against the small of her back, on the way his features softened and light danced in his eyes whenever she'd caught him off guard and he'd laughed. Not on those beady eyes watching her from the corner of this frightful pit. She shuddered. He would come.

The meager light within her cell slowly waned as she fought to stay upright, to believe. Too soon her cell was cast into deeper shadow as day turned to gloaming. Unable to deny the truth any longer, her legs exhausted and numb, she collapsed to the stone floor, the tears she'd been holding at bay for so long spilling, running hot down her cold cheeks.

Britt MacKinnon had known all along what would befall her. Why else would the heated look he'd given her before kissing her have been replaced by one of such profound sadness when he'd broken off the kiss and said good-bye?

She was as great a fool as Greer.

The moon rode high in the sky by the time Britt handed over his mount to his squire. With legs feeling like lead, he dragged up the stairs, then cursed, finding every bench occupied in Edinburgh's great hall and Lyle in a heated discussion with the Campbell. Resigning himself to waiting before he could seek out Gen, then dine, he hailed a passing serving lass. "Ale when you have a moment, lass."

Genny had done well to mask her fright when he'd left her hours ago, but not so well that he hadn't noticed the slight trembling of her hands when he'd brought them to his lips. Hopefully by now she'd put some of her fears to rest and made herself comfortable within the queen's apartment. He had, after all, promised to keep her safe until she could complete her mission, and so he would. The thought of her disappearing from his life after that—of his never seeing her dimpled smile or hearing her husky laugh again—caused an inexplicable tightening in his chest, and he pushed the thought away. Better he should be grateful for her presence now and take this gift one day at a time. That was all he could do, since Cassandra had yet to have had the good graces to die.

Someone tapped his elbow. "Here, m'lord."

Britt managed a smile for the harried serving lass holding out a tankard. He muttered his thanks, then downed its contents in long, lusty swallows. When he came up for air, he found Ross striding toward him. When Ross came abreast, Britt muttered, "I see the rats have come out of the woodwork."

"Aye, and more's to come." Ross leaned closer. "Did you find any evidence that His Majesty's fall was *not* an accident?"

"There were too many hoof prints near the ledge to discern if a rider had forced him over. By the time we snared his mount and hauled it up the cliff, it was too battered to know what, if anything, had wounded it or if it had simply taken a misstep, gone over of its own volition."

Looking somewhat relieved, Ross murmured, "Then we do no harm in telling all it *was* an accident. Only the Lord knows what might have ensued had you found solid evidence of foul play."

Britt could well imagine. "When will the Privy Council convene?"

"They're still waiting on Comyn, the Southerland, and a few others, but good news awaits them. Yolande has declared herself with child."

"Praise God." His countrymen should be greatly relieved, as would Gen. "Any notion of who they'll select to serve as regent?"

Ross snorted in derisive fashion. "None, and them coming to a consensus will take some time." A clamor arose. They looked left and found Alexander Comyn, Earl of Buchan, constable and justiciar of Scotland, entering the hall, followed by a large entourage. Lyle heaved a sigh. "I hate doing this to you, but I have need of your chamber again."

"As you lust." Britt had been kicked to the hall not but five months ago, thanks to the royal wedding. "I'll bed down at MacLean's. I need to check on Montre anyway."

At the mention of the queen's henchman, Lyle turned his full attention back to Britt. "Yes. And what, pray tell, goes on between you and the Armstrong wench? And don't tell me naught, for I read it on both your countenances when we met on the road."

"Truthfully, I wish I—"

A flash of blue near the stairwell caught Britt's eye. His heart nearly stopped seeing Yolande de Dreux and her court gliding into the hall. "When did Her Highness arrive?" And where was Genny?

"She arrived at midday. Why?"

Good God almighty. He must have been at the bottom of the cliff when her entourage rode past. "Excuse me." Without another word, his thoughts only on Genny, Britt strode to the stairs, waving off those who tried to draw him into conversation.

Reaching the queen's chamber, he nodded to the man standing guard. "Sir Britt to see Lady Armstrong."

The Frenchman shrugged. "She is not here."

Cursing under his breath, a hand grasping the hilt of his side sword, Britt shouldered past the shorter man. Finding the presence chamber vacant, he strode into the solar, his gaze raking every corner in search of Genny.

Where in hell could she be? He'd been very specific when he told her not to leave this chamber until he came for her.

Had she lost her courage when Yolande arrived and gone into hiding? Mayhap taken refuge in his chamber? Aye, that made sense, and any of the maids could have pointed her in the right direction.

He bolted around the corner only to find his chamber door open and his room's only occupant a maid. "Have you seen Lady Armstrong, lass?"

"Aye, this morn'."

"You've not seen her since?"

"Nay, though she was behaving most oddly for the bit that I did see her."

The hairs on his neck rose. "How so?"

The lass bit into her lower lip. "The woman usually primps the better part of a day, but this morn' she was in and out of her hip bath, hair whipped into a simple braid and gowned as fast as you please. And all with a 'thank you kindly' at the end." As if befuddled, the lass shook her head. "As I said, 'twas most odd for one usually as slow as snails."

Relieved to learn only Genny's hasty ablutions had caused the lass concern, Britt unlock the carved chest at the foot of his bed. Going about the room, he picked up Genny's bow and quiver, which he'd dropped in a corner, scooped up the few precious books he owned from the windowsill and tossed them along with his spare boots atop his clothing and relocked the chest. Satisfied he'd emptied the room of valuables, he said, "Please ask for my squire to carry this to the bailey."

He bid the lass good day and worked his way down the keep, checking each chamber, cubby and garderobe without catching sight of Genny. After checking the kitchen, awash with the scents of roasting meat, baking bread and boiling ham being readied for His Majesty's wake, he strode into the garden and, hands fisted on hips, looked about. To his right, two keening crones stood before Saint Margaret's chapel splashing whitewash—symbolic tears of a people in mourning—on its heavily carved doors. Soon slivers of hammered silver would be imbedded in the cracks where the tears from the more affluent would flicker in the sunlight. Without warning, the image of another, far more distant and simple chapel door, sparkling like a crown in the early glow of dawn, filled his field of vision. And beyond the door, a wee pine...

Tears sprang to his eyes, burned at the back of his throat. Dear God, no more. He'd thought he'd put this pain finally to rest.

He abruptly turned and tripped over one of the king's wolfhounds, kicked from the keep lest evil spirits embody them and steal the king's soul.

He gave himself a good shake. He had to focus on the living, not on the dead. On finding Genny. So, where the hell could she be?

Ah! The stable. Why hadn't he thought of it earlier? The woman had an unnatural affection for beasts and in particular that wee doe-eyed palfrey she'd ridden in on.

He wove his way through the torch-lit chaos that was now the upper and lower wards to the stable, where he grabbed a passing groom by the arm. "Have you seen Lady Armstrong?"

The lad looked up in alarm. "Been too busy with these mounts to notice a lady, m'lord."

"*Humph.*" Britt strode down the line of tethered destriers, some with sides still heaving, steam rising like ghosts off their slathered backs and haunches. Finding the gray sedately munching in a small enclosure but no Genny, he surveyed the bailey once again. Lord, she wouldn't have been so foolish as to just walk out alone, would she? Given what he knew of her, aye, she just might.

At the gatehouse, he asked his sentries, "Has Lady Armstrong passed?"

When both shook their heads, Britt huffed in exasperation. At least she was still within these walls. Well, there was no hope for it. He would have to ask the conniving witch where her lady-in-waiting might be found.

In the great hall, he bowed before the queen consort, who appeared hollow-eyed and tired. When she finally deigned to acknowledge his presence, he murmured, "My deepest condolences, Your Majesty."

"Thank you."

"I need ask where I might find Lady Armstrong."

She arched a thinly plucked eyebrow. "Her services are no longer needed."

Britt's breath caught in his chest. "She's been dismissed?"

"You of all people should understand why." She grinned without humor and turned her attention to John, Earl of Atholl, who stood not a foot from her elbow.

What the bloody—?

"When was this, Your Majesty?"

Yolande's exchange with the earl ceased for only a heartbeat—long enough for Britt to understand she'd heard his question—before resuming without so much as a glance in his direction. Jaw muscles twitching at being so summarily dismissed, Britt bowed and backed away.

If some harm had come to Genny—

He scoured the hall's perimeter, looking into every shadow, then bolted up the stairs, taking them two at a time before coming to a stop before the king's bedchamber, the only room he had ignored during his earlier search.

As he stood on the threshold—the door had been purposely left open so the king's soul might easily escape when it was wont to—he took a deep breath, readying himself again for the pain of seeing his once-vibrant liege still as stone. And despite the preparation, his breath still caught in his chest at the sight.

He pulled his gaze away and looked about the darkened chamber, praying he would find Genny lurking in a corner but finding only two of his most trusted guards. He asked, "Have either of you seen Lady Armstrong?"

When both shook their heads, he glanced again at Alexander and made the sign of the cross. He had only one place left to search.

Britt pulled one of the two lit torches from its bracket and crossed the room, where he removed the pin securing the secret panel. As the narrow door swung open, exposing the narrow escape route into the bowels of the keep, he said, "Should anyone ask, you've not seen me."

Under ordinary circumstances, a lady-in-waiting had no reason to know about the passage, but then Greer Armstrong had been the king's mistress, had used the passage to move unnoticed betwixt the queen's chambers and the king's. And what Greer knew, so likely did Genny.

Britt thrust the torch into the gaping blackness, his hope of finding her huddled on the narrow plank walkway betwixt the two royal chambers dissolving, seeing it vacant. His hope then sprang back to life, seeing a faint glow at the bottom of the stairs where the door stood ajar and where a few stools, a table and a pallet could be found for a guard on those rare occasions when a prisoner needed a constant watch...or their king was on the prowl. At the moment, there was no reason for the lower chamber to be lit. The cells were empty, their last prisoner having been found guilty of murder, then unceremoniously tossed over the castle mount wall, where he fell to his death in the moat some four hundred feet below.

Behind him, MacDougall, the larger of the two guards posted in the room with the king's body, murmured, "Be careful on yon stairs."

Britt nodded. "Close the door behind me, but do not lock it."

The steep stone steps, only a palm's width in depth, appeared to undulate under the torchlight dancing about the close walls and sloping ceiling. Knowing his shoulders were broader than the pathway, Britt twisted sideways and made his way down.

At the bottom, he pushed wide the door. "Damn it." The passage was vacant. He pulled on the door to the central staircase and found it locked as it should be. So she hadn't gone that way. Bile churned in his gut. "So where the hell are you, Geneen Armstrong?"

As his voice echoed down the damp stone walls, he heard a soft thud. Then another.

"Genny?" *Please God, don't let the thudding be my imagination.*

Thinking she might have taken refuge in a cell, he pulled on the iron ring on the first cell. Rusty hinges screeched as he jerked the thick door open. Finding the cell empty, he raced to the next. "Genny!"

"Hello?" The voice, decidedly female, was little more than a muffled croak.

He ran to the last cell. "Genny!"

Hands beat on the door. "Help!"

Please, St. Bride, let her be unharmed. He jerked on the iron ring. Locked! Cursing, he turned to fetch the key and saw that the peg where the key usually hung was empty. He slid the wooden cover from the viewing window and peered into the cell, blocking out what little light he had. "Genny?"

"Britt! Thank God. Please let me out."

"I would, but the key's gone."

Ignoring that important detail, she said, "You came back."

"How could you doubt I would?" His fingers reached through the bars for her. "Woman, I've been ill with worry. Come closer so I might touch you, know that you're all right."

She reached through the bars. He closed his fingers over hers and was alarmed to find them cold.

"I'm well," she told him, "but I've been so frightened. The queen ordered me seized. They grabbed me—"

The queen. His fingers squeezed hers. "You can tell me the details after I get you out of here. Do you know which guard has the key?"

"The queen told the guards to bring it to her."

He swore under his breath. Taking the key from a guard would have presented no problem. Taking it from Yolande, however...

"Do you have food and drink?"

"Nay, but why will I need such now that you've found me?"

He had no choice but to tell her the truth. "It may take some time to get you out of here." He would have to go before the Privy Council, which had yet to convene, but then the constable and justiciar of Scotland was above stairs.

She shook her head in vehement fashion. *"Nay,* please, you can't leave me here."

"Hush, *a ghraidh.* I know you're frightened, but take heart. You're a Scot and innocent of any crime. Comyn will hear me out. The queen will have no choice but to hand over the key."

Blue eyes still wide with alarm, she asked, "How long might this take?" She turned from the wee window to look behind her and mutter, "The rats..."

"Mayhap an hour or two. 'Tis all." An hour that would likely feel like a lifetime for her.

She rose higher and pressed her cheek to their entangled fingers. "You've been naught but kind and brave. I'm so sorry."

He frowned in confusion. "For what?"

She nibbled on her lower lip. "I thought...nay, I feared that you kenned what might befall me but knew you could do naught when you kissed me good-bye. You'd looked so forlorn, and then this happened, and being locked away in the dark..."

"How can you even think—" He took a deep breath. *"Tha gradh agam thu."*

"What? I don't understand."

His heart thumped heavily within his chest. "You have not the *Gaidhlig,* then?"

She shook her head. "I'm sorry, no."

Praise God. He'd told her he loved her. At what point his feelings had shifted from pure lust to so much more, he could not have said. They just had. Worse, had she understood his words, then she would hold him in no higher regard than she did their dead king when she finally learned the truth about Cassandra. Of that he had no doubt. Losing her high regard he could not bear. 'Twas all he'd ever be able to claim, truly have.

He managed a smile. "Woman, how can you be a Scot and not ken your native tongue?"

She laughed, husky and sweet. "'Tis because I'm Scot, you heathen, that Scot *is* my tongue."

He laughed then. "Brave talk for a lass behind bars."

"Aye, and I'd much appreciate you putting an end to it."

He kissed her fingers, all he could reach with a four-inch-thick door betwixt them, then reluctantly stepped away. "*A ghraid,* I shall get you out if I have to tear down the walls with my bare hands."

As his footsteps echoed down the corridor, Genny sniffled back the tears that had been threatening to spill since hearing Britt shout her name. How could she have ever doubted him? What a goose she'd been to think he'd abandon her after all they'd already been through. "'Twas just fear making me as addle-brained as Greer."

She put her back to the door, thankful Britt had left the wee window open, and looked about her filthy cell. How many had anguished, wasted away and died here?

Praise God and the saints, Greer, by now safely at Benbirk with their aunt, would be enjoying far better accommodations. Had her sister been the one locked away...

Genny shuddered. Her twin, for all her teary blustering and being the elder, was at her core naught but a willful bairn who, afraid of the dark, searched for constant light and laughter. God only kenned how Greer, already frightened out of her mind, would have managed here.

Thank God she had Britt. Recalling how frightened she'd been when she'd first set eyes upon him standing so tall and proud on her stoop, she sighed. That he'd nearly been killed trying to protect her still set her hands to shaking when she thought on it, his chivalry and courage still astounding her but no more so than his kiss. Who could have guessed a kiss could turn one's legs and brain to pudding and cause one's blood to run so hot it seared the limbs? She sighed as the truth settled over her.

She'd fallen hopelessly in love with Britt MacKinnon, a man who'd sworn never to love again. Just her luck.

But then again, he did act most fond of her. She'd seen it in his eyes, felt it in each kiss and had heard it in his voice when he'd sworn to set her free. As importantly, his character and form made him the perfect sire for bairns she thought she never craved but now, for some mysterious reason, she dearly wanted...with him. She could well imagine them. Brawny laddies with the look of him, mayhap three, and then perhaps twin girls as fair as she and Greer.

Hmm. Given enough thought, she could quite possibly make this dream come true. All she had to do was convince him that he wanted their union as much as she did.

Out of long habit—and admittedly being not one easily denied once she'd set her mind to a task—Genny methodically divided her problem into logistical parts. When she had each neatly aligned in her mind, she asked the rat eyeing her from the filthy rushes, "So, first I must seduce him." Given the scarceness of priests, none cared—save those royal—if a couple tupped before signing their names to a ledger. After all, there was no church edict against tupping, for 'twas as natural as heather. There was only a law against adultery and with good reason. She sighed. Greer was certainly paying the wages for that sin and would keep on paying upon learning her lover was dead.

The yellow eyes watching her from the corner blinked.

"So you agree. But how exactly does one go about seducing a man?"

Chapter Eleven

"Twixt the stone and the turf." ~ Old Scottish Proverb

Britt entered the great hall, which had been emptied of all but two guards and thirty-two of the forty-plus liege lords who would eventually make up the full Privy Council. Leaning toward the battle-tested guard manning the main staircase, he whispered, "How goes it?"

Macpherson shrugged. "They've agreed on no less than six trumpeter heralds for the processional and to having one bagpiper from each clan preceding the coffin. They're now arguing over who shall serve as first pallbearers and for how long before the second and third teams take over."

Britt rolled his eyes, looked around the hall and found Ross, who, having already spied Britt, was making his way toward him. Coming abreast, his friend whispered, "We're in closed session, Britt."

"Aye, but I've a most urgent petition to put before Comyn."

Ross waited for an explanation. When Britt offered none, he frowned but walked over to the Earl of Buchan and whispered in his ear. Comyn nodded, which meant Britt would have his hearing, but he would have to wait.

Hours ticked by, men argued, men agreed and men yawned. Finally, Comyn signaled Britt forward. He bowed before the men who'd come together to decide Scotland's future, most of whom were earls but a few who were landed knights as he himself would one day be upon his father's death. After recognizing the assemblage, he said, "Our clanswoman, Lady Armstrong, has been locked below in Edinburgh's dungeon on orders of Yolande de Dreux without due process, without a public declaration of her offense and without redress. I humbly beg you order the queen consort relinquish the key to Lady Armstrong's cell forthwith, so she might be set free until such time as she—if need be—goes through a proper and public trial before the Privy Council."

Despite the assemblage considering themselves good and just men, Britt wasn't the least surprised that not one raised a hue and cry over the injustice he'd outlined. All understood the cause for Yolande's distaste of Greer Armstrong, and many felt it justified. What they didn't know, and Britt couldn't tell them, was that the queen had imprisoned the wrong woman.

Comyn, at least, had the decency to glare at those who snickered, then turned his attention back to Britt. "MacKinnon, we have far more pressing matters to deal with at the moment. When the Council officially convenes, we shall be happy to take the matter under consideration, but not until *after* we finish with the business of Scotland."

"But, Your Grace, 'twill be days before the Southerland and the MacDonald arrive and the full council can convene. Then more days shall be lost in endless discussion. Nay, you cannot let the lady languish so long in a dark, dank cell when she is innocent of any and all crimes. Your Grace, I know—"

Comyn held up a hand. "Sir, you have my answer. You are excused."

Teeth clenched, Britt turned on his heel. At the stairs, Ross caught up with him, and Britt hissed, "The outside of my loof to you all."

Ross grabbed his arm. "Whoa, now. Tell me what's going on, or I swear I'll have you tossed into the cell next to Lady Greer."

Britt glared at the steely fingers gripping his arm. "'Tis not Greer Armstrong in that cell."

Scowling, Ross released his arm and motioned for Britt to follow him up the stairs. Finding the first floor landing empty, he stopped, crossed his arms over his chest and leaned back against the wall. "If not Greer Armstrong, then, pray tell, who is she? I swear you've not been in your right mind since fetching that woman."

Britt took a deep breath and rolled his shoulders in an effort to ease the tension running up his neck. "The woman in the cell is not Greer Armstrong. 'Tis her twin, Geneen."

Ross, brow furrowing, straightened. "Ah, that explains her behaving so oddly."

"You see now why we need set her free? She's an innocent. I grabbed the wrong woman."

"So why did you not tell the Council this?"

Britt sighed. "'Tis complicated."

"*Humph.* What I see is that you've come to care for this Geneen, want her for yourself." When Britt didn't deny it, Ross grumbled, "As you lust, but do us all a favor. The moment she's released, take her somewhere private and tup her blind. Take a day or two. I don't care. Just get her out of your system, then send her home." Ross huffed and started down the stairs. "All hell is about to break loose, my friend, and I need you with a clear head."

Fists clenched, Britt watched his friend disappear. What to do now? He would love to do as Ross suggested, ached to do so, but 'twas impossible. He could not simply tup Gen, then send her on her way. Kissing her had been mistake enough. The simple act had given him a taste of what might have been had he not allowed himself to be led by the bollocks so many years ago. 'Twas too late to correct that mistake, but he'd be damned if he would make another. Should he be so foolish as to take Ross's advice—should he and Gen become lovers—Britt knew to his bones he would never be able to give her up. And that would destroy her.

He gave himself a hard mental shake, shifting his attention to the most pressing problem at hand. He had to somehow manage Gen's release on his own.

Regrettably, he had no advantage over the queen. And then there was the problem of Montre. Now that his king was dead, Montre had become a liability, one better dead than set free—

Or was he?

Britt thought back to the last time he'd seen Montre and Yolande de Dreux in whispered discussion on this very staircase. Yolande had been in an obvious royal temper, doubtless over something she'd seen in the hall betwixt her husband and Lady Greer. At one point, she'd burst into tears, and Montre had taken her into his arms, patted her back as he whispered urgently into her ear. After a moment, Yolande, apparently appeased, dashed at her tears and nodded. The moment she turned, Montre rolled his eyes as if to say, *Women! I'll never understand them.*

Or perhaps he'd done so because he knew her *too* well. As a father might his daughter.

They were not lovers. Of that he was certain. The ladies Campbell and Fraser would have reported such had they even suspected a liaison. Aye, there was definitely more betwixt Yolande and Montre than a simple relationship of chief guard and queen.

"Aye, and quite possibly I've found the other way to skin this fox."

He jogged up the stairs to the queen's apartment, where he found one of her guards before the door. "Sir Britt MacKinnon to see the queen consort."

The guard's bored expression shifted to one of distain. "Her Highness is not to be disturbed."

"Tell her I bring word of Montre."

Within two breaths, Britt was ushered into the presence chamber, where he found Yolande standing pike straight before her perpetual fire, the door to her private chamber and nosy court closed. "You have news of Montre, sir?"

"Yes, Your Highness." He looked over his shoulder to be sure the guard had closed the apartment's exterior door behind him.

Sweat that had little to do with the stuffy room trickled betwixt his shoulder blades. The stakes were high. If his instincts were correct, what he was about to say could very well so unsettle their queen that she could lose the bairn she carried, the heir Scotland so desperately needed, but there was no hope for it. He could stand guard at Gen's cell door for days on end if need be, provide her with food and drink, but he could not protect her from the rats' nightly forays. One bite and Gen could die of purulence and fever before the Council had time to hear her case.

"Your Highness, Montre has been in my keeping since he and his two henchmen attempted but failed to kill Lady Armstrong and myself."

Yolande blanched. "This is outrageous! You must bring him to us immediately."

"I shall...after you give me the key to Lady Armstrong's cell."

Yolande gaped at him, her cheeks now sporting vivid red blotches. "No! You shall bring Montre to me this instant. I am your queen. You shall do as I order."

Britt snorted. "You are naught but a queen consort, one who—the Council would be most interested to learn—has tried and failed to kill two of His Majesty's subjects without his knowledge or consent whilst he still lived." Britt blew through his teeth. "My king is now dead, but soon too will be your bodyguard if you do not hand over that key to Lady Armstrong's cell."

Yolande staggered back, hands blindly reaching for the chair behind her. Collapsing onto it, she hissed, "You would not dare."

"I not only would dare but *will*, since none would be any the wiser, for only I and Lady Armstrong know he did not meet his end on the road but is now my prisoner." A blatant lie, since Ross, MacLean and Hildy also knew he held Montre, but she had no way of knowing this.

"Is he well?"

"He is injured, Your Highness."

Tears welled in her eyes. "Grievously?"

"With proper care, he will survive."

As she ruminated, gnawing on her trembling lower lip, Britt, his middle churning, waited. Finally, she reached into her pocket and pulled forth the large iron key he sought. Holding it close to her sparrow's bosom, she said, "I have your word that Montre is alive and that you shall bring him to me?"

"He is alive, but I shan't bring him here, for that would raise questions you doubtless do not want asked. I shall bring him to a safe place where your men may find him and then take him to Kinghorn, where he can be tended to properly and in private."

"But how shall I know where?"

Britt weighed his safest options. "I shall send word of the locale through my squire."

His quiver empty, Britt held his breath. He could do naught now but pray. Finally, she held out the key. "Take it, but know I shall not suffer Lady Armstrong in my presence. You must send her away."

Hell, he'd not anticipated that. Taking the key, he said, "Your Majesty, our custom demands Lady Armstrong remain within Edinburgh until *after* the funeral." In truth only Scotland's chiefs and those clansmen from within one hundred miles were expected to show their respects by attending the burial.

Eyes narrowing, Yolande came to her feet, her regal posture restored. "As you lust, MacKinnon, but hear well, if you fail to keep that slut from my sight..."

Without another word, she spun, threw open her private chamber door and disappeared.

Britt blew through his teeth. "Well, that went better than expected."

Heavy footsteps echoed through the hall. Gen raced to the door, the threat of her furry companion forgotten in the hope of seeing Britt. She stood on tiptoes and craned her neck, only to find a thick, squat shadow moving toward the cell.

Oh God, 'twas one of the queen's men coming to take her away.

Or kill her.

Breath hitching in panic, she scrambled backward, tripped over her satchel and pressed her back to the wall. Instinctively, she slipped her hand into her pocket for her *sgian duhb*, only to recall Britt still had her blade. Augh! Claw and scream as she might, it would be to no avail. No one was close enough to hear.

Metal scratched metal and shadow blocked the door's wee window, throwing the cell into complete darkness. "Gen, I have the key."

"Britt!" Genny ran to the door. The moment it opened, she threw herself into his arms, pressing her face against his massive chest.

His arms tightened about her, his hands warm and soothing at her back and neck. Pressing his lips to her hair, he whispered, "Shhh, shhh, there's no need to greet. You're free."

She managed a jerky nod, still not sure she believed it. When she did catch her breath, she muttered, "What took so long?"

He laughed. "'Tis a long tale that can wait until you've had something to eat and drink." He took hold of her right hand and, grinning, brushed a loose lock from her cheek, then wrinkled his nose. "And a bath."

She smiled at that. She did reek to high heaven, her hair was a tangled mess, and Greer's favorite gown was torn and soiled beyond repair, but she didn't care. She was free and with Britt. 'Twas all that mattered, all that would likely ever matter again. "I'm past ready to take my leave."

He retrieved her satchel and, taking her hand again, headed for the door at the end of the hall. "We need go through the kitchen."

She followed without question until she found he'd led her into the crowded lower bailey, what he called a ward. Realizing they were heading for the stable, she pulled back. "Wait. We can't leave the castle."

"But we must."

"But my—" She looked about, then crooked a finger, bidding him come closer. When he bent, she whispered, "The moon is full."

"So?"

Feeling heat rise up her neck and infuse her face, she muttered, "My courses—I am *due* any day."

When understanding finally dawned, he turned the color of a fresh-cut beet. "Oh. But not yet?"

"Not yet."

"Then we have time to worry about how we'll get you safely within the queen's company later. Right now, we have a more pressing problem."

Was he not listening? "What could be more important than protecting Greer's bairn?"

"Montre."

"Oh?" In her distress, she'd completely forgotten about him.

"I promised the witch his safe return in exchange for the key."

The admission took her breath away. Here she'd thought the Council had ordered her release, but instead 'twas due to Britt's risking his own freedom to garner hers.

He tugged her forward. "Come. We've no time to waste."

From the window high above the lower bailey, Yolande, hand to her heart, watched the whore and MacKinnon race for the stable.

How had MacKinnon gotten the upper hand like this?

She needed Armstrong's infant, needed it desperately, but she would not lose Anton in the process.

Now she had no choice but to trust that MacKinnon was a man of his word, that he wouldn't kill Anton now that he had what he wanted.

Just the thought made her ill.

She'd been given no choice but to trust her instincts. She'd seen the way MacKinnon's lip had curled in derision whenever

Lady Armstrong had flirted and her husband had made a fool of himself. Knew there was no love lost there. In fact, MacKinnon had done his utmost to keep her lustful husband and whore separated. Why he should now take up her cause was beyond her understanding. Unless...

Oh Lord, unless this had all been a ruse.

Her heart hammered against her hand. Could MacKinnon have wanted Armstrong for himself all along? If so, she'd just placed the nails in Montre's coffin.

No, she would not believe that. MacKinnon, a man of few words while around her, was also a man uncomfortable with dissembling.

"My queen, are you all right?"

Ignoring her cousin's question, Yolande said, "Please summon Duval."

"Of course, but first let me see you to rest. You've been standing before this window for so long—"

"Now, Evette!" Startled, her cousin jumped back a step. After she rushed away, Yolande turned her ire on the rest of her court. "Leave. We wish to be alone."

No sooner had her ladies disappeared than Duval bowed before her. "Your Highness."

She gave Montre's second in command a much altered and abbreviated version of her conversation with MacKinnon. "If MacKinnon speaks the truth, then soon he will send word through his squire as to where Anton will be found. Bring him to Kinghorn and tend to his every need until I join you." She took a shuddering breath, then squared her shoulders, a queen in command. "If, God forbid, you find Anton dead, then I want MacKinnon's head severed and brought to me on a pike. Take every guard we have, but *do not* return without word that Anton is alive or with the other."

Britt looked about Hildy's personal chamber in shock. "Are you sure this is the only room left?"

MacLean's lady, hands on her ample hips, rolled her eyes. "'Tis the only bed left in the town. Take it or leave, love."

Growling under his breath, Britt dropped a mound of coins—what Hildy claimed would be three days' lost wages—onto her outstretched palm. The coins disappeared before he could blink. Hildy then turned her attention to Genny. "Hot water is on the way. The hip bath is behind yon screen."

When the door closed behind her, Britt muttered, "At least 'tis clean."

Genny grinned. "'Tis more than I can say for myself at the moment." She sighed and looked about the room. "I can honestly say I've never seen anything quite so...red."

Hildy's boudoir was not simply red but shockingly so from floorboards to ceiling, thanks to beet-colored stenciling and yards of scarlet drapery and bedding. Even the sheepskin pelt beneath his feet had been dyed blood red.

Genny tested the thickness of mattress. "I dare say, she must do...uhmm, very well for herself."

"Apparently." The room's appointments, as lavish as any he'd seen in Edinburgh and certainly more than any within his home, could have come straight from a Persian palace.

Genny kicked off her slippers and, giggling, took a flying leap backward and landed in the center of the bed with a pleasant thump, her arms above her head, her breasts thrust toward the ceiling. God's teeth!

Laughing, she patted the counterpane. "Come. You've never felt the like."

He shook his head. Not only would he have "never felt the like", but would in all likelihood roll atop her, kiss her breathless, then love on her 'til neither of them could think, much less feel. To distract himself and the growing discomfort betwixt his thighs, he said, "I need go."

Genny sat up, a frown marring her normally smooth brow. "What's wrong? Have you suddenly taken ill?" She gasped. "'Tis your wound, isn't it? Has it festered?"

Worry etched her lovely face as she slid off the bed and reached up to touch his forehead, but he stepped away. "Nay, I'm fine. I just need to leave." Before he gave in to desire.

She reached for his breastplate. "If 'tis so, then let me see your wound."

He rolled his eyes. "I'm fine, better than fine, but if you must check something, here." He took her hand and placed it on his cheek. "See. No fever."

"You aren't fevered. Then you must be worrying about the meeting. Please tell Ross at the least what you're doing. If something should happen—"

He pressed a finger to her lips. "The fewer who know I've coerced the queen, the better." And the safer for Genny. There were many in the queen's court who, thinking Gen to be Greer, would gladly bring her down.

"Then promise to be careful."

"Aren't I always?"

"Nay. If memory serves, you rarely are." She placed her palms on his chest. "I've been most ungrateful, have yet to thank you. Were it not for you..."

The earnest expression in her eyes, the soft swell of her lower lip and sweep of her thick lashes as she looked up at him caused his heart to thud erratically, and without thinking, he pulled her close. Could she feel the chaos just looking at her caused within his chest? Could she hear the roar of his blood? "I'll return once the queen's men find Montre and take him away to safety." Of that he had to be certain.

Heaving what sounded like a resigned sigh, she slipped her hand from beneath his and backed away. "Then you'd best be off, but keep in mind I shan't rest until your return. Then we shall break fast together, and hopefully you can get some sleep."

He nodded, knowing he'd be fortunate to get any. He'd be sleeping in the stable, in Montre's cell, if need be. Anywhere but next to lovely Geneen Armstrong.

In the stable, Britt forced his reluctant destrier betwixt the poles of MacLean's cart, then struggled into the too-tight homespun tunic he'd found in a corner. He had no time to find anything else. His squire was already making his way to the queen.

His disguise finally complete, he opened the door to the secret room and found his prisoner just as he'd left him: bound, battered and bruised. "You're a lucky man. Her Highness has negotiated your release."

Montre glared at him through his one good eye.

Britt bent, unlocked the shackles securing Montre's arms behind the pole, then pushed his prisoner forward and secured his wrists again. "Listen carefully. I'm bringing you to your men. They will take you to Kinghorn, where you will remain. Her Highness will join you there after the funeral. Should you take it into your head to disobey and leave, then I'll have no choice but to relate the whole sordid tale of Her Highness's duplicity— how she took it upon herself to order the executions of two of His Majesty's subjects without His Majesty's knowledge or consent—to Ross and Comyn, neither of whom is a forgiving man. Do you understand?"

From his expression, Montre was apparently surprised Britt hadn't already done so, but he nodded.

"Then off we go." Britt jerked Montre to his shackled feet. "Into the cart and lie down."

The moment Montre was in, Britt buried him beneath a mound of straw, then jumped onto the driver's seat.

To his annoyance, the roadway out of Edinburgh was clogged with citizenry, cattle and heavily laden wagons. Britt didn't begrudge those who would make a handsome profit from his liege lord's demise—life did go on—but he was also most mindful of those who would soon give chase and couldn't help but grind his teeth in frustration. He had to deposit Montre and then be away before the queen's guards arrived at the shielding.

Finally the roadway cleared before him, and Britt braced his feet against the footboard before shouting, "Hie now!" His destrier, none too happy about the cart poles shafting his powerful sides, tried to run out of them.

Ten miles later, the isolated shielding he'd chosen for Montre's rescue came into view. Britt pulled back on the reins and guided his agitated mount up the narrow, rutted path, then around the shielding and into the nearby piney copse, where he dropped the reins and jumped to the ground. Reaching under the straw, Britt took firm hold of Montre's ankles, hauled him off the cart and onto his feet. "To the shielding. Move."

Montre, his stride limited by the foot of heavy chain, hobbled forward. The minute they were under cover and in shadow, Britt hit Montre between the shoulders, pushing him to the ground. When his prisoner, growling, flipped over onto his back, Britt pointed to the thorny brush to his far right. "I'll leave the key to your shackles in yon weeds." Finding the key would take Montre's guards some time, enough at least for Britt to take his leave unnoticed.

As he turned to leave, he stopped and looked back at Montre, who was now sitting up. "Should Her Highness ever again try to take her revenge out on Lady Armstrong, upon *my* honor I will see Yolande de Dreux dead."

Britt returned to the copse, unwound the leather straps securing the cart to his mount and pulled him free. Grabbing a fistful of mane, he vaulted onto his horse to wait and none too soon. No less than a dozen of Montre's red-clad soldiers came around the hillock and thundered up the road. Spying the shielding, the man in the lead—likely Duval—pointed, and the riders turned as one and came racing up the hill. Britt, mission accomplished, turned his mount in the opposite direction.

While Hildy dried her flame-colored hair in what breeze could be found within the mews, Gen paced before her. "'Tis well past gloaming. MacKinnon should have been back long by now."

"Back from where?"

Gen shrugged. "That I don't know."

Hildy waved a dismissive hand. "Then you're acting the fool. For how can he be late if you have no notion of how far afield he's gone?"

"True, but—"

Hearing hooves clip-clop behind her, Gen spun around. "Britt!" Entering on foot, leading his mount, he grinned and held out an arm in welcome. She ran to him. "I've been so worried. Did all go well?"

He slipped his arm about her waist and gave it a squeeze as he led his destrier to the stable. In a whisper he said, "Aye. Montre is safe, and Her Highness has been informed."

"Wonderful. When shall we return to the castle?"

"On the morrow, but only if you promise to keep from Yolande's sight."

Genny's steps faltered. "But how? I must return to court. You ken why."

"I do, and we shall ponder the how of it after I've board and rest."

"Of course. How thoughtless of me. I shall see to your meal while you tend to Valiant."

"To who?"

Grinning, she pointed to his destrier. "Appropriate name, don't you think?"

He rolled his eyes. "You're daft. You ken that, aye?"

She laughed. "No more than you, sir."

Genny waited until Britt, muttering, disappeared into the shadows of the stable, then ran into the hostel in search of food. She'd been unable to eat what with all her fashing, and now that Britt had arrived unharmed, she too was famished.

Finding no kitchen inside, she looked out the back door. Spying an outbuilding spewing fragrant smoke, she peered inside and found a rotund balding man stirring a pot simmering over the fire. "Hello?"

He glanced over his shoulder, then rose. "Hello. What can I do for you?"

Gen crossed the threshold. "I'm Lady Armstrong. Might that wonderful scent be hotchpotch?"

He smiled, his gaze raking her from braids to slippers. "Aye, m'lady, 'twould be. I'm Alan MacRae."

"Good eve. Might I beg some dinner for myself and Sir Britt MacKinnon? He has just arrived and—"

"Why didn't you say so, lass? Wait right here."

MacRae disappeared into the hostel and returned with two loaves of brown bread. Using quick, deft fingers, he dug out the centers, and ladled a huge serving of the fragrant, mutton-rich stew into each bowl. Handing them to her, he said, "My compliments to MacKinnon." He then peered out the door. Turning his attention back to her, he whispered, "And you'll find MacLean's best ale in the hidey-hole beneath the stairs."

Genny laughed, thanked him and carried her booty up to Hildy's boudoir. By the time Britt, his hair wet and road dust knocked from his person, arrived, she also had two round-bottomed kelties of MacLean's finest in hand.

Taking a seat at the small table in the corner, he took one of the tall glasses from her hand. "Bless you, woman."

Noting she had no blade, he dug in his sporran and pulled out her *sgian duhb*. Gen gladly accepted her blade back and, after saying grace, asked, "So what took you so long? Did you take Montre to London?"

Britt grinned around a mouthful of mutton, which tasted as divine as it smelled. "Worried were you?"

"Aye, since you insisted on going alone. I spent these many hours fearful you'd been waylaid by any number of the queen's guard."

"I was quite safe. I brought Montre to a shielding rarely used except during the droving season. His men arrived shortly thereafter and took him away. I then had to be sure the queen was informed her pet was in safe hands. May I?" he asked, indicating her uneaten bread.

"Please. Take it."

He sopped up the last of his hotchpotch, then said, "Ross knows who you are."

Her pulse quickened with dread. "How?"

"I told him. Now there's no need to scowl. He demanded an explanation for my coming to your defense before the Council, and to be honest, I thought you could do with another friend within Edinburgh's wall, should anything happen to me."

Her supper suddenly felt like a stone weight. "Did you tell him the reason for my being here?"

Britt shook his head. "Like you, I'm still of the opinion the fewer who know that another heir is in the offing, the better for all involved."

Relieved but still shaken, she said, "Tell me more about Ross." Britt's friend struck her as a man of strong opinion and not one of a particularly compassionate nature. "He's painfully gaunt. Is he ill?"

"Nay, and if you think him gaunt now, you should have seen him when we broke him out of Rothwell."

She'd heard of the borderland fortress. According to her father, wars had been fought over it many times. "Had he been a political prisoner?"

"In a way. He'd had the misfortune of falling in love with the wrong woman, a Sassenach lass who apparently had second thoughts about her elopement."

Oh! She loved tales of gallantry, and since meeting and becoming enamored with Britt, the more romantic, the better. Elbows on the table, her chin resting on her hands, she leaned forward ready to be enthralled. "So, what happened?"

"When Ross arrived at their secret meeting place, her father's men were waiting for him. He spent the next four years in Rothwell's dungeon."

Having suffered through only one day, she found four years beyond imagining. "How did he get out?"

Britt leaned against the wall and stretched his long legs before him. "Upon learning of Lyle's capture, the king ordered John Talbot and me south to negotiate his release. We returned empty-handed and with even less liking for the Earl of Rothwell. Annoyed, His Majesty sent us back, fully expecting us to return with a ransom offer. We rode south again and were denied entrance. Learning of this, His Majesty, now incensed but hesitant to start an all-out war, offered a most handsome ransom for Lyle's return, but when we brought the offer to the earl, he rejected it out of hand. 'Twas very apparent Rothwell was far more interested in making Lyle suffer for daring to reach beyond his station than he was in lining his pockets."

"Oh dear."

Britt nodded. "Aye. At this point, I'm well past ready to go to war and told Talbot I would recommend such to His Majesty. Lyle Ross was—and still is—my closest friend. Talbot, an odd sort but a thoughtful man much interested in the nature of things, said nay, we should advise caution, that a long-drawn-out siege would do no one—particularly Lyle—any good.

"I was still seething the next morn when we left. Moments later, Talbot reined in on the riverbank across from the castle and pointed up toward it. He asked if I saw the main difference betwixt Edinburgh and Rothwell. I said I saw only similarities. They were both impenetrable, standing on high promontories surrounded on three sides by cliffs and water. He smiled, then said, 'Aye, but Edinburgh stands on granite, whereas Rothwell stands on sandstone. Sandstone, my friend, we can tunnel into if we were of a mind and had the right men.'

"It took several weeks before we could find experienced under-the-curtain-wall tunnel borers. Using the ransom we'd brought with us, we engaged three borers, one of whom was very familiar with the castle. Talbot headed home, and I set to work with the men, digging only at night."

"How long did the digging take?"

"Two backbreaking years, but we managed to break in and rescue Ross, who by that point was near death."

Gen shook her head. "And he suffered all that because he'd loved and lost." No small wonder Britt remained unwed. He'd not only suffered Cassandra's rejection, but his best friend had been deceived. Well, she certainly did have her work cut out for her, but then she was made of hardy stuff. She knew to her bones precisely what she wanted, and it was sitting directly across from her.

As if on cue, Britt stretched and yawned. "Augh, I'm tired."

"The bed is there for the taking," she murmured, knowing he would decline, insist that she take the bed and that he sleep on the floor. She would remind him that he had the harder day and insist she take the floor. Chivalry would demand he argue, and then she would suggest they compromise. She would suggest she sleep below the covers and he above. She had no doubt that as tired as he was, he'd relent. Sleeping beside her should get him thinking about how pleasant sleeping together forever would be and make him ponder the possibilities. A perfect plan!

Instead, he blinked like an owl and, if she wasn't mistaken, paled just a wee bit. He abruptly rose. "I need check on my horse."

She came to her feet. "But you just said—"

"With all these strangers about, I will not rest until I check."

He was out the door before she could catch her breath. "Well! That certainly didn't go as planned."

At the window, she sighed, watching him walk to the stable. But sooner or later he would return, and then she could get on with her plan.

And she waited.

And she waited.

Only when it became painfully apparent he was not returning did she huff in exasperation and gut the candles. She took off her gown and slipped under the scarlet, down-filled coverlet, sinking into the feather mattress.

Sir Britt MacKinnon had no idea what he was missing.

A cock crowing above his head brought Britt out of his fitful sleep. Opening his eyes, he found his destrier staring at him and sat up. As he knocked the straw from his hair, his mount snorted in derisive fashion. "I know. I'm a fool."

But had he remained in that bed chamber, Britt had no doubt he would have ruined her.

He and Gen had spent far too much time in each other's company for him not to recognize the signs. Gen Armstrong was a woman falling in love. And a woman in love paid no heed to the threat around her. She didn't question the obvious, didn't listen to her inner voice that warned of danger.

Had she, she would have asked him days ago, "Why are you not married?"

He scrambled to his feet and shook the straw from his tunic. He would have told her the truth. To spare her—and him, if he were truthful—further heartache. But did she ask? Nay. She focused only on what her heart desired. And coward that he was, he'd let sleeping dogs lie, taking what joy he could from each passing moment, knowing too soon she'd be gone from his life.

His mount nuzzled his chest, and Britt ran a hand over the sleek black contours of its head. "She named you Valiant. Did you know that?" A most appropriate name for the beast. The stud had proved his worth many a time, had seen him through thick and thin. "You think me a coward, huh?"

Behind him Gen said, "Good morn'."

Mustering a smile, he readied to face her ire, but to his surprise found her smiling at him.

"You neglected to say good-night," she said.

"I apologize. It shan't happen again." His gaze raked her as she stood before the door in a pale blue gown, the dawn's light creating a halo around her. She did take one's breath away. When he could breathe, he told her, "You look lovely."

"Thank you, and your apology is accepted." She peered into the stall. "Comfy was it?"

Ah, she wasn't letting him get away so easily after all. "I've slept in worse."

"Hmm."

"Have you broken fast yet?"

"Not yet." She said no more as he tended to his destrier's needs. When his mount was fed and watered, he asked, "Are you ready to face the dragons?"

She squared her shoulders. "Aye."

He grinned. "Then let us find something to eat and be on our way."

After a bit of bread and cheese, he held out his arm, and she placed her hand upon his wrist. The walk up the high street was pleasant enough, the roads having dried out after a day of sunshine. He had to lift her out of harm's way only twice, once from before a dray wagon and then out of a sodden sot's reach.

Spying a greening rosebush, she pointed to it and murmured, "Mine should be blooming by now."

She obviously missed her home. "Where shall you go when you've accomplished your mission?"

"To Ireland, I suppose... To be sure Greer is safe."

"Then shall you return to Buddle?" Why this was important for him to know, he dared not ponder.

She shook her head. "By now someone about Buddle will have notified the earl that I've left and that my parents are dead. A new factor will be sent to occupy our cottage."

"I'm sorry."

She looked up at him. "Why? 'Tis not your fault that I'm homeless. If 'tis anyone's, 'tis that of Greer and His Majesty, for if they hadn't dallied, Greer would not now be with bairn, I'd not be here, and you'd not be racing about risking life and limb trying to set matters to rights."

"I haven't minded in the least and would do it again."

She studied him for a long moment, her rich blue gaze warming his blood, before mutely turning away.

Edinburgh's stairs and gate loomed high before them. Feeling her slight tremor, he covered her hand with his and smiled down at her. "No faint of heart won fair battle, my lady."

"Nor fair lady, my lord."

He couldn't help but grin. "Touché."

Entering the great hall, Gen sucked in a deep breath and squared her shoulders. Let them stare and whisper behind their hands. She'd done nothing wrong. The queen and her sister, aye, but not her.

Across the room, Ross, his surprise in seeing her apparent, excused himself from the group with which he spoke and made his way through the close masses to greet them.

Bowing before her, he said only, "My lady." He then turned to Britt. "How did you get her out? Never mind. I don't want to know, or I'd likely have to toss *you* into the dungeon."

Britt didn't deny it. "How goes it?"

Ross looked at her. "My lady, will you please excuse us?" Without waiting for an answer, Ross hauled Britt by the arm behind a nearby pillar.

Gen looked about the crowded hall in hopes of finding someone who looked as lost as she felt. She dared smile at the few who glanced in her direction, but all abruptly turned their backs to her. She'd never felt so alone in a crowd. She was about to withdraw into a corner when someone tapped her arm. Thinking it Britt, she smiled automatically, only to have it dissolve finding herself looking into the steely eyes of Lady Campbell.

"You must have bollocks the size of my husband's prize bull," Lady Campbell hissed in a whisper, "to return here after Her Highness has dismissed you."

Taken aback but in her heart of hearts having expected something of the sort, Gen kept her temper. "She dismissed me from her court. As a Scotch subject, I have every right to be within these walls and shall remain until I pay my last respects to His Majesty."

The woman curled her lip in derision. "One would have thought you've paid quite enough."

"I beg your pardon?"

"Everyone and their cat knows you were in his bed more often than you were in your own."

So this was the sort of abuse heaped upon her sister? "And you and the cats ken this how exactly? Did you see us together?" Gen jabbed a finger at the women's chest, forcing her, alarmed, to take a step back. "How dare you accuse me of committing the sin of adultery when here you are bearing false witness? I'll have you ken I was never in His Majesty's bed, and I defy *anyone* to prove otherwise."

The woman, mouth agape, blinked like an owl for several heartbeats before running off, her skirts clutched in her hands.

Gen, hands shaking, clutched the silver cross that hung at her breast. She shouldn't have lost her temper like that, should have bit back her retort, but then...it served the witch right.

"What was that about?" Britt asked from behind her.

Startled, her heart still thudding from her confrontation, Genny managed a smile. "Nothing of import. What did Ross want? I hope he's not sending you off on a mission." Not only did she not want to be left alone among these vipers, but she had little enough time left with Britt to accomplish what was beginning to feel like an impossible task: getting Britt MacKinnon to ask for her hand.

"Ross wanted to know how I garnered your release."

Oh no. "You didn't tell him the truth, I hope."

"I had no choice."

"I see." Now Ross would be angry with her too. How on earth did her sister tolerate living with all this hostility? She should say as much to Greer when next they met. Perhaps her voicing some compassion would help close the gaping glack that now stood betwixt them.

Britt's hand settled on the small of her back. Propelling her forward, he said, "You looked like you could use some fresh air. Let's go outside."

"But we just got here."

"And we shall return."

Once in the bailey, he guided her toward the stable. "Shall we visit your palfrey?"

"That would be lovely." She hadn't had the opportunity since she'd arrived, and patting the beast might help restore her shattered confidence.

Spying her, the gray nickered and came to the fence, making her laugh. "He recognizes me."

Britt ran a hand along the gray's neck. "He should. You're his mistress."

"Not after a week, although I would dearly love to someday own such a horse. He's truly lovely."

"And what would you name him?"

"Silver. 'Tis the color of his mane and tail in sunlight."

"As good a name as any, I suppose. Very well, then. Lady Armstrong of Buddle, please make the acquaintance of Silver, once of His Majesty's royal stable and now of Lady Armstrong's stable."

She laughed. "If only it were true."

"He's yours, Genny. You now own him."

The saints preserve her! He was serious. "But how?"

"Ross agreed that the gray would serve as fair compensation for you being falsely imprisoned. And he's taking the next week's board out of Her Highness's allowance. "

"Oh Britt!" She threw her arms about his neck, not caring that others were around. His arms came about her, and to her already excited heart's delight, his lips met hers. Warmth spread through her veins, and the world withdrew. Only Britt existed. His taste, the feel of his tongue as it swept past her lips, the feel of his strong hands as one slid to her neck and the other slid to her waist, pressing her firmly to his core.

Too soon his lips left hers and his arms fell away, taking with them the heat and scent she'd come to love and associate with him. Reality returned as he cleared his throat, looking everywhere but at her. "We need go in."

Feeling unaccountably bereft, she nodded.

He said not another word until they were again in the hall reeking of meat, sweat, perfume and intrigue, whereupon he hailed a serving lass. "Ale for my lady and me."

She sighed. Would she ever understand this man?

The lass returned with two lead tankards in hand just as lilting piping started and a lute-strumming troubadour began a sad lament, extolling King Alexander's virtues and legacy. Britt handed her a tankard and guided her to a long, fully occupied bench, where only a look from Britt caused men to rise, making room for Britt and her. Genny, thinking his action rude, murmured her thanks to those who gave up their seats.

Britt settled beside her and whispered, "Why did you do that?"

"Because now they must stand."

"As well they should when a lady is present."

Why was he now so grumpy? "I was simply being polite."

He made a thick sound at the back of his throat, then studied those about them. "On your right in the dark green *breachen feile* is the MacDonald, Lord of the Isles. To his left is his second son. To his right, Magnus, Earl of Orkney. The man laughing is Comyn, and the man next to him is James, steward of Scotland."

So many and so regally dressed. She'd never seen the like and could well imagine herself enjoying the spectacle had it been under other circumstances. She looked about the room, trying to find an older version of Britt. "Is your father here?"

She looked up at him and found his countenance darkened. "He and I agreed long ago to never again be in the same place at the same time."

Oh dear. What on earth could cause such a rift? She'd had no love lost for her father but still managed to tolerate his presence while he lived. Deciding now was not the time to ask, she said, "Have all of these chieftains come just for the funeral?"

"That and to decide who among them will now be regent."

"I thought Longshanks was destined to be regent."

He looked at her blankly for a moment. "Ack. In the rush to set you free and tend to...our other problem, I forgot to tell you the queen is with child."

She gasped. Had he turned into a goat before her eyes he could not have taken her by more surprise. "Oh my, this is the best of news. God's many blessings upon her." She must write to Greer as soon as possible. The news would greatly ease her mind.

Or would it?

What if their roles were reversed? What if it was she carrying Britt's bairn? Would she feel better knowing that whilst he professed love to her that he'd made love—and a bairn—with another woman? Nay, she most certainly would not. But then again, she—unlike Geer—would never have lain down with a man who could not commit to her.

She heaved a sigh. By now her sister was settled and growing plump and pink under their aunt's care. To tell Greer about the king's heir apparent would serve no purpose, possibly only cause her distress. So, better that she forget the letter. When the bairn was safely born would be soon enough.

At her side, Britt whispered, "Your reaction surprises me, given what the queen tried to do. You must be kindness itself."

She smiled. "The babe is an innocent, unlike me. I've been accused of being one who could pluck and dress a bevy of quail before their blood had a chance to cool." He laughed, and she arched an eyebrow. "Trust me on this, MacKinnon. I'm quick to anger and slow to forgive...if ever."

At least whilst I'm in my world.

Here it would behoove her to speak from her head and not from her heart, the Lady Campbell being a hard lesson learned. The woman was doubtless now berating her character from one end of the hall to the other.

A guard approached, and Britt stood to speak with him. Hearing only Gael and losing interest, Gen looked about and caught the eye of the strumming troubadour. He winked and started a new ballad. Deciding he had a lovely voice, her thoughts returned to Greer. Oh, how she missed her sister's voice. The woman could put a nightingale to shame. She struggled to recall the last song she'd heard Greer sing, but the words to the troubadour's song intruded. As she listened more closely, the fine hairs on her neck rose. He was singing not only to her but *of* her, extolling her—actually, Greer's—voice and beauty!

Alarmed, she flapped her hands, signaling him to stop the nonsense, and looked about. To her horror, others had taken note. Too many were obviously as displeased as she, albeit for a far different reason.

Not knowing what else to do, she tapped Britt's arm. She made a quick apology to the man with whom he spoke, then pulled Britt close. "Please make him *stop*."

Britt bristled, his chest expanding. "Him who?"

"The troubadour. Listen."

Britt did, apparently for the first time. Before she could catch her breath, he was looming large over the singer, appearing ready to separate the man's head from his shoulders.

Oh, nay, Britt! A fight will only make matters worse.

Around her, the room grew still. Without looking, she knew all eyes were on the pair. Waiting. Watching.

She strained to hear what Britt was saying, but failing, prayed it had naught to do with the severing of limbs. When he reached out and only patted the man on the back, her relief knew no bounds. The troubadour managed a shaky laugh, and the room let loose their collective breaths. There would be no fight on the second eve of His Majesty's wake. Leastwise, not one over her presence.

Britt, a smile in place but his eyes still shooting flames, returned to her side and, bending toward her, whispered, "He apologizes for any discomfort he caused and shall refrain from any further reference to you."

She swallowed the tears of embarrassment burning at the back of her throat. "I only made matters worse by soliciting your help, didn't I?"

"Nonsense. You did the right thing, and as you can see, all has returned to normal." He raised a hand to hail Ross across the hall, who nodded in response. "If you'll excuse me for just a moment, I need speak with Ross about this eve's security."

"Of course." Every liege lord in Scotland, friend and foe alike, would soon be standing shoulder to shoulder in the chapel for the requiem mass whilst their many guards, bristling with steel and sot with ale, milled outside it.

Britt followed Ross into the privy chamber and closed the door. "Someone, determined to start trouble, paid the troubadour a handsome sum to sing about Lady Armstrong."

Ross rolled his eyes. "Why am I not surprised? Your lady draws trouble to herself as fast as shit draws flies...no insult intended. Did the troubadour say who his generous benefactor was?"

"He claims not to know the man but describes him as being about my age, a head shorter and having brown hair, which describes half the men in the hall. I asked the color of the man's *breachen feile*, and he had no idea. He's blind to color."

"So we know nothing. Grand. In any event, my thanks for remaining calm. I had visions of an all-out war in the hall when you strode toward the fool."

"I'm sure some were hoping for it."

"Have you yet told your lady I know the real reason she's here?"

"Are you daft? She'd have my head. And she's not my lady, and you knowing why she shall never be, please do me the courtesy of refraining from calling her such." Britt raked his hands through his hair. "Never in my wildest dreams did I ever expect to be in so untenable a position."

Lyle, appearing sadder than Britt had seen him look in a long while, shook his head. "Women will rot the soul if given half a chance, and well you know this."

"Not Gen. She's here not for herself but to protect her sister, and in doing so also protects Scotland."

"And in doing so, she's also turned *you* into a shipwreck."

"'Tis not so bad as all that."

"Isn't it? The whole of Scotland sits only feet away—the most important of them in any event—and are you among them forging bonds so you might someday rise above knighthood? Nay. You're in here, your gut in knots, your head full of golden tresses, blue eyes and skirts." Lyle heaved a sigh. "Just tup the woman, will you? Please. For God and country, if not for yourself."

With that, Ross walked out.

Britt returned to the hall and found Gen hadn't moved, although even from a distance he could see how uncomfortable she was as others kept their distance for fear friend and foe alike might think they'd befriended her. To the casual eye she appeared neither angered nor frightened by their disapproval. If anything she looked quite regal as she sat in her borrowed gown with her back arrow straight, her hands in her lap and her countenance serene. 'Twas heartbreaking, really.

He strode to her and, smiling, held out his hand. "Come, my lady."

Somehow she managed a radiant smile as she placed her hand on his wrist.

Hildy looked at Genny as if she were daft. "You're not going to watch the funeral procession?"

"Nay. I already paid my respects at the mass for the repose of His Majesty's soul." God kenned his soul would need all the prayers it could garner, given what a knave the man had been, and all while she hid in the back of the little chapel after Her Highness unexpectedly arrived, taking her place upon the raised dais where her husband's ornate coffin sat before the altar. Gen, having been nearly caught once, dared not tempt fate again by having Her Highness spot her in the crowd.

Hildy placed her hands on her cocked hips. "Oh, but you must go! 'Twill be grand, I promise."

"I'm sure it will be." Her countrymen did tend to celebrate death as they did life. The processional would be quite a sight to see, the vendors would be out selling their wares, and there'd be drummers, pipers and trumpeters...

"When Queen Margaret passed to her heavenly reward, the processional was more than a mile long." Hildy bent in the sunshine and ran her fingers through her wet waist-length curls in an effort to untangle them.

Oh, to have hair like that instead of her horse-straight mane. "You have lovely hair."

"Thank you." Hildy straightened and, eyeing her, grinned in mischievous fashion. "So tell me, how is it that you've gone from being the king's mistress one minute to being MacKinnon's the next? Have you gold tucked betwixt those thighs? Or were you tupping both without the other kenning?"

Ack. "MacKinnon and I do not... He has yet to hitch." Not yet, at any rate. "And you, mistress, are the *last* person to be casting stones."

Ignoring Gen's insult, Hildy said, "Hitch?"

"To promise, propose marriage." Hildy, born in Oban and having learned Gael at her mother's knee, spoke Scot and French but neither perfectly. Since Gen spoke no Gael, the women had to keep shifting betwixt French and Scot to make themselves fully understood.

Hildy laughed, filling the small courtyard with her full, throaty sound. "Men like MacKinnon do not handfast. They marry or they don't."

Suspicion skittered up Gen's spine. "Ken him that well, do you?"

She smiled. "Not in the way you mean and not for my lack of my trying, I can assure you. He's easy on the eye." She winked, then shrugged. "What I meant to say is men like MacKinnon need to take wives to beget legal heirs but only *rent* mistresses. You've seen my boudoir. You'd do well to get what you can whilst you can." A smile played about her lips, then abruptly disappeared. "I'm not being cruel, my lady. 'Tis simply that I can tell you're new at this, despite you having been with the king. I guess what I'm trying to say is that your pretty face won't last forever, any more than mine will. You need keep that in mind as you pick and choose whom you bed."

Oh dear Lord, she thinks I'm a whore...like her!

Gen opened her mouth to correct the woman's dreadful misconception, then, thinking better of it, clamped down on her tongue. Here was the perfect opportunity to learn something of value, something she needed...but she must be very careful acquiring it.

Hildy cocked her head. "You want to ask something. Go on. No need for shyness betwixt birds of a feather."

Augh. Gen took a deep breath. "All right. How does one ken for certain that you've...uhmm, garnered a man's interest? That he wants you?"

Hildy looked at Gen as if she'd sprouted feathers. "Oh my, you *are* green as grass if you need ask that."

Gen waved a dismissive hand. "I ken when a man is in..."

"Rut?" A grin danced about Hildy's full lips. "And how might you ken that exactly?"

Feeling heat rise up her neck, Gen made a vague motion below her waist. "His...uhmm—"

"Cock?"

"I *was* going to say rod."

"Ah, as in 'his rod and his staff, they comfort me'."

"Hildy!" Lord God and Saint Bride preserve her. Talking to this woman was impossible. That she even knew the psalm was shock enough.

Gen turned on her heel to leave, but Hildy reached out and grabbed her wrist. "Stay. Please. I kenned what you meant and was only taunting you. Please stay. I've so few women to talk with as it is."

Gen huffed. She did want answers. "As you lust, but be warned, not another word of blasphemy, or I leave."

"Not another word, I hitch." She grinned and patted the cottie stool beside her. "Sit and tell me what has you so...*perplexe.*"

Gen settled on the stool, her thoughts in a tumble as to where to begin. "I ken the nature of breeding. Do ken which parts go where, as it were, but ken aught about the...heart of it. He lusts, aye." She grinned sheepishly, recalling her and Britt's mutual discomforts while riding tandem. "But he has yet to speak a word of his feelings, nor has he tried to bed me."

"Hmm. Could it be that he thinks of you only as the king's property?"

"Nay, he has kissed me."

This was apparently of great interest, for Hildy stared at her. "Has he now?"

Unable to keep from blushing, Gen looked away. "Aye, and on three separate occasions." But not once since their time at the stable, and certainly not last night nor the night before.

"My, my. In my experience, kissing usually leads to bedding. Leastwise with the furry ones."

Gen didn't want to ask but couldn't help herself. "What furry ones?"

"You ken the ones donning fox, ermine and such. They like their kissing before they sink their coc—rod." She shrugged. "The burghers, on the other hand, are usually in a hurry and prefer it like their whisky—quick and neat—but they pay well, so who am I to complain."

Good God's porridge. What a life this woman leads.

"So what, precisely," Hildy asked, "has you fashing?"

In for a copper, in for a pound sterling, my lass. "Do you swear not to tell anyone what I'm about to tell you?"

"Oh aye!" Hildy made the sign of the cross on her ample bosom.

"All right, then. I love Britt MacKinnon and wish to wed him."

She told Hildy about her well thought out, step-by-step plan and her failed attempts to get Britt in bed with her. Hildy murmured a few *hmmms* on occasion but otherwise kept her own counsel. When Gen came to the end of her sad tale, she, elbow on a knee, rested her chin in her hand. "So there you have it, the whole tale. Two well-planned attempts and two miserable failures. I'm truly a sorry excuse for a woman."

'Twas no doubt about it.

Grinning, Hildy patted her back in motherly fashion. "M'lady, there's naught wrong with you or what you're wanting. 'Tis the way you've gone about it."

Gen straightened. "How have I gone wrong?" She'd spent hours ruminating over each and every step.

"Well, to start—and I mean no offense—you've been acting the vestal virgin instead of the determined woman who kens what she wants."

"I have *not.*"

Hildy snorted. "For heaven's sake, you were planning on *bundling* with MacKinnon."

"Not so." To bundle, she and Britt would have had to have been cocooned to the neck in a linen bag whilst fully dressed. She'd planned to simply lie beside him with her hair loose and in her nightshift beneath the counterpane whilst he lay next to her atop the counterpane. Sensible and safe for her whilst being thought-provoking for a man of Britt's apparent appetites.

"Close enough," Hildy insisted, "and a charming custom for the young, but we both ken you and MacKinnon are well past first blush."

She was? MacKinnon certainly, but...

Gen sighed, deciding the woman might be right. "So what do you suggest I do instead?"

Grinning, Hildy said, "You take advantage of his every weakness and take no prisoners, m'lady."

Genny seriously doubted Britt had any weaknesses, but she was also at the end of her creative tether and had naught but Britt and her happily-ever-after ending to lose. "Tell me what I need do."

Chapter Twelve

"The man that wants must take the trouble."
~ Old Scottish Proverb

"Angus, a word, if you please."

Britt's second in command—chosen as much for his brawn as for his level head, followed him into the shadow of the curtain wall. "Aye, MacKinnon?"

"How goes it?"

"Just two fights thus far resulting in a few cuts and severed wee finger, but little else."

"Good. I need a boon."

"Whatever you lust."

"I need you to keep an eye on Lady Armstrong, see that no harm comes to her whilst I attend the funeral." Had women been allowed, he'd have insisted Genny go with him, but such was not the case.

Angus arched a brushy dark eyebrow. "Hmm, seeing Lady Armstrong walking about, I thought the tiff with Her Highness— the one that resulted in her spending a day's penance in the dungeon—was behind them. Do you anticipate more trouble betwixt the two?"

Relieved the rumor he'd put forth had been accepted as truth, Britt said, "Where our queen consort is concerned, I prefer leaving nothing to chance."

She and Montre had yet to speak face-to-face, so Yolande had no idea on what fragile ice she treaded. That Britt *would* make good his promise to Montre and see her dead should she move against Gen again.

Presently, the only thing the conniving witch feared was the Privy Council learning of her duplicity, which in his absence might not prove enough to hold her in check. Fearing she might arrange a kidnapping, then claim innocence, Britt said, "Assign Lady Armstrong a constant guard. She's not to walk out these gates unescorted. Since being dismissed from court, she's staying at MacLean's. Do you know the place?"

A brow arched, and a twinkle caught his eye. "Oh, aye, I know the place well."

"Obviously I pay you too much."

Angus laughed, then sobered as he looked about the crowded ward, at the hundreds of lounging warriors eyeing one another in suspicious fashion. "You can never pay me enough."

"True." Angus would have his hands full keeping this lot occupied and away from each other's throats. "Soon they'll be gone."

"And none too soon."

Britt nodded. "Any questions?"

"How long will you be gone?"

"Three days at most."

When Angus nodded, Britt bid him good-night and made a final tour of the north wall and upper ward. Satisfied all was as it should be—that his men were well fed and as content as could be, surrounded by too many warriors they neither liked nor trusted—he crossed the ward to Saint Margaret's Chapel, where his king lay.

Inside, he ignored those kneeling in prayer and looked at the coffin now illuminated by dozens of candles, and his gut churned, whether from the reek of burning incense or from the sight, he wasn't sure.

On the morrow, he among many others would take their turns carrying Alexander upon their shoulders out of Edinburg. Upon reaching the Firth of Forth, they would place his coffin on a waiting ship and escort it across the water, and then carry it and their king to his final resting place at Dunfermline Abbey, a striking edifice of flying buttresses, columns and spires. 'Twould be a fitting place for a good but headstrong king who died, tragically, before his time.

Britt, sighing, made the sign of the cross, and left. As much as he hated the need to do it, he'd delayed the inevitable—his heart-to-heart conversation with Genny—as long as he dared.

He shouldn't have kissed her again. But seeing her joyous countenance upon learning she owned the gray, seeing the look of admiration for him in her eyes, he'd been hopelessly lost. Wanting to share in her joy—nay, *needing* to share in her joy since he had so little to call his own—he'd pulled her close. And she'd melted into him, dissolving what little resolve he'd earlier mustered.

But no more.

He'd fallen in love with her, of that he had no doubt, but no more kissing. No more hugging. Hell, no more simply holding hands. He could no longer give in to his baser needs. He had to stand firm, or he'd hurt her beyond all forgiveness or redemption.

As he reached the gatehouse, someone called his name, and he stopped to find the petite Lady Campbell standing in the shadows. "Good eve, Your Grace."

"Good eve, MacKinnon. I need ask a boon. May we speak in private?"

Tonight was apparently the night for boons. "Of course."

Seeing the nearest gatehouse room vacant but well lit, he guided her in and closed the door, whereupon he discovered her cheeks were blotchy and her bonnie brown eyes red-rimmed. Concerned, he said, "Your Grace, how may I be of assistance?"

"Uhmm"—she wrung her hands—"you know where Lady Armstrong is lodging, aye?"

The fine hairs rose on the back of Britt's neck. "I do."

She burst into tears. "I fear...I fear I've done something quite terrible."

Hildy pointed to the padded cottie stool before her mirror. "Sit and I'll brush out your hair."

Genny, clutching the sheeting tight about herself, her middle in turmoil, sat. Beeswax candles Hildy reserved for the best of clients glowed, filling the room with delicate scent. Rose petals floated in the steaming hip bath. A heavy wineskin full of rich burgundy hung by what she'd come to think of as Britt's chair. Looking at their simple supper of sausage, cheese and bread, she told Hildy, "I still think I should have made a stuffed pullet. He liked that very much."

"If he found midday fare awaiting him at this hour, he'd grow suspicious. Besides, a stuffed, satiated man sleeps, and you want him wide awake and thinking."

She did want him thinking...about her and a future together. "But what if he takes one look at me and bolts for the barn?"

Hildy snorted in unladylike fashion. "MacKinnon is a man. All man. If you do as I say, he won't be able to breathe, much less bolt."

"I pray you're right." On the morrow, he would leave and be gone for she didn't know how long. Meanwhile her courses would come, she'd make that known to the women who remained behind by groaning and whatnot, and then, with her mission accomplished, she'd have no reason to stay on. Not without his wanting her to stay.

She might never see him again.

An ache, deep and strong, took her breath away. Hunching forward, she wrapped her arms about her waist.

Hildy knelt before her and parted the hair falling over Genny's face. "Are you all right?"

If only she could tell Hildy the truth, but she didn't dare. "Just a wee bit frightened."

Hildy smiled. "Ah, I see. He is rather brawny, but 'tis no reason to fash. He's experienced, has doubtless run into this problem before and will take care."

Good Lord, that wasn't what she meant at all. But now that Hildy had brought up the matter of size—

"Listen!" Hildy jumped up. "Someone's coming."

Hearing gravel crunch underfoot in the yard, Gen stood, her legs suddenly quaking. Oh dear. 'Twas now or never.

Hildy peered out the window. "'Tis MacKinnon!" She grinned at Gen and flapped her hands. "Hie now, into the bath. And remember, men are like bairns. Give them a glimpse of the sweets, and they'll come back for more. I'll leave the door open just a wee bit so you'll hear the tread squeak. When it does, rise, and he cannot help but get an eyeful." She gave the room a final glance, then blew Gen a kiss. "Good luck, m'lady."

"Good eve, mistress." Britt's gaze roved over Hildy in appreciative fashion. "You look most fetching tonight."

Hildy, smiling broadly, preened. "Why thank you, MacKinnon. I hope my gentleman thinks so, as well."

He laughed. "I'm sure he will. Is Lady Armstrong above?"

"Aye. I do hate to say hello and good-bye in one breath, but I really must go, else I be late for my rendezvous. Have a good evening."

Before he could wish her well, she was gone, the door thumping closed behind her. Despite her occupation, Hildy truly was truly a good lass at heart. 'Twas sad knowing she'd soon be having a hard row to hoe thanks to her having already lost that blush of youth and innocence that Genny, a good few years Hildy's senior, still retained.

As he climbed the stairs, the notion of leaving Gen to her own devices—even with an armed guard—gnawed at him. She'd proved headstrong on more than one occasion and might prove too much for the man. She'd certainly proved too much for Lady Campbell, and the countess wasn't easily cowed. He, on the other hand, could handle Gen. Would gladly shed blood for the privilege. If only he could relive his life and start anew, but alas...

Beneath his boot, the stair tread screeched like a cat with its tail caught in a dog's jaws. He really must remember to speak to MacLean about getting the damn thing fixed.

At the landing, he found the door to Gen's chamber slightly ajar, the sliver of light spilling out as if in welcome, and he smiled. Two long strides and he pressed his palm to the door, then froze.

Sweet Mother of God and the Holy Trinity.

Seeing Gen rise from her hip bath, her back to him, he gulped, his breath catching in his chest. Unaware of his heated perusal, she, humming quietly to herself, lifted her hair from her neck and arched her back. Water, sluicing like liquid diamonds off a sheet of gold, rolled over the gentle swell of her hips and glistening hurdies—as round and firm as polished silver globes in the candlelight—then fell in gentle streams down the length of her long, white thighs.

Blood thundered toward his groin. His mouth went dry. He envied the water. Wanted to run his hands and tongue over the very paths it took, then lap up whatever drops remained from her pale skin made pink by the warm water.

In an effort to breathe, he cleared his throat. She jerked at the sound and looked over her shoulder, her lush lips forming a perfect surprised O. Blushing scarlet, she immediately crossed one arm over her breasts, and the other slipped down to cover the golden apex of her thighs. She looked from him to the toweling sheet tossed out of reach on the bed.

"Uhmm," she said, in an obvious quandary.

Had he been gallant—or of loose tongue—he would have apologized and backed out, closing the door behind him. But then he was neither. He'd spent too many wakeful nights imagining Geneen Armstrong in a state such as this.

He walked into the room and closed the door.

Chapter Thirteen

"It was supposing that destroyed the lady."
~ Old Scottish Proverb

Oh dear! Genny gulped when Britt dropped the bar locking the door behind him. His gaze slid from her to the toweling lying next to her modest gown and shift on the large, inviting bed. She held her breath as he took his time picking up the toweling, then, with eyes hooded, crossed the too-small room toward her. A predator on the prowl.

Sir Britt MacKinnon was definitely not adhering to the plan she and Hildy had set forth!

Britt was *supposed* to have spied her rising like some Celtic goddess from the sea, and then, being a chivalrous knight of girth and sword, he was *supposed* to have quietly closed the door. He was to think upon what he'd seen out in the hall whilst she quickly dressed, and then he was *supposed* to knock, and she'd bid him enter. They would dine. He would bid her good-night as he was wont to do and go to the barn where he'd be unable to sleep. He would then return to her, profess his love and hitch to wed. She, in turn, would profess her love and bid him take her...body and soul. Getting Hildy to share *those* intimate secrets had been a bit of a headache. Genny did hate speaking ill of the dead but had had no choice but to lie and claim the king bedded her only to suckle...his wife being so sparrow-breasted and all. Hildy, grinning, had thought on this and said, "Aye, I've had one or two of those. Odd ducks, aye?"

And what Hildy had told her about bedding! How she could get the most pleasure. My goodness, who would have ever kenned?

So she'd planned and prepared well for everything...but this.

"My lady?" He stretched out his arms, making a neck-high screen of the sheeting so she might step out of the hip bath.

Not kenning what else to do, Gen tried to snatch the sheet from his hands. "Please let go."

To her annoyance, he grinned, keeping tight his hold. "Now why would I lust to do that? I rather like what I've seen thus far."

She huffed in exasperation, stepped out of the water and reached around the sheeting for her shift. Before she could grasp it, his arms closed about her, enfolding her in the soft fabric.

"Do you taste as good as you smell?" he asked, lifting the wet strands clinging to her neck and back from beneath the sheeting. He pressed his lips to her neck, sending the most astounding skitters down her spine. "Ah, you do, *a ghraidh.*"

She was most pleased he thought so but had bigger doves to pluck. Trying to ignore the delicious flutters tripping down her limbs, she looked over her shoulder, focusing on his countenance, hoping to discern more than simple lust. "You've called me *a ghraidh* before. What does it mean?"

"It means..." He hesitated as if pondering whether or not to tell her, then murmured, "My love."

Delighted, she rotated in his arms to face him. "Truly?"

His hands slipped to her hips, pressing her to him. Feeling his arousal, she had no doubt of his body's needs, but what of his heart's?

"Truly," he said. "Were circumstances different, I would have made my feelings for you known long before now and despite my having wanted to throttle you on more than one occasion." She grinned, as did he; then he sobered. "I think us

151

very well suited, Geneen Armstrong, but my life is in shambles. A total ruin." He took a deep breath. "I've no right to even speak to you thus, much less hold you in such an"—he glanced down to where her breasts pressed his chest—"*intimate* manner." A smile twitched at the corners of his mouth, then just as quickly disappeared. "May I ask you something?"

"Ask anything you lust." Ask for the moon. She would try to grant it. He loved her! The saints be praised, he loved her.

"Do you lust for a home of your own and bairns?"

He looked so forlorn, her heart lurched. She reached up and stroked his cheek, marveling that the dark shadow coating his wonderfully strong jaws wasn't scratchy as her father's had been but felt delightfully soft to the touch. "I do." She ducked her chin. "I've been so bold as to imagine our bonnie sons, both with your countenance and stature, and mayhap a daughter or two for me to fuss over and you to fash over."

When he said naught, she looked up and instead of finding him grinning at her silly fantasies, she found his expression most grave. Before she could ask why, he said, "Then, *a ghraidh,* you must forget about me and find a better man. One who'll be able to give you such...for I cannot."

"But—"

Dumb ox! She had no need to ask why he said such things. She already kenned. How could she be so thoughtless, so dense?

With Alexander dead, Britt now had no means by which to provide for a family. Whomever the Privy Council chose as regent would want his own man as captain of the guard. Britt, estranged from his father, would have no choice but to become a sword for hire, a mercenary. Something men of character are loath to do. Should none of the chiefs hire him, his choices would be reduced to starvation or going on crusade.

Suddenly, place names—Syria, Damietta, Antioch and Tripoli—and horrors beyond description from her father's many tales ran riot through her mind. The very thought of Britt dying in one such godforsaken place made her pulse race, her blood run cold.

She clasped his face betwixt her hands. "Britt, I need you to promise me something."

He grinned. "Anything you lust."

She thumped his chest with a palm. "'Tis serious."

He covered her hand with his, pressing it to his chest. She felt his heart take an erratic thud before he murmured, "All right. What is it you would have me promise?"

"Promise me that you will never go on a crusade."

His brow furrowed in confusion, but his heart steadied beneath her palm. "Upon my honor, I promise never to go on crusade."

"Thank you." Much relieved and having taken care of that fear, she readied to broach her greatest. What she would do or say should his answer not be what she wished to hear, she dared not imagine. She could only pray for dignity, to take the blow without falling apart. She took a deep breath. "If your circumstances were different, would you still wish me to find another?"

The muscles along his jaw twitched, and his arm tightened about her. "Nay, never." He ran a finger along her lower lip, his expression dark. "Upon my honor, if I were free to do as I lust...if I could change what is, I would take you to wife before the cock's crow."

'Twas all she needed to hear. He loved her! And now to put his fears to rest.

"You admired my cattle and sheep, aye?" When he nodded, she said, "I bred them. I ken husbandry as few others do. I've the best wool. We can breed your destrier. I ken just the mare. Their foals will be the finest, fetch small fortunes. And we can trade for a few of the earl's lambs."

Her mind filled with possibilities. Together they had the skills to turn any holding, no matter how humble, into not only a loving home but a profitable one. He would never again have to raise his sword save for in defense of hearth and clan. And who kenned, mayhap she and their bairns might even become a force in bridging the rift twixt Britt and his father.

Heart soaring, she rose on tiptoes and boldly pressed her lips to his. He groaned and deepened the kiss, taking control, his tongue sweeping past her lips as his hands swept over her in urgent fashion, setting her blood afire and her bones to pudding.

'Tis glorious, this meeting of mind, heart and body.

This was what she'd been longing for on those long, confusing nights in Buddle when she hadn't been able to sleep. A man to love.

Too soon he ended the kiss and released his hold. Smiling down at her in wistful fashion, he took a step back. "As much as it pains me, I need go, *a ghraidh*. Else I make the biggest mistake of my life."

She blinked in confusion. He had no cause to leave. She loved him. He loved her. He'd said so. He wanted her. She wanted him. So how could his staying and bedding her be a mistake? "But...?"

He shrugged as if to say he didn't understand either and, sighing, turned away.

She clutched the sheet to her aching breast. Tears burned at the back of her throat and pooled in her eyes as he reached for the latch. "Britt?"

His hand froze. With his back still to her, he said, "Please...I beg you."

"I'm a woman of few wants who loves you. Please look at me." She released her hold on the sheeting and let it drop to the floor so he might see her as she truly was, a simple woman who loved and wanted to be loved, without care for trappings, so he might put his pride aside and listen to his heart. When he finally turned, she saw hunger and an unaccountable longing in his eyes.

Heart tripping, she whispered, "Was our king not proof that gold can't purchase happiness? Was his death not proof enough that we can't count on a morrow? That all we have is our here and now?"

They stared mutely at each other for what felt like a lifetime.

Undone by the tears streaming down her cheeks, Britt closed his eyes.

This woman he had no right to love had bravely put forth on the line of battle every weapon in her arsenal. Her hopes, her fears and her pride. She'd held naught back, then committed to battle without hope of escape. How could he now deny her her victory?

He could not.

Heart thudding a hard tattoo against his ribs, Britt closed the distance betwixt them and took her into his arms. "There's no need to weep, *a ghraidh*, for I do love you."

With every ounce of my being and knowing full well this love sets my place at hell's table.

He scooped her up and carried her to the bed, where he laid her down gently, then brushed the tears from her cheek. "You're certain?"

She nodded. "Most certain."

His gaze roamed over the lush curves he'd so often dreamt of but never dared believe he might actually one day touch, as he tore off his breastplate, his *breachen feile*, mail and shirt and tossed them aside. Standing naked before her, letting her drink her fill of him, he waited with bated breath. More than one woman had found his proportions intimidating. He had to be sure that if Gen found them so as well—had a change of heart— he gave her ample time to bolt. To his relief, she, nibbling her bottom lip, patted the ticking next to her.

Lying down beside her, he caused the mattress to trough. She, warm and flushed, rolled toward him and wrapped her arms about his neck. "I've dreamt of this."

He pulled her close and draped a thigh over hers, cocooning her. "I've longed for this moment since first setting eyes on you."

She grinned in shy fashion. "I fear I can't say the same."

Not a talker in bed but suspecting she needed time, he asked, "So when was it that you started to fall in love with me?"

155

"You'll laugh."

He kissed her brow. "Nay, tell me."

"When you drank the milk, looked like a pup with a mouthful of stink bug."

He grinned. The stuff had been foul. "And when did you ken for certain?"

"Whilst in the dungeon, when I feared I might not live to see you again. The very thought was more terrifying than any impending torture or death."

He'd expected her to say when he'd gifted her with the gray. What a curious creature she was. Truly guileless and wonderful. "I kenned the same, finding you behind those bars...but now you're here."

She murmured *hmmm,* and he brought his lips to hers, taking his time memorizing the soft, smooth contours, his hands doing the same over her back and hurdies. Her hands burrowed into his hair as she pressed closer, her breath coming in shorter and shorter heated pants.

Aye, she wanted him, but he would not cross *that* line. He would bring her to the ultimate pleasure, then, satiated, she would fall asleep, and he, as much as it would pain him, would take his leave.

He rolled, taking her with him so that he rested on her, his heart's desire. Looking into her bonnie blue eyes, he silently told her, *Oh, but that I could make you mine before God and man.*

He kissed her as if such were the case, trailing kisses down her body from graceful neck to glorious breasts, then lower still as he rocked above her. To his great pleasure, she grew feverish, her breath coming in quicker and quicker gasps. Sooner than he expected, she began to moan and clutch at him. He rolled to his side so he could stroke her most intimate place, bring her to her pinnacle. She gasped at his touch and, keening his name, arched. Kenning where she soared, wishing with all his heart he could follow but not daring, he delved deeper into her mouth, relishing the warm confines, capturing her ragged breaths...

"Oh! Oh! Britt!"

As she shuddered and slowly fell back to earth, he froze.

Somehow, some way during their lovemaking, she'd cocked her leg above his hip, and he, in the heat of passion, had come to her, was now well within her. Fully engorged and throbbing.

Oh shit!

How on God's green earth had this happened?

She nuzzled his neck and rocked her hips. Wrapped in warm, delicious slickness, his shaft slid deeper. Gasping, he grabbed her hurdies. "Do *not* move."

Oh God, he was in so much trouble. The thought was immediately replaced by a more pressing one. He arched back to better see her face. "Did I hurt you, lass?" She grinned up at him, her hand gently stroking his chest. "Nay, Hildy gave me her special oil."

Hildy. No small wonder he slid into Gen with such ease. He was going to kill that woman. Genny, sighing, rocked again. Teeth grit, he locked her hips against his. "I said stop that."

He had to extricate himself very carefully, or he'd shoot his full quiver, but how? Mayhap if he tried to relax, counted the painted grapes on the walls, he'd go flaccid. Anything was worth a try at this juncture. Dear Saint Bride, why did he have to think *juncture*?

He looked down and found her watching him through glazed, half-opened eyes. "Hmm," she murmured, "Hildy said you would like it when I moved thus."

"'Tis precisely the problem." He liked it far too much. And Hildy, bless her conniving little heart, was definitely not long for this world.

Genny sighed, causing her breasts to jiggle ever so enticingly against his heaving chest, then licked her lips. "What of this, then?"

To his utter astonishment, her satin sheath, wet and hot, pulsed repeatedly around his engorged shaft.

Oh Lord God, he was bound for hell.

Blood thundering in his ears, his mouth closing over Gen's, he exploded with a roar on the next heartbeat, deep within her.

Britt flopped onto his back, carrying Gen with him. She, more content than ever she could recall being, rested her head on his chest. Listening to the slowing rhythm of his heart, she ran her fingers through the dark, silky hair that made a delightful triangle on his chest, then tapered to a thin line down his abdomen. This magnificent man was hers. Needing to share the wonder she felt, she whispered, "I love you."

"And I you." After a moment he asked, "Are you sure you're all right? That I did not hurt you?"

"I'm sure. 'Twas ever so lovely. Truly." And to think she'd yet to experience all that Hildy had told her she had in store! Amazing.

His chest muscles, which had been rigid beneath her cheek, relaxed, and his hand slid from the small of her back to her bottom. Stroking her, he murmured, "Aye, 'twas definitely that."

"Is tupping always so grand?"

"Nay, not in my experience."

Hmmm. She would not ask what went on betwixt him and that Cassandra witch. 'Twas no concern of hers. Britt now loved her, and 'twas all that mattered. And speaking of love...or rather a lack thereof. "Britt?"

"Hmm?"

"I need tell you something." She really didn't want to, but...

"What?"

"I had words with Lady Campbell. I fear I was rather caustic."

"I know."

She lifted her head from his chest and gaped at him. "You do?"

Eyes still closed, he grinned. "Aye, she took me aside this evening and asked me to tell you she's most sorry for what she said."

'Twas the last thing Gen had expected to hear. Dare she trust this change of heart? "Did she say why?"

He stroked her back. "Only that sisters of the Gaul need stay together."

"Of the Gaul? How odd. I'm obviously of Saxon blood, not Plantagenet."

"I thought her comment odd as well. In any event, she said you have a friend in her at court, and I lean toward believing her. Lady Campbell is not only astute but a good woman. She makes no bones about whom she dislikes, but if she befriends you, she has the reputation for proving a friend through thick and thin. She begs an audience with you before the funeral procession leaves on the morrow and gave me a packet to give you as proof of her sincerity."

"What's in it?"

He shrugged. "'Tis in my sporran."

He started to rise, and she placed a hand on his chest. "Nay, I'll get it."

Her curiosity piqued, Gen pawed through the mound of clothing Britt had tossed on the floor in his rush to bed her and came up with his sporran, his pouch made from an otter, head, paws and all.

From behind her, he said, "Open it, *a ghraidh.* I've naught in there that will bite. Her gift is the package wrapped in silk."

Gen pulled out the grass green packet secured by a fine cord of silver. "This?"

"Aye. She said 'tis a treasured heirloom and would appreciate its return in the morn."

Gen sat on the bed and untied the cord. "You're sure this lady can be trusted?"

He rose on his elbow, his curiosity apparently also piqued. "I'm quite certain."

She parted the silk and found the finely crafted silver shell the size of an egg the lady had been wearing just the day before. Dangling the small globe by its delicate chain, she said, "'Tis lovely. Do you think it a reliquary?" From what little she kenned of them, she expected a glass window so one could see the sliver of saint's bone or hank of hair within, but the shell had none.

"Mayhap. Try to open it."

Genny ran her finger along the fluted edge opposite the hinge and found a wee indention. Placing the shell flat on her palm for fear of spilling whatever it might contain, she held her breath and carefully separated the halves. "Oh my."

In the bottom half in a puddle of solid silver sat two perfect cream-colored pearls of identical size nestled side by side. On the other half, she found an inscription.

Iona et Isla

I, V, MCCXXX

Iona and Isla, the 1st of May in the year of their Lord 1230.

Genny's heart stopped and then kicked hard before resuming a harried beat. Two pearls, two names, one date.

Twins.

She snapped the shell closed. "Do you happen to ken Lady Campbell's Christian name?" *Please God, don't let this be so.*

Peeking over her shoulder, he said, "Mary, I believe."

Ack! Half the woman in Christendom had been baptized Mary—Mary Louise, Mary Agnes, Mary Elizabeth. Given the date, Lady Campbell could be Mary Isla or Mary Iona. But then again, Lady Campbell looked to be no more than thirty. Mayhap her mother had been a twin. Highland lasses were rumored to often wed upon having their first course.

He took the shell from her numb hands and examined the exterior carving. "What a lovely wee treasure. Italia made, I think."

Oh dear God in heaven, what if Lady Campbell kens I'm not Greer?

Britt held the locket out to her, and she took it with shaking hands. He sat up and draped an arm about her waist. "Is something amiss? You look like you've seen a ghost."

He might trust the lady, but did she dare? "I'm just surprised Lady Campbell would part with this even for a wee while. Do you not find anything odd about it?"

When he shook his head, she kissed his cheek. "Mayhap 'tis just my imagination."

"And what are you imagining?"

"That she kens I'm an imposter."

Heavily muscled arms enveloped her. He pulled her close and, looking most serious, assured her, "She has no means to ken who you truly are, Gen. Ross would not have told her, and I certainly didn't."

"You're right. I'm being foolish." When he continued to scowl at her, she forced a smile. "Truly, I'm fine."

At least she hoped to be, once she found out what the woman wanted. If Lady Campbell had blackmail on her mind, the woman was about to be sorely disappointed. Genny hadn't a brass plack's shaving, much less a piece of silver, to her name...but then she did have the silver-and-jet necklace. Surely Greer wouldn't fault her for using it to protect them both if need be.

Genny wrapped the shell back in its protective silk, stood and placed it in the deep pocket of the kirtle she planned to wear on the morrow, then took a steadying breath. Soon enough she would learn what was on the lady's mind. Until then she would distract herself with positive thoughts about her and Britt's future together. Which would now take a good bit of planning.

She'd been so distraught finding Britt on her doorstep that day and then so distracted getting Greer to safety that she'd left Buddle with very little. Not only had she left her mother's thimble, horn spoons and tongs, but she hadn't given a thought to the linens she'd managed to adorn in the event she should marry. They were still in the cedar marriage box beneath the eaves. And then there were her flax combs and the spinning wheel.

Well, they could get them when they retrieved the lambs. But first things first. There could be no wedding until after they'd posted banns.

Finding Britt studying her again with hungry appraisal, she swatted his arm. "Cease that."

Grinning, he reached for her. "Cease what?"

"You ken wh—eee!"

Strong arms scooping her up, she tumbled onto his broad chest. Before she could catch her breath, he flipped, and she was on her back with Britt nestled betwixt her thighs, looming over her. "You were saying?"

Laughing, she tugged on a lock of hair that had fallen over his handsome face. "You're incorrigible."

"Mam said much the same thing, but she loved me anyway."

She rolled her eyes. "Mothers tend to do that."

His good humor suddenly dissolved, his mouth shifting into a hard line. "Not all."

She frowned, wanting to understand. "Why do you say that?"

He shook his head as if to clear it, then smiled. "Best we not dwell on the past."

"As you lust." She would get the information out of him later. Hoping to regain their lighter mood, she asked, "We shall think only of the future. What say you to a date?"

"For what?"

"To marry, you goose. Do you think it necessary to pay the cryin' siller in both your kirk on Skye and to mine? I should think paying and posting banns in one should be sufficient." Bigamy was rampant in Scotland, and kirk officials were doing their utmost to curtail it, but since neither she nor Britt—

"Gen, we can't post banns right now."

She studied his grave countenance. "Oh, how thoughtless of me. You've yet to lay Alexander to rest, are still grieving, and here I am making marriage plans."

Britt brushed a lock from her forehead. "'Tis not that, *a ghraidh*."

He rose and sat on the edge of the bed. She touched his back and found it as rigid as steel. "Britt, what is it? You're frightening me."

"I'm sorry, I don't mean to, but you need ken something."

"What?" Could he not have bairns? Was he in debt? What?

"A decade ago, when I was but eight and ten years—"

Bammm! Bammm! Bammm!

Britt was on his feet with sword in hand facing the door before Gen, startled near to death, caught her breath.

"MacKinnon! Are ye there, sire?"

Britt blew through his teeth and relaxed his stance. Looking over his shoulder at her, he murmured, "'Tis only my squire." He waited until she dove under the covers, then opened the door. "What is it, Ian?"

His squire, breathless, said, "MacLean bids ye come. *Now*, m'lord. The Gunns and the MacDougalls... They were gaming, then fists were flying. Then the MacDonalds joined the fray, and the lieges... 'Tis awful, m'lord. Tall Angus bids ye hie."

She heard Britt rumble a curse, then say, "Wait below."

Hearing the door close, she threw back the bedcovers and found Britt already in his boots and shirt. "I'm sorry," he said, reaching for his chain mail. "I've no notion of how long this will take." The mail chattered down around him. He then drew his *breachen feile* about him, secured it with a weighty broach and broad belt, then slung his scabbard and sword onto his back.

Pulse racing, she knelt, pulling the bedcovering about her. "Promise to be careful."

He leaned over and quickly kissed her. "Aren't I always?"

Kenning the opposite to be true, she shook her head. "Come back as soon as you can." She'd not rest easy until she was sure he was safe and they'd finished their conversation. He'd been on the verge of telling her something important, something she greatly feared she didn't want to hear.

Britt stroked her check. "I shall. Lock the door after me."

The moment the door closed, she rose and saw that he'd left his breast armor on the floor.

Dear God, protect him.

Chapter Fourteen

"One funeral is worth twelve communions."
~ Old Scottish Proverb

Hearing the ring of steel on steel and men shouting, Britt took the stairs into Edinburgh two and three at a time. Whoever started this mayhem would be spending a month of Sundays living on naught but bread and water.

He pulled his broadsword free as he passed beneath the raised gate and into the lower ward, where he found no less than one hundred men in armed combat, while others stood on the sidelines cheering them on. To his right he saw Angus knock the wind out of one warrior, then clout the fallen man's opponent over the head. As the man dropped like a stone, Angus looked up, spotted Britt and shouted, "Nice of you to come."

Britt grabbed his squire by the arm. "Tell MacFee to get up there." He pointed up to the top of the curtain wall. The bagpipe's drone would get these bastards' attention as nothing else would.

As Ian took off running, a pair of combatants crashed into Britt's back. Without a thought to who was who, he slammed the hilt of his claymore into the closest man's head, then, spinning, swung his blade, pulling back just as the steel made contact with the other warrior's chest. "Move and I swear I'll cleave you in half." The man, a full head shorter than Britt and chest heaving, froze. "Drop the blade and sit."

Teeth bared, the Gunn warrior did as he was told, collapsing next to his opponent.

Britt strode to the next battling pair, which, having dropped arms, were rolling on the ground pummeling each other. He kicked the top man's arse to get his attention. When he reared back, fist at the ready, Britt pressed his blade to the man's neck. "Enough!" He nodded to his right. "The pair of you to the wall. Sit and don't you dare move."

Cursing under their breaths, noses and mouths bleeding, the men moved off.

As he engaged the next warriors, MacFee, forty feet above him, let loose on his bagpipe. The ear-piercing battle drone echoed around the curtain walls, and every man's head came up on the alert, each one thinking a new enemy approached.

He waved at MacFee to stop, and the man thankfully pulled the drone from his lips. As the last moan escaped the bag and echoed around them, Britt shouted, "Have you no shame? 'Tis the eve of your king's funeral." Grumbling rose to his left. Glaring in that direction, he said, "Stand quiet! I don't give a snake's arse which one of you started this. 'Tis *over*. And the next man who raises his hand in anger within these walls will spend a fortnight in its dungeon. Is that clear?"

More grumbling rumbled around the ward but with less venom. "Good. Now go back to your places. Sir Angus, a word if you please."

When Tall Angus made his way to him, Britt asked, "What in hell happened?"

"Some of the men were playing dice. One accused another of cheating, then fists were flying."

Britt looked about the ward and, seeing only two chieftains, asked, "And where were the rest of their lieges whilst all this was going on?"

Angus nodded in the direction of the keep and shrugged. "Drunk on their arses within?"

Ah, the Scots celebrating death. "All right. How many did we lose?"

"One that I ken, but we may have others."

"Dare I ask what happened to you?"

Angus gingerly touched his right cheek and grinned. "A well-aimed foot, which shan't be usable in the foreseeable future."

They spent the next few hours striding among their own men, pressing on wounds to stem the flow of blood, carrying those who could not walk to the upper ward, where they'd find Auld Sadie, their healer, and then congratulating those who'd held their own against superior forces.

Seeing all tended that needed tending, Britt looked about the lower ward. "I need speak with the archbishop...if he's sober."

Angus clamped him on the shoulder. "Good luck with that."

In the great hall, Britt found the Archbishop of St. Andrews, rich embroidered jerkin and robe askance, eyelids barely open, listing in his chair. "Your Grace, may I have a word?" When he got no response—the man had apparently mastered the art of sleeping with his eyes open—Britt poked him in the shoulder.

The man jerked and peered at Britt through one gimlet eye. "Mac...Mac?"

"MacKinnon, Your Grace. I need ask a boon—"

The man's eyes closed. Britt poked the archbishop again to roust him and got a snore in response.

Ack. The archbishop was the only man in the room with the information he needed, kenned the cost and process by which to obtain a papal bull. Looking at the slumbering archbishop, Britt toyed with the idea of throwing water in the old man's face but then tossed the idea aside. Garnering the man's ire would not serve, archbishops being some of the most powerful men in the realm.

Perhaps if I sat him up. Britt reached beneath the man's red robe and hoisted the bishop up by the armpits, repositioning him against the back of the chair, then none too gently slapped the man's face. "Your Grace!"

To his annoyance, the archbishop only groaned, and then, head lolling, began snoring in earnest.

God grant me patience.

If only his father had prosecuted the bitch as Britt had asked—nay, begged. But nay, his sire, fearing her family's wrath, wouldn't hear of it, claimed Britt had no proof. What more proof did the bastard need than a dead bairn?

He shuddered, the old pain washing over him.

He would put an end to this madness today if it meant tying His Grace to his chair and forcing water down his gullet.

Britt crossed the hall and took the stairs to the kitchen. Aye, he would get his papal bull and one day return to Skye with Gen by his side. Cassandra could go back from whence she'd come or to hell, for all he cared.

In the kitchen, he ignored the questioning looks of the scullery lasses and filled the largest tankard he could find from the water buckets awaiting their turn over the coals and returned to the hall.

As he tipped the water to the archbishop's gaping mouth, Ross asked, "What are you doing?"

"Sobering him up."

Ross, looking a bit green, yawned as he watched the water Britt poured sluice down the archbishop's front. "Not happening, my friend. Best you leave him be."

"I can't. I need speak with him."

Ross shrugged. "Today drunk, tomorrow on water. You do know he drained a full budget and was working on another before..." He made a vague motion toward the archbishop, then yawned again. "Do what you must, I don't care. 'Night."

As Ross stumbled away, Britt sniffed the goblet at the archbishop's elbow. The best wine in Edinburgh's cellar, of course. Ross was right. The man would be out cold for hours. He would have to reconcile himself to waiting, since there was no way he could return to Gen—and their conversation, which he sorely dreaded—without the information he sought. Calculating how he might pay for the bull would keep him occupied until then.

Hearing someone rap on the door, Gen woke from her fitful sleep with a start and found sunshine streaming betwixt the shutters. "'Tis about time he returned."

She bounded out of bed, wrapped the sheeting about her and lifted the latch, a smile on her lips.

"Good morn'!" Hildy, grinning, breezed by her with a wooden tray laden with bread and cheese in hand. Looking about the room, she frowned. "Has MacKinnon left already?"

Gen collapsed onto the bed. "He was called away late last night." And before finishing what he had to tell her.

Hildy shrugged and plopped down on the nearby stool. "So, tell me. How did it go?"

Gen felt heat rise up her neck, then bloom in her face. "Better than expected."

Hildy clapped her hands. "I kenned it!"

"You did?" She certainly hadn't. The whole evening had been one shock after another.

"He's a man, isn't he? So, tell me. Did he hitch?"

"Aye, and a good bit more."

Hildy gave her a knowing smile. "I thought as much. You've turned beet red. So, are you sore?"

Gen thought on that for a moment. "Nay, not really."

"You're most fortunate, then. I couldn't walk nor piss right for two days."

"Hildy!"

She shrugged. "Hey, 'tis the truth, but then I was but half your age and had no clue what the man was about."

Gen gaped at her. Hildy wasn't more than two and twenty years now. "You were a bairn?"

Hildy helped herself to a wedge of cheese. "Aye, about eleven summers, but that's the way of it sometimes. He needed a new mam for his bairns, and my da had too many mouths to feed. So we were handfast, and off I went. A year and a day later, I'd had my fill of his fists and his brats and said *adieu*. I've made my own way since."

"I'm so sorry." Gen couldn't imagine being pawned off, then brutalized. Oh, she'd heard such did happen, but she'd never met anyone to whom it had.

"Nay, don't be. I'm happier and wiser for it." She reached up and patted Gen's knee. "So, was it all ye expected?"

Gen felt fresh heat infuse her cheeks as she nodded. In truth, their coupling had been more than she could ever have imagined.

Hildy sighed in wistful fashion. "You're a lucky, lass, then. MacKinnon will make a good husband."

"And I've you to thank. He'd have spent the night in the stable again if not for your plan."

Hildy laughed. "Oh, he'd have gotten around to speaking his mind sooner or later. A dolt could see that just from the way he looks at you and always finds a reason to place a hand on you. We just gave him a wee push along the path he was already taking."

Hildy rose, opened the shutters and peered up at the sky. "'Tis a fine day for a funeral procession. We should have cartloads of fun."

Oh good heavens! Genny had forgotten all about her meeting with Lady Campbell. Jumping off the bed, she asked, "Do you ken when the processional will start?"

"Nay, but the trumpets will sound when it does."

Genny grabbed the pitcher and splashed cold water into Hildy's washbowl. "I need leave. I have an appointment."

"Ah, is there anything I can do?"

"If you would, might you be kind enough to do something with this hair of mine? I should be wearing it up now that I'm, well...bedded, and I've no such skills."

Hildy laughed. "Dress and I'll tend to it."

Gen made quick work of her ablutions and was dressed before Hildy finished digging in her basket for pins and cauls, then sat drumming her fingers and tapping her toes as Hildy ran a brush through her tangled tresses, then parted, roped and trapped her hair within silver net cauls on either side of Gen's head. She then placed the silver coronet on top. Stepping back, she said, "You look lovely."

Not really caring, Gen popped up and gave her friend a hug. "Thank you!"

The trumpets had yet to sound when Gen ran into the crowded bailey, what Britt called the upper ward. She looked about in hopes of finding Britt as she hurried toward the keep. Not seeing him, she decided it was just as well. She would have more to tell him after her meeting with Lady Campbell.

In the great hall, she skirted dozens of men leaning on elbows or out cold on their backs on benches with their mouths agape as she made her way to the staircase, but still caught no sight of Britt.

Reaching the level of the royal apartments, Genny's feet faltered. How was Lady Campbell to ken she was here? She couldn't go in nor could she have her presence announced. She'd likely end up in the dungeon again.

As she pondered what to do, the door to her right opened, and Lady Campbell came through it. Greatly relieved, Gen quickly curtsied. Lady Campbell, smiling, took a firm hold of her elbow and whispered, "Hie now. Her Highness could be coming out any moment."

They rushed down the stairs, Lady Campbell leading the way. At the ground level, she turned left and strode down a corridor. When Gen—having visions of the cell room—hesitated to follow, Lady Campbell stopped and smiled over her shoulder in kind fashion. "Fear not. We only go through the scullery to the garden, where we might have some privacy."

Catching the scent of baking bread, Gen decided she spoke the truth and followed. They rushed into the hot scullery, passing the busy lasses, and out a door. Entering a fallow garden, Gen gulped the cool air. So far, so good. The lady had not led her astray.

Lady Campbell took a seat on the low stone wall and patted the stone next to her. "Come. We've not much time." Gen sat but several stones away, and the lady grinned. "Did you bring the locket?"

Gen pulled it from her pocket and held it out. Taking her treasure, Lady Campbell said, "Do you understand why I shared it with you?"

Studying the woman at close range, seeing the tiny lines about the countess's eyes and lips, Genny was forced to put aside her earlier wishful thinking. "You're a twin."

"Aye, as are you." Gen opened her mouth to deny it, and Lady Campbell held up a hand. "Nay, do not deny it. I understand the risk you're taking and shall keep your secret. You see, I have secrets of my own that involve my twin." She opened the locket. Stroking the pearls, she sighed. "I was born Iona but have answered to Isla for the last twenty years."

Taken aback, Gen asked, "Why would you do such?"

"As lasses, Isla and I were inseparable yet different as day and night. I was quiet and subdued, quite content to watch life from a distance, whilst Isla was the just the opposite. Bold and energetic, she was always on the lookout for our next adventure. She was truthfully everything I was not but secretly longed to be.

"Then it came time for us to wed, and I, being the eldest, was betrothed first. To a bold, aggressive chieftain who frightened me. Frightened me so much that I balked on my wedding day. Isla did her best to reassure me, but seeing she was failing, said she would take my vows for me." She caught her lower lip betwixt her teeth. "You have to understand she kenned as well as I that father *needed* this marriage alliance. Initially I told her no, she could not, for I sensed something was terribly wrong about John, that I believed he hid his true nature behind a civilized façade. She laughed, saying that was precisely why she found him handsome and exciting. That if anyone could bring the rogue to heel, 'twas her.

"In the end, she insisted, and coward that I was, I allowed it. She donned the gown I was to wear and signed my name in the ledger when she exchanged vows with John. And to my astonishment, no one took note that we'd switched places. Not even our mother. We got through the wedding breakfast, Isla slightly subdued and I a total wreck. And then they left, and that was the last time I saw her. Alive."

Gen edged closer, a hand pressed to her breast. "Oh no! What happened?"

"I married soon after to Lord Campbell. Almost a year had passed and then we received a missive from the monster saying Isla, distraught over the loss of a bairn, had thrown herself off the curtain wall. Mother fell apart and I...I simply refused to believe it."

Tears shimmered in Lady Campbell's eyes as she looked at Genny. "My sister loved life as few do. She would *never* have killed herself. Him possibly, but never herself. I told my husband this and that I had to go to Glencoul and see for myself that she was in fact dead.

"To my horror, I found it to be true. While I was there, others whispered in my ear that it was by *his* hand and not hers that she died." She took a shuddering breath, and the tears the countess had been fighting cascaded. "As I wept over her grave, I swore I would see the bastard dead."

Teary-eyed, easily imagining killing to protect her twin, Genny reached out and carefully brushed the tears from Lady Campbell's cheek. "And did you?"

She shook her head. "Fate got to him before I could. He broke his neck when his mount, having had enough of his whipping, reared and flipped over onto him."

She reached out and took Gen's hand in hers. "I made another pledge to Isla that day. I swore I would live my life as she would have...had she been given the chance. And as much as it has frightened me at times, I've kept that pledge."

"And your parents never guessed?"

"To Father, we were little more than pawns, and I couldn't tell Mother. She'd nearly died from grief thinking she'd lost her *gentle one.* I couldn't tell her that she'd lost her favorite."

Gen heaved a sigh, unable to image carrying such a burden for so long. "You've never told anyone?"

"There's been no need until now." She dashed the tears from her cheeks and, squaring her shoulders, smiled. "I'm again keeping my pledge to my sister by telling you that after much thought, I believe the reason you are here and not Greer is that she is *enceinte...* thanks to Alexander."

The saints preserve me!

Blood roaring in her ears, Genny shot to her feet and tried to pull her hand away, but Lady Campbell held firm. "Fear not. I tell you this only because I want to help you...as I could not help *my* sister."

She then released Gen's hand, and Gen stumbled back. Dare she believe this woman? "What makes you so sure I am an imposter?"

Lady Campbell pointed to Gen's right hand. "Shortly after your sister's arrival here, I admired the silver band she wore on her index finger. She told me she always wore it to mask a scar she garnered as a bairn. And then last night you, enraged, poked my breast, and I noted you wore no ring nor did you bear a scar."

Genny's heart tripped in panic. She'd not given a thought to Greer's broad band, no longer even registered its presence on Greer's hand since Greer was never without it. The ring had become so much a part of her.

Acknowledging defeat, Gen collapsed onto the stone wall, her gaze dropping to her shaking but perfect hands. "We were but seven summers when a spider bit her. It festered, and Mam, fearing Greer would lose the finger, packed the wound in bog mud for weeks. When it healed, Greer was left with that awful scar. She hated it."

Lady Campbell settled next to her. "I can understand why, having seen it." She grinned. "You did rattle me yesterday—I was accustomed to a far more flighty but harmless Greer—so it

173

took a wee bit for me to realize what I'd seen. I then had to wonder why. Kenning what I do of your twin, 'twas not difficult."

"So now what? Will you tell the queen?"

"Good heavens, nay. The woman is a viper."

And this woman didn't ken the half of it. "On that we can agree."

"Besides, I trust Ross's judgment. He said MacKinnon is much taken with you, and after speaking with him, I do believe he's right."

Gen nodded "And I with him."

"Hmm." She watched the men pacing atop the curtain wall for a bit, then said, "May I ask what you planned to accomplish here?"

"To protect Greer, I need to bleed my courses, prove to all that I—or rather Greer—is not with child. I then plan to take my leave." Whereupon she would go to Greer, to be with her at the birthing, then join Britt, wherever that might be.

"I see." After a moment, she asked, "And when are your courses due?"

"Any moment now."

"Good, for I fear the queen will not tolerate you being around much longer. She's still incensed that you've remained after she dismissed you."

"She never dismissed me. She threw me into the dungeon, then lied about the dismissal. Britt, kenning why I would never have left of my own volition, hunted for me and somehow garnered my release."

"So Britt kens Greer is carrying an heir."

"Aye. He discovered he had the wrong woman on the way here. Then we were attacked and—"

Lady Campbell, surprised, held up a hand. "By whom?"

"The queen's men."

"I see." Lady Campbell gnawed on her lower lip for a moment. "So she does suspect you—or rather your sister—is with child. That would explain much."

Alarmed, Gen clutched Greer's ponderous crucifix. "Explain what?"

Lady Campbell waved a dismissing hand. "You have enough to fash over right now without worrying about her nibs. Leave that intrigue to others." She then smiled. "Here we've been sharing our most intimate secrets, and I've yet to ken your name."

"'Tis Geneen."

"Hello, Geneen."

Gen managed a smile. "Hello, Iona."

"Have you heard yet that Yolande plans to retire to Kinghorn immediately following the funeral procession leaving?"

"Oh nay!" Her Highness's leave-taking would do more than seriously hamper her plans. Her taking her leave would destroy them. She couldn't follow the queen. She'd been banned from not only her court but from her sight.

"To see your goal met, it might behoove us to push the actual course of events up a day or two." She thought for a moment, then said, "I shall return to Her Highness's apartment immediately and ask Evette if I may borrow a few of her special rags. All within court ken I'm well past childbearing, so she'll be curious as to why I would need such. I shall tell her—in great confidence, of course—that I need them for you. The queen will hear of it before either of us can take our next breaths. Meanwhile, you'd best not take a step within view of others without your hand pressed to your middle as if you were in great discomfort. Should any of the ladies be bold enough to ask after your welfare, you know what to say."

Gen nodded. "How can I ever thank you?"

They rose, and Lady Campbell wrapped an arm about Genny's waist and kissed her cheek. "Name a daughter after my sister."

As they walked toward the kitchen door, Gen asked, "What did you mean when you told Britt we were sisters of the Gaul?"

Lady Campbell laughed. "Is that what MacKinnon told you? Men. I said *caul*, not Gaul."

"Ah, the veil of birth."

"Aye." She laughed. "Men can prove so ox-brained sometimes."

Just before they parted ways, Lady Campbell whispered, "I think you should ken"—she tapped the crucifix hanging at Gen's breast—"that this was crafted from the plate silver Yolande brought into her marriage. Alexander had several pieces melted down in order to make it for your sister. I ken this only because my cousin was the silversmith and told me of the de Dreux crest."

"Gen!" Britt, excited that he'd finally gotten the information he needed out of the archbishop, took the inn stairs three at a time. The amount of coin required to make Gen truly his before God and man was exorbitant, and the task and time it would require was daunting, but he *would* see the task done.

He would resign his post and return to droving. Ross would remind him the work was more than dangerous, then doubtless call him insane, tell him the work was now beneath him, but they both knew there was coin to be made if Britt proved canny and if the weather and seas remained on his side. Now, he just had to convince his ox-headed father that he, his heir—and not their MacDonald cousins—should take over the cattle of Skye and drive them to the southern markets.

If he left within the month, he could be on Skye by the end of May, before the prime droving season—

"Good morn', MacKinnon."

Britt's plans flew out of his head at the sound of Hildy's voice. "You! I have a bone to gnaw with you, woman." Chest expanding, he thumped back down the stair.

Hildy, suddenly looking alarmed, backed toward the door. "Uhmm, later, MacKinnon. I need go."

"Oh, no you don't!"

The lass was quick but not quick enough. He caught her in the busy courtyard, taking tight hold of her wrist. When she tried to kick him, he grabbed her about the waist and hauled her over his arm like a sack of grain back inside. What he had to say to Hildy was not something he wanted bandied about by those standing about gaping at them.

Once inside, he slammed the door closed and let her go, whereupon Hildy scrambled to maintain her footing.

Arms out and palms up before her—as if *that* could hold him at bay, she said, "Now, MacKinnon, calm yourself. All went well last night. Lady Armstrong told me so herself."

"I am calm. What I am *not* is happy with your interference, your coaching of Ge—" Good Lord, he'd almost told the wench Gen's real name. "Of Lady Armstrong.

She batted her lashes as if she hadn't a clue what he was going on about. "What coaching?"

Hands fisted on hips, he loomed over her. "You gave her special oil."

"Oh that." She waved away his concern. "You can pay me later."

"Hildy! Are you daft, woman?" Gritting his teeth, he raked his fingers through his hair to keep them away from her throat. "She was a virgin and would have remained so had it not been for that damn oil."

Brow furrowing, Hildy now looked up at him as if he were the one who was daft. She poked a stiff finger in his chest. "I did not put you in that room, MacKinnon. You went in of your own accord." She poked him again. "I did not put you in that bed. You did that on your own as well. You told her you love her." When his eyebrows shot up in surprise, she nodded. "Aye, she told me. More importantly, she loves you fiercely, so I do not for the life of me understand what has you so frigging out of sorts."

Surprised to find himself on the defensive and unable to tell her the truth, he continued to glare and took a different track. "What of that muscle thing?"

"Huh?"

"You ken." He made a vague motion toward her crotch.

When the light finally dawned on Loch Lomond, she said, "Oh. That." She then grinned. "I threw that in for free, her being inexperienced and all." As his jaw dropped, she turned on her

177

heel and said over her shoulder, "But you still owe me two pence for the oil."

God's teeth! The woman was impossible. Before he could think of a rebuke, she was gone, leaving only a hint of perfume lingering in the hall. Roses and lavender. Genny.

He raced up the stairs. Finding the room empty, he cursed. He'd totally forgotten she had an appointment with Lady Campbell and had doubtless headed for the castle alone, since he'd yet to leave and MacLean had yet to assign her an escort. Had he not told her *not* to leave without an escort for fear the queen might take her revenge out on her again?

Praying he would find her safe within Edinburgh, Britt ran down the stairs and out the door, where he was again accosted by the sounds of villagers readying for the celebration of life and death. Dodging ox-drawn wagons and harried merchants shoving pushcarts into what they hoped would be prime viewing spots along the processional route, Britt wondered not for the first time why he'd allowed Genny to get under his skin and ease her way into his heart. This traipsing off was the very kind of erratic behavior that drove him insane. Women could never be trusted to do what you told them. High above him, the first blast of trumpets sounded, and he quickened his pace.

He entered Edinburgh's lower ward huffing and found dozens upon dozens of place-holding squires and grooms being lined up for the processional by the castle chamberlain. When the second blast of trumpets sounded, their head-aching liege lords would make their way out of the keep to take their places as dictated by position and protocol before the casket, which Britt and others would carry out of the chapel and through the gate of Edinburgh.

He entered the great hall as the trumpeters let loose again. Seeing most of the lieges stirring, he looked around for Genny and spotted her in the far right corner. Thanking God that she'd come to no harm, noting she appeared calm after her interview with Lady Campbell, he made his way toward her only to stop midstride seeing Yolande de Dreux and her court enter the hall.

His gaze immediately shot to Genny. He was greatly relieved to see she, also spying Yolande, had already started easing to her right toward the tapestry-draped staircase at the opposite end of the hall. When she ducked out of view, Britt released his breath and followed. Halfway across the hall, he heard Ross hail him, but Britt kept on walking. Ross could wait.

He ducked into the cool darkness of the stairwell and spotted her sitting above, on the first landing. "Gen, a word if you please."

Rising, she smiled at him, flashing her dimples, which eased his mind considerably. He'd feared Lady Campbell might have inadvertently let slip something about his past.

"I was hoping to see you before you left," she whispered.

How could he *not* take the time to say good-bye after last night?

Britt raced up the stairs, where he pulled her close, then placed a palm on the right side of her face. "*A ghraidh,* you cannot be running about without an escort. 'Tis far too dangerous."

"I hadn't intended to, but I was late for my appointment with Lady Campbell. She's the most extraordinary—"

He placed a finger on her lips, not caring why she'd done it. "Promise me you'll not go about town like that again, that you'll always wait for one of my guards or ask Angus MacLean to escort you." He'd be gone days, and God only knew what trouble might befall her.

"But..." When he glared, she huffed, then muttered, "I promise."

"Thank you. Now you can tell me about your meeting."

Light danced in her eyes, the corners crinkling in the way he loved as she smiled. "You will not believe this. Lady Campbell is a twin herself, and she kens I'm not Greer."

Interesting and unsettling. He'd not expected them to become bosom friends, but out of caution had extracted a promise from Lady Campbell that she would not discuss him— beyond his work and saying he was of good character—as a condition of his helping her. "Did she question why you're pretending to be your sister?"

Gen shook her head. "She'd already guessed why but promised to keep our secret."

Humph! He had the highest regard for Lady Campbell, but should something untoward happen to the queen, the lady might feel compelled to tell others about Greer's infant. "Do you truly believe she'll hold to that promise?"

"I do, but I can't explain why. She swore me to secrecy, and I shall abide by my promise, but I do trust her. She's already helping me. Now, your turn." She caught her lower lip betwixt her teeth and slipped her arms about his waist. "You'd started to tell me something important last night before we were so rudely interrupted by your squire."

"I fear this is not the time or this stairwell the place." Definitely not, considering she'd either be shouting like a fishwife or keening like a banshee once she heard what he had to say. "However, before I left I wanted to reiterate that I do love you."

Her hands slid up his chest and slipped about his neck. "I'm most happy that you do, since your feelings are reciprocated."

"MacKinnon!"

Britt sighed, looked over his shoulder and found Ross, hands on his hips, glaring up at them from the foot of the stairs. "Yes?"

"Didn't you hear me call? We need you in the chapel."

"In a moment."

"Now. The other pallbearers are already in position."

"All right." To Gen he said, "I'm so sorry. We'll talk when I return in four or five days' time. Remember, go nowhere without a guard at your side."

"I shan't. Return soonest. I'll miss you."

"I will, and I'll miss you as well." He kissed her thoroughly as if it might be their last, hoping to impart all he felt for her.

Reluctant to leave her, he pulled away and whispered, "I love you."

Soon, God willing, she would know just how much.

Spying Evette and Lady Campbell with their heads together before the chest in which the ladies of her court stored the strips of muslin used during their monthly courses, fearing they might have noticed the level dropping, Yolande said, "Evette, if you please."

Evette looked over her shoulder, and Yolande crooked her finger.

When Evette came to her side, Yolande nodded toward Lady Campbell. "What are you two doing?"

Her cousin blushed. "Lady Campbell had need of some rags."

Yolande blinked in surprise. "At her age?"

Evette caught her lower lip between her teeth. "Not for her, Your Highness, but for...Lady Armstrong."

Not believing her ears, Yolande staggered backward.

Evette grasped her arm. "Have you taken ill?" Without waiting for an answer, she started to raise a hand to summon Helene.

"*Non.* I'm fine." Or she hoped to be once her heart steadied and the blood roaring in her ears ceased. "You must be mistaken. Please bring the Scot to me."

Too much rode on the whore being with child.

When Lady Campbell stood before her, Yolande managed a smile. "Is it your time of the moon, Lady Campbell?"

Her lady-in-waiting grinned. "Thankfully, I am well past that, Your Highness."

"So who are those for?" She pointed to the wad of strips in Lady Campbell's hand.

Her lady-in-waiting gnawed on her lip, then huffed. "I'm sorry, Your Highness, but I couldn't just let Lady Armstrong bleed all over the hall. Bad enough she stained the back of her gown."

"You saw this?"

"Aye. I took her to the scullery and cleaned the spot as best I could."

Yolande managed a nod. "That will be all."

Greer Armstrong was not with child. How could this be? Had the slut lost it by bedding MacKinnon? Or had Helene and the scullery maids been mistaken from the start?

At this point, it mattered not. There would be no babe for Scotland. All would soon know she, their queen, was barren, and the heartless heathens would toss her out.

What was she to do now? God help her, she had to get to Kinghorn and Anton. He would know.

Unfortunately, she had to remain here—at least for one more day. She had a faithless husband to bury.

With her thoughts on Britt and his profession of love, Gen made her way to the keep's uppermost opening onto the curtain wall and peeked out. Finding only guards and the trumpeters, she made her way to the first crenel and peered down in wonder at the crowded bailey and town of Edinburgh. Never in her life had she seen so many people in one place. Hundreds ringed the courtyard and thousands lined the roadway as far as the eye could see.

As she squinted against the wind searching for Britt, she couldn't help but wonder how many of those murmuring below were truly grieving the loss of Alexander, the man. Britt, certainly. He'd guarded the man day and night for ten years. And Ross, as well, but how many others would truly missed *this* man in particular? She would wager more were grieving their loss of a ruler, a king. Particularly those beyond these walls who'd had only glimpses of Alexander in life and kenned him naught beyond those rare sightings and the tales and ballads they'd heard.

And then there were those who were grieving not so much Alexander's passing as they were grieving the passing of their own good fortunes and holds on power. She might be the novice at court, but she'd seen enough anxiety within the hall to suspect more than a few were. Which left the rest, those grieving as she did...for Scotland and its people. Would the transition to a regency government be a smooth one, or would greed overcome common sense?

War.

She pulled her sister's cloak more tightly about her. With war came heartache and pain, widows and starving bairns.

As if to echo her thoughts, the trumpets blasted, jarring those assembled on this cold, clear morning into dead silence. The archbishop, dressed in scarlet regalia and carrying a golden staff, stepped out of the chapel. Behind him followed eight pallbearers carrying the gold-and-red-draped casket of their king. Spying Britt's jet-black hair, she brushed the tears from her cheeks. She had to believe he would survive whatever was to come, and so would she and those she loved.

As pipes commenced their moaning, those wielding the most power in Scotland led the processional through the gates with their standard-bearers before them. Ever so slowly, the rest followed, the last being those bearing their fallen leader, and behind the casket, the queen and her guard.

Gen watched until Britt had passed through the gates, then turned toward the keep. She had one more thing to do this day while the queen was otherwise occupied. She had to return what was by all rights Her Highness's. The silver necklace.

Flanked by her own guards, Yolande, her rosary beads hanging slack in her hands, could do naught but watch the men bearing her husband to his last resting place pass through the gates without her.

Blocking her path stood four of MacKinnon's men with their lances crossed.

Fear blooming in her chest, she raised a hand. Without a word, Duval marched forward, spoke with the guards, then returned to her side, looking as confused as she felt.

"Your Highness, he says 'tis unseemly and unhealthy for the wife to follow beyond the gate. Wives must prepare for the *dairdgie*."

"What, pray tell, is that?"

He shrugged. "Some sort of feast."

"But..." She looked about in panic in hopes of finding someone who understood the heathens, who could make sense of this madness.

"Your Highness, may we be of assistance?" The ladies Fraser and Campbell stood at her side. Lady Fraser, apparently noting her mounting distress, immediately said, "Oh dear, there's no cause for alarm, Your Highness. Look about you. We too must remain."

For the first time, Yolande truly did look at those both near and far. She was surrounded entirely by women. The only men about were the guards. "But I'm his *wife*. His queen. Surely...?"

Under her breath, Lady Campbell muttered something about Ross in their barbaric tongue. Already at the breaking point learning the whore was *not* with child, that she'd not get her hands on the babe she so desperately needed, still furious over what befell Anton, Yolande snapped, "In *French*."

Lady Campbell dipped in a quick curtsy. "My apologies, Your Highness. I just said Ross should have explained our traditions to you days ago...so as not to upset you like this."

Beside her, Lady Fraser said, "Your Highness, our customs dictate that only men attend a burial. That we women remain behind and prepare the after-funeral banquets for the liege lords and the bread and alms to be given to the poor upon the men's return."

Looking from one Scotswoman to the other, Yolande couldn't decide whether they'd just sprung some sort of elaborate trap or not. God, she missed Anton's council. He wouldn't have had to guess. He would instinctively know.

As if reading her mind, Lady Fraser held out a velvet-draped arm. "Your Highness, there is naught to fear. Come to the gate so you might see for yourself."

Yolande placed a tentative hand on her lady-in-waiting's outstretched wrist. As they approached the guards, Lady Fraser said, "Step aside so Her Highness may have a clear view."

When the men did as bid, Lady Fraser whispered, "See below? Only women and children now mill about. All the men now accompany their liege." She pointed to the long processional line snaking north. "Some men will by necessity return by gloaming, but most will follow the processional all the way to the cathedral."

True enough, there wasn't a man to be seen in the village. Greatly relieved, feeling her heart slow, Yolande murmured, "In Scotland is this always so when a man dies...or just upon a king's death?"

"In small villages, wives often follow the coffin as far as the cemetery gate, but never are they allowed beyond it. Some believe evil spirits will corrupt our fragile souls, whilst others believe we might go mad or die of grief at sight of the open grave. Your Highness being with child, the Privy Council is being most cautious."

"And what do you believe?"

Lady Fraser leaned close and whispered, "I believe men use funerals as an excuse to get drunk as lords, but, wishing us to remain ignorant of this fact so we will not harp, they make use of superstitions to keep us home."

"Ah." Given the rate at which the men had recently emptied the castle's cellar of wine casks—many of which having been part of her dowry and intended to last for years—Yolande had no doubt whatsoever that Lady Fraser was right in her assumptions. "So what do we do now?"

"We use this time to see that the bread gets baked and make pouches for the coins we shall collect and the lieges, in their largess, will toss to the poor who come to the gates."

Yolande heaved a sigh. "Which won't be for days yet."

Exhausted from the hours of kneeling in prayer and emotionally drained, she turned her back on the distant processional and headed toward the keep, her court in tow like dutiful goslings following their goose. As the doors were opened before her, she placed a hand to her traitorous and again bleeding womb. "Lady Fraser, I need to retire. This babe takes much from me. Please tell the others I wish them to remain below and do whatever they wish...need to do. I shall join them later. And thank you. You've been most kind."

Smiling, Lady Fraser dipped in a curtsy. "Rest well, Your Highness, and God's blessings upon you."

Leaving her court in the great hall, Yolande didn't feel the least blessed taking the stairs to her apartment. She had to retire to Kinghorn forthwith to see to Anton, to garner his council, and to hell with these heathens' practices. And should any dare to question her, she would simply state it was imperative she start her lying-in, for a change a most convenient lie.

For heaven's sake, which of these chests holds the witch's jewelry? Genny, having gone through eight chests, stared at the dozens more piled shoulder-high about the queen's solar. Never had she ever imagined so few women owning so much.

Well, she'd best keep looking since she couldn't leave the necklace lying about. The queen, spying it, would immediately ken Genny had been nosing about the room. The woman was angry enough with her as it were. Only if she failed to find the jewelry chest would she toss the crucifix into one of the chests and pray whichever lady owned it proved honest.

Spotting a silver-trimmed chest in the corner that looked promising, Genny wormed her way through the maze and knelt before it. She raised the latch and lifted the lid, only to freeze, hearing someone enter the adjoining presence chamber.

Oh, please, Saint Bride, please let it be only a maid.

The presence chamber door closed with a soft thud, shutting out what noise came up the stairwell, and the footfalls grew louder, came into the solar. Gen's throat went bone dry. Then the solar door closed. Genny's breathing went ragged. She could think of no reason for a maid to close the door. Worse, she couldn't escape without opening it.

Fabric rustled and what sounded like light chain tinkled to her right, a chest lid squeaked, then thudded closed, fabric again rustled, then footsteps sounded again as if hurrying toward the fireplace. Praying she'd find only a lady-in-waiting, preferably Lady Campbell, and that the person's back would now be toward her, Genny rose ever so slightly and peered betwixt the chests.

Heart hammering, she gaped at Yolande de Dreux's back as she stood before the fire.

The saints preserve her! And what was that in her hand?

Dear God! Not believing her eyes, Gen rose just as Yolande threw the evidence of her monumental lie into the fire. "So, we both bleed?"

At the sound of Gen's voice, Yolande de Dreux spun and, seeing Genny, blanched to the color of whey. Propelled by righteous indignation, Genny came out from behind the chests. Her Highness's gaze darted to the fire and the smoldering evidence of her monthly courses. When her hand shot out, reaching for the poker, Gen hissed, "Back away or I'll scream walls and the truth down around you."

Her Highness, taking her at her word, turned to stone; then her gaze shot to the door, in an obvious quandary as to what to do next. Finally she took a step back, and Genny snatched the poker from its hook and knocked the bloody wad from the flames and onto the hearthstones.

Cringing, Yolande asked, "What are you going to do?"

Genny was sorely tempted to let the witch stew like an old pullet above hot coals, but thought better of it. Her Highness's guard was only a breath away. "Keep your secret."

The queen shook her head as if to clear it. "Why?"

Genny ignored the question. "I still can't believe this. Here you are playing the poor grieving widow, whilst all this time you've been lying to the entire country." Genny flung out her arms. "I've been on the receiving end of your wrath on two occasions and suffered for it. I dare not even *ponder* what else have you may have done."

Yolande put a hand to her throat. "Again, I ask why?"

"Why? Unlike you, you conniving bitch, I happen to *care* about Scotland." She took a deep, steadying breath in the hopes of controlling her rage. "I shall keep your secret only because it buys time. None within the realm want Edward of England to gain control. Without your babe, war *is* assured, make no mistake about that, but so long as the Privy Council thinks an heir is forthcoming, none will dare make a move." Britt would remain safe, as would her sister and her bairn...at least for a while.

Yolande de Dreux, squaring her shoulders, clasped her hands before her. "As you lust."

"If that were the case," Gen snarled, "you would indeed be carrying the king's heir, and all this would be naught but a nightmare." She reached into her pocket and pulled forth the silver necklace Greer so prized. "I came into this chamber to return this to you."

She held the necklace out, but Yolande, looking at the necklace as if it were a cow flap, shuddered and took a step back.

"Fine." Genny shrugged, pocketed it and headed for the door. Her sister could melt it down for species, for all she cared.

Behind her, Yolande said, "Before you take your leave, I've one more question."

Gen stopped on the threshold. "Yes?"

"Why is it that women like you can never find men of their own? Why is it your lot are only drawn to married men?"

"What are you talking about?"

"You understand me. I've seen the way MacKinnon looks at you and you at him."

Something clamped about Gen's heart, taking her breath away. The once solid floor beneath her shifted. Reaching for the door frame to steady herself, she asked, "Are you saying Britt MacKinnon is *married*?"

"Ah, from the look on your face, I gather you did not know." Chuckling to herself, Yolande turned and looked out the window. "Good-bye, Lady Armstrong."

Chapter Fifteen

"A man can survive distress, but not disgrace."
~ Old Scottish Proverb

The queen's laughter followed Genny into the corridor, where she had to grasp the stair's rope railing with both hands to keep from falling headlong down the steps.

Britt was married.

Nay. Yolande de Dreux was a liar! Hadn't the witch proven that time and again?

In the great hall, she would find Lady Campbell...and learn the truth.

Britt could *not* be married. He wouldn't have kissed her, much less made love to her, if he was. He kenned good and well how she felt about adultery. They'd spoken often enough about it on the way here. For God's sake, he'd wiped the tears from her cheeks as she'd spoken about Greer and her disdain for the king.

The witch lies!

She only said that because she had no other means by which to lash out and hurt me.

She lied.

Aye, she lied.

But mayhap the witch just misunderstood our custom of handfasting. That must be it. Handsome as he was, Britt could well have been handfast, then terminated the relationship. Aye, that must be it.

Finally reaching the first-floor level, Genny stopped, took a deep breath to steady her racing heart and dashed the tears from her cheeks. She would not make a spectacle of herself. She kenned in her heart—in every fiber of her being—that Britt was a good and honorable man. She would keep that firmly in mind when she questioned Lady Campbell. So she might laugh when the woman confirmed what Genny already kenned to be true.

Composure partially restored, she squared her shoulders and glided as Greer was wont to do into the great hall, where she found Lady Campbell in conversation with Lady Fraser.

Noticing her approach, Lady Campbell smiled for a brief moment before her expression grew serious. To Lady Fraser, she said, "Please excuse me for a moment."

She then rose, took Gen by the arm and guided her toward the far end of the hall. Once out of everyone's hearing, she whispered, "Whatever is wrong? You're as pale as snow."

So much for her putting forth a brave face. "I apologize from disturbing you, but I need to ken if..." There was no tactful way to ask. "Is Britt MacKinnon married?"

Lady Campbell's mouth gaped open; then she looked away. "Uhmm...oh dear."

Oh good God above, 'tis true.

Genny's legs turned to liquid beneath her. As the air left her chest, only Lady Campbell's quick wits and strength kept her from hitting the floor.

The woman eased her onto the nearby stool, then drew up another and sat beside her. With an arm about her waist, she whispered, "Take a breath, dear."

Genny tried. She truly did, but the bright flashes dancing before her eyes wouldn't stop and no air would come. A dark, thick pain now lurked where her heart should beat.

In her ear, Lady Campbell growled, "Genny Armstrong, you are better than this. Do as I say before others take note. Open your mouth and breathe."

Gen opened her mouth, and air whooshed in on a gasping keen.

"That's the good lass. Now again."

Genny tried once more. Air rushed in, the bright flashes dissolved, and the pain within her chest eased a wee bit. Slowly she straightened and was able to hold herself upright of her own accord.

Apparently satisfied with her progress, Lady Campbell loosened her hold and whispered, "Now tell me what all this is about."

Genny managed to choke out the tale of her and Britt's relationship and what the queen had told her.

At her side, Lady Campbell sighed. "I had hoped after speaking with you that your and MacKinnon's liaison was more of the romantic but chaste sort...like those so many at court seem to be dabbling with these days."

"Unfortunately, nay." She never would have lain with him had she kenned the truth. "How long has he been married?"

Lady Campbell thought for a moment. "I suppose there's no harm in telling you. He's been married to Cassandra some ten years now."

Cassandra, the very woman Britt had claimed he'd loved and who had lied to him. And married ten years ago. Genny's wee hope for him walking away from an ill-fated handfasting shattered.

Dreading the answer but needing the final piece of the puzzle, she asked, "Have they many bairns?"

"That I do not know."

But they most probably did after ten years of marriage, which would explain Cassandra remaining on Skye...to tend hearth and family.

Britt MacKinnon had certainly done a masterful darg of keeping his personal life away from court a secret from her. And how many other lies had he told her?

Lady Campbell reached into the tapestry bag at her feet. "Here." She handed Genny a thick pile of cloth strips. "I spoke with Evette as I collected these for you. Within moments, the queen was informed you are *not* with child."

Genny buried them in her pocket. So, her mission was now completed. Her sister and bairn would be safe to live out their lives as they chose, and none save a few would be any the wiser that the bairn was Alexander's heir apparent.

And she had no reason to remain.

Gen rose on shaking legs, and Lady Campbell reached for her hand. "Where are you going?"

"I need some air, some time alone to think."

"As you lust. I'll be here should you need me. And, dear, please keep in mind that MacKinnon is a good man. I'm sure he'll have a very reasonable explanation for all this upon his return."

She mustered a smile. "I'm sure he will."

But she wouldn't be here to hear it.

He'd done the unthinkable. He'd turned her into what she most loathed. An adulterer.

She managed to cross the hall without stumbling and carefully took the stairs down to the bailey, where the high winds and castle life whipped about her as if all was still right in the world, as if her life hadn't just crumbled to dust. At the stable, she hailed a groom.

"Please saddle my gray."

The ruddy-cheeked lad doffed his cap. "Aye, my lady. I'll summon your guard as soon as 'tis done."

"No need. I'm merely going there"—she pointed to the tallest building she could see in the village below—"on a mission for Her Highness. I shan't be but a moment before returning."

Frowning, the lad scratched under his cap. "Are ye sure, m'lady? MacKinnon said you're always to have—"

Damn MacKinnon and his edicts. "He meant should I travel any distance, which I shan't be."

The lad shrugged. "If you're sure, m'lady."

"I am." Sure as she had ever been about anything in her life.

The moment the lad had Silver ready, Genny mounted and headed her gray toward the gatehouse. Relieved the portcullis had yet to be lowered, she sat proud and smiled as she approached the guards, as if her leaving were perfectly normal. It worked. They smiled in turn and let her pass unchallenged. Heads would doubtless roll when Britt learned of it, but then that wasn't her concern.

She traveled down the high road at a leisurely gait, knowing the guards watched. The moment she rounded the brew house which blocked the guards' view of the road, she kicked Silver into a trot, anxious to get to MacLean's before Lady Campbell discovered her missing and sounded the alarm.

The moment she reached the hostel, she dismounted, tethered Silver to the nearest post and raced up the stairs to Hildy's room. Britt's words crashed to mind as she stared at the huge bed still disheveled from their night of lovemaking.

Upon my honor, if I were free to do as I lust, if I could change what is, I would take you to wife before the cock's crow.

Bile rose in her throat. She, in her need and loving him, had taken his words at face value. Had thought he worried over how he might support them now that their king was dead and he'd lost—or would soon lose—his position and livelihood.

Why? Why hadn't he told her the truth whilst they were on the road, before she could fall in love with him? At the very least, why had he not told her the truth when she stood naked before him? Why hadn't he simply picked up her gown, draped it over her, then taken her by the shoulders and spoken? Why?

Edinburgh was naught but a hateful liars' lair.

Oh, sure, she'd come to this place with a ready lie on her lips too, but not for her own sake. Nay, she'd come to protect her sister and Greer's unborn babe. These people, on the other hand, lied for themselves. The king lied to bed Greer. The queen was lying to save her sorry hide. Britt lied to garner what he wanted from her. Even Lady Campbell was living a lie.

She grabbed Greer's satchel from under the bed and took a steadying breath. God, what he must think of her? She'd been such a honey-eyed fool. At least she could take comfort in the fact that she'd not been one intentionally. Unlike Greer.

"There you are."

Jerked out of her reverie by the sound of Hildy's voice, Gen dashed the tears from her eyes and reached for Greer's brush and comb. "You may have your room back. I'm leaving."

"So soon?" Hildy came around the bed and craned her neck to look at her. "What's this? Why are you weeping?"

She took a deep breath. "MacKinnon is married."

Hildy, dressed in a dandelion yellow kirtle which did naught for her pretty, pale pink complexion, gasped. "No! Truly?"

Gen pulled the gown she'd intended to wear on the morrow for Britt's possible homecoming from the wall peg, carefully folded it, then stuffed it into the satchel. "Aye. If I owe you rent, please ask Br—MacKinnon for it, for I've no coins of my own."

She'd have to survive on air soup and shadow pudding until she could convert Greer's necklace into species. How many coins it would garner her, she hadn't a clue. Hopefully, 'twould be enough to purchase her and Silver's passage and a bit to spare.

Sounding alarmed, Hildy asked, "Where are you going?"

Having had a belly full of lies, she muttered, "Home." Home now meant her sister.

Hildy, her lower lip caught betwixt her teeth, thumped down onto her dressing stool.

"Where might that be?"

"Ireland."

"'Tis so far away! Have you family there?"

"My aunt, Lady Margaret." She'd blurted the name without thinking, but then Ireland was a big place, so it mattered naught if Britt learned of this or not. If anything, he'd likely think himself lucky. No ugly confrontation.

195

As Genny pulled her bow and quiver from behind the pile of Britt's armor and set them next to the door, Hildy said, "Are you sure you want to do this? MacKinnon being married doesn't mean he doesn't care deeply for you. In fact, I ken that he does. This needn't be the end of—"

"Hildy, I'm sure. I love—*loved* MacKinnon and thought he intended to take me to wife—but no, he played me for a fool." She stuffed her sister's coronet into the satchel and looked under the bed for her boots.

As she kicked off Greer's silly long-toed slippers, Hildy sighed, then, voice cracking, said, "I'm really going to miss you."

"Oh Hildy." Gen dropped the slippers and held out her arms. Hildy rushed into them. Holding her new friend tight, she assured her, "I'll miss you as well. You've been a true friend." The first she'd really ever had, other than her sister. Thanks to Britt's lies, she was losing not one person she'd come to care about, but two.

Fearing she'd fall apart, Gen stepped away, picked up the slippers, and shoved them into the satchel atop the gown. "I really need go before those at court realize I'm missing."

Hildy, looking quite miserable, murmured, "I'll walk you to the door."

Outside, Gen tied her satchel to Silver's saddle and gave Hildy a final hug. "Please say thank you and good-bye to MacLean for me."

"I will." Hildy reached into her décolleté and pulled out a small velvet pouch. Taking Gen's hand, she placed the pouch in her palm. "Here. You'll need this."

Realizing she held a small fortune in coins, Genny tried to give the pouch back. "I can't possibly—"

"Nonsense." Hildy closed Genny's fingers over her wages and winked. "I can always earn more. And I ken you'd do this for me were our positions withershins." She waved Gen toward her mount. "Now away with you and God's speed."

Stunned by the woman's generosity, Genny clasped Hildy to her breast a final time. "I promise to return them."

Hildy, tears streaming, murmured, "I never doubted."

Genny hauled Silver to the mounting block. Once settled onto the side saddle, she mastered a wee smile to assure her friend that she would be fine and waved good-bye. Ahead lay the unknown.

At the end of the mews, she turned the gray toward the tall masts marking Edinburgh's seaport and couldn't help but wonder if Britt would also find it ironic that she was making good her escape on the very gift she now suspected he'd given her in the hopes of binding her—his mistress—to him.

Britt couldn't recall the last time he'd been so pleased to see Edinburgh Castle standing proud above the mist that so often clung to the stinking moat surrounding the castle mount. High above the stench, he'd find Gen, the love of his life, the woman he would take to wife.

He kicked his rented mount in the sides in the hope of getting the swaybacked beast to pick up the pace and, as with every past effort, the lop-eared sumpter ignored him. Any other time he would have purchased a quality mount, but now, mindful of his purse and the coins he'd need to garner his freedom, he'd bartered for the cheapest cattle in the stable.

The sumpter stumbled, and Britt rolled his eyes. "I could run home faster than this, you miserable excuse for a horse."

Halfway up the road, well within view of the castle gates, the sumpter suddenly sat...like a dog. Cursing, Britt slid off and glared at the beast. "What the hell do you think you're doing?"

He jerked on the reins, trying to pull the animal to its feet. In response, the sumpter only rolled his eyes and turned his head. "You miserable—"

Britt dropped the reins in disgust. The beast could follow, should he have a mind, or rot where he sat. Britt no longer cared.

Approaching the gate, he heard laughter and glared at his men. "Enough! One of you fetch that sorry excuse for a horse and put him in the stable."

He would decide on the morrow which of these laughing jackals would have the pleasure of returning the beast to its owner. Right now all he cared about was finding Gen, who, given the hour, should be taking her midday meal.

Entering the hall, he scoured the room for her and, not finding her, strode over to where Lady Campbell sat among the queen's court. "My ladies, pardon my intrusion, but do you happen know where Lady Armstrong is?"

"Sir Britt, so good to see you." Lady Campbell rose and said to her companions, "If you'll excuse us." She placed her hand on Britt's wrist and hissed, "We need speak in private."

The fine hairs on his neck rose. At the far end of the hall, he asked, "Has something happened to Genny?"

"You could say that. The queen told her you were married, and she did not take this well."

Oh Lord, no. He would kill that bitch. He truly would.

Lady Campbell, obviously annoyed, slapped his arm. "Why didn't you tell her? You are a sore disappoint, MacKinnon."

"Never mind that. Where is she?" He could make this right. He had to.

"I've no notion. She said she needed a breath of air. When she didn't return after several hours, I went in search of her and learned from the guards she'd ridden out on what she told them was a mission for Her Highness, which we both know was a lie. I sent one of my clansmen—"

Without waiting to hear more, Britt raced across the hall. At the stable, he learned Genny had taken the gray. Praying she'd gone to MacLean's to lick her wounds, he strode down the crowded line of horseflesh and untied Valiant, shouting to the closest groom, "Get my saddle!"

The moment the groom arrived with his saddle, he snatched it from the lad's hands. "Get my tack. Hie now!"

Before the lad could catch his breath, Britt was riding through the gate at a breakneck speed, slowing only to make the turn into MacLean's mews. Without waiting for Valiant to come to a full stop, he jumped off and ran into the hostel.

Please let her be here!

Upstairs, he found the door open and Hildy hunched in the middle of her bed, weeping her eyes out. Seeing Gen's gowns and female doodads gone, his heart sank. "Where is she? Where's Lady Armstrong?"

Dashing the tears from her cheeks, Hildy straightened and glared at him. "I can't believe you did this! You broke her heart, MacKinnon. How could you?"

"'Twas never my intent." And why was he justifying his actions to Hildy?

"Right." Sniffling, she crawled off the bed. "You're just like all the rest. Love 'em and lose 'em is the only thing your ilk know."

He raked his hands through his hair and ground out, "Hildy, where has she gone?"

"Home, if you must know."

"To Buddle?"

"What Buddle? She's gone to Ireland, you rutting heathen. To her aunt's."

Ireland? Why the hell would she go—ah, her sister! She'd gone to be with Greer. "What's the aunt's name?"

"Why do you care?" She tried to brush past him, and he grabbed her by the arms. Bending at the knees, he looked her in the eyes. "Listen to me carefully. I love her beyond reason and intend to make this right if it kills me, but I need to know where she's going in order to do so. What's her aunt's name?"

Hildy, cheeks blotchy and her nose red as a berry, studied him for a long moment. "You'd best not be lying to me, MacKinnon."

"I swear to God I'm not."

Hildy sighed. "All right, then. Her name is Lady Margaret."

"And her surname?"

"How should I know?" Hildy tried to pull away. "She only said Lady Margaret."

Christ's blood. There could be two hundred Lady Margarets in the whole of Eire, for all he knew. "By which way is she traveling?"

"By horse."

"By which *road*, woman?" If Gen was taking the route they'd taken to get to Edinburgh, he could catch her but could only pray that he'd do so before she was set upon by thieves.

Hildy shrugged. "She turned left at the end of the mews, and I saw her no more."

East? Oh God, she was heading to the harbor and a ship. And she had a full day's lead on him.

He wrenched Hildy to him and pressed a kiss to her salty cheek. "Bless you."

Britt thundered down the narrow stairs.

Minutes later, Britt would have trampled a dozen guilders, merchants and fishmongers if not for their agile feet in his rush to reach the crowded harbor. Praying the ship Gen had booked passage on had yet to weigh anchor, he dismounted and grabbed the nearest stout bairn he could find. "Are you honest, lad?"

The lad, his ragged jerkin a good two years' growth too small, bristled at the question. "I am."

"Grand. Keep watch on my destrier until my return, and you'll earn yourself three bawbees."

The lad blinked in surprise, then grinned from ear to ear at the thought of earning what was likely for him a month's wage unloading fish. "Three? Aye, then I will."

Britt tossed him Valiant's reins and started down the waterfront dotted with stone quays, past dozens of storehouses reeking of tar, hides, wool and spice. Good Lord, there were so many ships.

After asking at the first three ships and learning they were bound for ports of call other than Ireland, he spotted a prosperous-looking man scribbling in a ledger before a stone storehouse. "Sir, might you know which ships are bound for Ireland?"

"I do." He bowed. "MacPherson, port's chandler. What name does she go by?"

Britt shrugged. "I've no idea. I'm looking for a fair and fulsome lady"—he held out a hand to mid-breastbone—"of this height, with blonde hair, who wants to book passage to Ireland. She may have a gray palfrey with her." If Gen hadn't sold the gelding to garner her passage. "Have you seen her?"

"A lady with a gray palfrey." He thought for a minute and then nodded. "She passed by last eve, as I recall."

"And the ship?"

He checked his ledger. "I've no means to know, but the *Galway* left on the even' tide, and the others, the *Fian* and the *Turoe*, should be weighing anchor as we speak."

Praying she hadn't left on the *Galway*, he asked, "Which quays?"

The man pointed to his left, and Britt ran. The *Fian* had raised its gangplank but had yet to be towed from its berth and into the Firth of Forth where it could catch the wind. Calling up to the captain, Britt shouted, "Have you a Lady Armstrong onboard?"

The captain leaned over the rail. "No ladies, m'lord. Only coal."

Damn. "Do you know the *Turoe*?"

"To your right, fifth down. She's as green as Eire. You can't mistake her."

Britt thanked the man and, his hope rising once again, ran. His heart sank when he reached the quay. A good hundred yards out in the firth floated the green cog, *Turoe*, her huge square sail already unfurled and beginning to billow as she caught the wind, her towboat oarsmen already heading for shore. At mid-ship on the rail, he could see a woman, her long blonde tresses flying.

'Twas her! He would recognize that carriage, that wonderful hair, anywhere.

Waving like a madman, he jumped at the end of the quay. "Genny! *Genny!*"

His heart leapt when she shielded her eyes and looked directly at him. Thank God she'd heard him. Frantically waving, he again shouted, "Genny!"

If it took his every coin, he would get the oarsmen to bring him out to her. She had to hear the whole sordid truth about his marriage from his lips and learn what he was now doing to rectify it. But first he had to get her to stop the cog's forward progress. Get the captain to drop sail. "Gen! Hail the captain!"

To his horror, she put her back to him, bent forward as if in pain and covered her ears.

"*Nay!*" She had to listen.

The *Turoe* chose that moment to catch the wind and surged forward, waves breaking around her proud bow.

Nay! He would not lose her like this. She couldn't leave without knowing the truth, ugly and painful as it was.

Determined she would listen, Britt shouted until blood thundered in his ears. Shouted until his burning eyes felt they would bleed, waved until his heart was near to bursting, and still she kept her back to him. The *Turoe* and its crew, mindless of his anguish, continued their forward charge, the ship seemingly shrinking in size with his every breath.

Gasping, he stared at the cog and the wee blue spot that was Genny.

He'd lost her.

Heart splintering, Britt collapsed to his knees on the hard stone and head thrown back, roared, "*Genny!*"

Chapter Sixteen

"Lights are not meat, nor buttermilk milk." ~ Old Scottish Proverb

Why on earth had Britt followed her?

Throat raw from crying, Genny clutched the ship's thick rail with both hands as the *Turoe*, its sail bulging, surged over another wave and broke free of the Firth of Forth, entering open seas.

Why could he have not just let her go in peace? Was it not bad enough that he'd broken her heart? Shattered the dreams she'd come to cherish? Of them working side by side, forging a home and creating a family together? Why had he come, then stood there screaming her name? Had he no pity at all?

A firm hand settled at the small of her back, startling her.

"Here," said a masculine voice, but one not as deep and rumbling as Britt's. Looking over her shoulder, she found the man who had welcomed her onboard holding out a handkerchief. Taller than she by a hand and blond, he'd told her his name, but distracted and heartsick, she'd not paid any heed.

Murmuring her thanks, she took the handkerchief—hers was so wet with tears she could have swabbed the deck with it—and dabbed her nose.

His short jerkin opened to the wind as he moved to her side, where he placed broad, tanned hands on the rail. In a lilting cadence, he asked, "Who might the blackguard be?"

Sandy Blair

She saw no point in asking to whom he referred. Britt had been bellowing like a skewered bull, his voice carrying across the water like thunder for any and all to hear. "No one important." Not anymore. So why did her heart feel like a crushed thing heavy in her chest?

"Hmm. Well, *no one important* has certainly caused ye to keen. Any more tears and we'll be bailing for our lives."

Sniffling, she nodded. She had been carrying on—acting more like Greer than herself—and that simply would not do. "My apologies. This has not been one of my better days."

She tried to hand him his handkerchief, but he shook his head. Blue eyes crinkled at the corners where only moments before white lines that paid tribute to days at sea had radiated over his clean-shaven cheeks. "I've a feeling you may have more use for it."

Pride stiffened her back. Oh no, she wouldn't. She was quite over that lying behemoth, Britt MacKinnon. And mayhap if she said this often enough, not only would her head believe it, but so too would her aching heart.

"Hmm," he said, "think he'll follow ye?"

"Nay." Britt wouldn't dare.

"Given the way he was bellowing, I dare say he will." He turned to his crew of eight and shouted, "What say ye, men? Will the giant follow the lassie or nay?"

Good Lord! Was he trying to do what her broken heart could not? Embarrass her to death?

To the man, they all laughed and shouted, "Aye, Captain, he will."

Looking from one weathered brown face to another, noting the look in the men's eyes as they laughed at her expense, as their collective gazes swept over her body, Gen felt the fine hairs on the back of her neck quiver. She slipped a hand into her pocket and grasped her *sgian duhb*. She'd been in such a hurry to get away from Edinburgh and gain passage to Ireland, she'd not given a moment's thought to whom else might be onboard the *Turoe*. She was the only female in sight. And would be for days.

204

Had she, in her hurt and fury, just jumped from the skillet into burning coals?

"Leave the lassie be, O'Neil!"

Genny spun at the sound of a female voice. A plump woman of mayhap thirty years, her curly titian locks flying in all directions in the wind, stood wiping her hands on a soiled apron in the doorway of the cog's forecastle.

Grinning, the woman crossed the deck on steady legs, shooing the men in her path away. Taking hold of the rail next to Gen, she dipped in a brief curtsy. "Darby O'Neil, m'lady. Ship's cook and wife"—she cocked her head in the direction of her laughing husband's back—"of yon lout, the ship's captain, Brian O'Neil."

"My great pleasure to meet you." The woman would never know how great. "I'm Lady Armstrong, formerly of Buddle."

The woman beamed at her. "Lovely to have ye onboard, and please, pay no heed to the men. The oafs mean ye no harm."

She could only pray so. "I will...I mean I won't."

"So are ye for Dublin or Cork?"

"Dublin. Do you know how long the journey will be?"

Mrs. O'Neil inhaled, looked to west, then toward the northern horizon. "If this fair wind and weather holds, we should make Dublin in six days."

Not so long before she could make her way to her aunt's home. Mayhap this woman could direct her. "Do you ken the O'Learys of Benbirk?"

Darby O'Neil frowned. "O'Learys, you say. Hmm. Are ye sure ye'll not be wanting to go on to Cork? 'Tis the O'Leary stronghold."

"Are you sure?"

"Quite."

Oh, Saint Bride and Columba preserve her!

She raked her memory for tales she'd heard at her mother's knee, hoping for clues to exactly where her sister might be. Of her aunt being wed to an English baron assigned to a castle that had been built a century before by some Norman earl in an effort to keep the peace. Greatly relieved to come up with something, she said, "Mother said Castle Benbirk—a tower keep—was in a place called Kilkenny."

Darby grinned, "Ah then, 'tis well beyond what the English call *the pale.*" When Gen frowned, she said, "Beyond Dublin's walls...in the wilderness." She patted Gen's arm. "No need to fret. If Kilkenny is where ye're bound, then Dublin or Cork makes no never mind as to where ye disembark. The place ye seek will be betwixt the two, likely on or near the River Nore, which is but a week's ride from either port."

Gen sighed. 'Twould take her a week to get to Dublin and then another week—this time alone—going through wilderness. Suppressing a shudder, she asked, "Have ye wolves in this wilderness?"

She could bring down a single wolf with her bow, but a pack...?

The woman laughed, "Only the two-footed kind." After a moment, she said, "Which brings us to me asking ye why a lady of obvious means should be traveling unescorted?"

Genny looked down at the borrowed clothes she wore. A plausible story immediately began to take shape, but, sighing, she cast it aside. She had quite enough half-truths, polite falsehoods and outright lies to last a lifetime. "I didn't have time to properly prepare for this voyage."

"Which means no one is meeting you. Hmm. He did ye that wrong, did he?"

Oh aye.

The image of Britt cradling her in powerful arms, his thick, raven hair spilling over his wide forehead, a look of pure hunger in his eyes, filled her field of vision. Then the queen's hateful words echoed in Gen's mind, and the woman in Britt's arms was no longer her but a laughing auburn-haired beauty. The world tipped. As sparks burst inside Gen's head, exploded before her eyes, her breath caught in her throat.

Gen, do as Lady Campbell instructed and quickly, before you fall on your face.

Gripping the rail, she opened her mouth, desperate to grasp the wind making whispery horsetails high above, brushing relentlessly against the endless waves, sweeping them into foam-topped hills. Her chest expanded, and slowly the world righted itself. Feeling more herself, she looked at Darby and found her staring. Marshaling a resigned smile, Gen said, "'Twas never meant to be."

'Twas all. She'd loved and lost. Nothing thousands upon thousands hadn't done before her and would likely continue to do, more's the pity for them. But not her. Never again.

Damn him.

"Well, enough about foolish men," Darcy said. "Ye've yet to see where you'll berth." Darcy bent to pick up Gen's satchel and nearly toppled lifting it. "Good gracious, m'lady, are ye tottin' stones?"

Gen felt heat bloom in her cheeks. She'd scoffed Britt's armored gauntlets. Why she'd bothered, she couldn't imagine.

"There you are. I've been searching high and low for you."

At the sound of Ross's voice, Britt, leaning into his storage chest, looked over his shoulder. Finding his friend standing outside the stable frowning, he straightened and handed the last of his heavy armor to a young guard who'd just earned his spurs, saying, "Sorry, I can't find the gauntlets. You'll have to ask the smithy to make you a pair."

The young man, his arms weighted down, beamed. "I can't thank you enough, MacKinnon. I've long dreamt of possessing fine armor someday, but never so soon or of the likes of this."

Britt waved away the compliment. "Wear it in good health and vigor."

As the younger man walked away, his prizes clanking with every step, Ross came to his side. "What the hell are you doing?"

"Lightening my load." He'd sold all but his broadsword, Valiant's light armor and his own chain mail. The fancy livery, lances, pikes, mauls and now his heavy armor were all gone.

"Why?" Lyle asked, knowing it would take another lifetime to replace it all.

"She left." Without a word. Without giving him a chance to explain. Tearing his heart out.

"Her Highness has already returned to Kinghorn?"

Britt blew through his teeth. "Not her. Genny."

"And why should this be cause for you selling your armor?"

"I'm leaving, Lyle, returning to Skye." He reached up and secured the ties on his saddlebag.

"Forgive my stupidity, but what does her leaving and your going home have to do with any of this?"

"Lyle, I'm not coming back. I've already talked with Tall Angus. He's past ready and most anxious to take over my responsibilities."

His best friend stared at him opened-mouthed for several heartbeats, then said, "This is cattle shit. You can't leave. Whoever takes over as regent will still need your sword arm. Hell, I need you." He raked a hand over the ruddy stubble that dotted his hatchet jaw. "I understand you're grieving Alexander's loss—"

"'Tis not my loss of Alexander I'm grieving, Lyle, but my loss of Gen." When his friend continued to scowl in obvious confusion, Britt heaved a sigh and leaned against Valiant. There was, apparently, no getting around the truth.

"I love her, Lyle. I am frigging hopelessly in love with Geneen Armstrong and want—nay, *will*—take her to wife, and she felt the same until our bitch of a queen told her I was married. Hurt to the bone, thinking I'd been using her as Alexander had used her sister, she ran." He straightened. "Now I'm going to do what I should have done nine years ago. Rid myself of Cassandra."

"All right." Lyle nodded and, after a minute's thought, said, "You kill your wife, but then what? Are you then going to kill your father as well, in order to take over his stronghold and sept? I know you, Britt. You're a man who needs work to keep sane...not that I think you are at present."

"I don't intend to kill either of them, much as they both deserve it. I'm going back to droving." He knew the routes, the safe crossings and pastures and several southern buyers, having assisted his elder brother many a summer during his youth.

Aghast, Lyle stared at him. "You have gone mad."

"Not in the least. The archbishop said he'd convene the Bishops' Court on my behalf once the affairs of state were settled, but my annulment would only be granted on two grounds: bigamy or consanguinity. Apparently murder, like rape and adultery, does not qualify as grounds." Had it, he'd have been a free man a decade ago.

"I intend to go through every kirk record in the Isles if need be to prove Cassandra and I are either directly related—which will guarantee my annulment—or collaterally related up to the fourth degree. If the later proves true, the archbishop warned my petition will, in all likelihood, still be denied, since a MacDonald heir sits on the court and would be loath to dissolve a marriage brokered by the lord of the isles. Should that happen, I'll have no choice but to appeal to Rome and likely *will* get the annulment, but that, I'm told, requires far more coin than I have or can earn here." Which also explained how the kirk could afford to build so many massive edifices such as that in Dunfermline.

And not until he'd exhausted his last legal option would he consider alternatives, tempting as they were at the moment.

"Droving? God's teeth, Britt! Your brother died whilst droving."

"I don't need reminding on how Ian died. But droving is the only way I can garner the coins I'll need, should the Bishops' Court vote against me."

"I can't talk you out of this?"

"Nay." He would wed Genny come hell or high water...when he could find her.

Lyle heaved a sigh heavy with regret and resignation. "As you lust, then. When do you leave?"

Britt examined his saddlebags, then looked at his longtime friend. "Just need a bit of food and I'm away."

Lyle clasped him by the shoulders and pulled him close. Thumping his back, he murmured, "God's speed, my friend. I shall miss you."

"That's it!" Darby rolled out of the narrow berth she and Gen shared, taking her warmth with her. A hinge squeaked in the dark, flint scratched flint, and suddenly their wee cabin was awash in the soft glow from the oil lamp. Gen dashed the tears from her eyes, rolled over and found Darby, her hands on her hips, scowling at her. "For four days, you, Geneen Armstrong, have done little but mutely stare out to sea. For four nights, you've done naught but weep and toss. I want to know why. You're not carrying a bastard, for I know you bleed. So what, pray tell, could possibly be so god-awful wrong?"

Genny, mortified, sat up. "I'm so sorry. I hadn't meant to disturb you."

"That I understand. What I don't understand is why all the wretched and silent sobbing."

Genny sniffled. "Tis naught that bears repeating."

"Let me be the judge of that." Darby sat on the edge of the berth and patted Genny's knee. "The telling will be hard, I've nay doubt, but you'll feel better for it. So talk, tell me why neither of us is getting a wink of sleep."

Genny marshaled a resigned grin for the woman who had tossed her husband from his bed so Gen might feel safe and have a sound sleep, not that she had slept. "Idiot that I am, I fell in love only to learn the man had turned me into an adulterer. I left."

Darby's brow furrowed. "I wasn't plucked from the kale patch yesterday, dear. A woman doesn't carry on as you are unless there's a lot more to the tale. And start from the beginning."

There was more to the tale. A great deal more, but more puzzling was why she should be suffering this niggling guilt, which had no basis, since she was the injured party in all this.

Mayhap if she did talk about what had happened betwixt her and Britt with another woman—one a bit older and married—she might be able to put all that had happened these past weeks into their proper perspective. Talking wouldn't ease her pain over being deceived, but it might put to rest this constant unease now gnawing at her.

Mindful she still had to protect Greer and her babe, she said, "MacKinnon escorted me from my home in Buddle to court in Edinburgh. On the way, we were accosted by three men who meant us serious bodily harm."

Darby's eyes grew wide. "How dreadful."

Genny nodded and told her how Britt had put her in hiding, then slew two before being injured by the third man, who then came after her. She went on to tell her how she'd found Britt, already making his way back to her and despite the arrow in his side, and how, at his insistence, she'd removed it.

Darby shivered. "I might well have fainted too, and 'tis about then that he kissed you for the first time?"

Heat crept up Genny's neck. "How did you know?"

"The circle of life, dear. So how did you feel about him kissing you?"

"Confused."

"But you liked it."

"Very much."

"So then what happened?"

"We reached Edinburgh and learned the king had died. We were both most distraught. Britt in particular. He is—was—Captain of the King's Guard."

"Ah, he'd lost not only a king but likely a friend. And he kissed you again, this time with more passion."

Genny blinked in surprise. Who was telling this story? "Aye, he kissed me again."

"And who broke it off, ye or he?"

"He did."

"Hmm. And you never thought to ask him during all this time alone with him if he—a handsome and virile man by your account—was married?"

"Uhmm." No, she hadn't.

Darby just shook her head and said, "Then what happened?"

Since it had become more than apparent Darby was more interested in the personal aspects of her and Britt's relationship than anything else, Genny skimmed over the why and wherefores of the queen's distaste for her but told Darby she'd ended up in the cell.

"And he came to your rescue?"

"Aye. He first tried to gain my release through the Privy Council. They agreed to hear my case but had more pressing problems to deal with first, so he confronted the queen and made her see reason."

"And why would he do this?"

"Because I'd been falsely imprisoned."

Darby snorted. "'Tis not the reason."

Genny cocked her head in question. "I beg your pardon?"

"His king is dead. The queen, angry with you, has no reason to do as he bids, so why would he risk her wrath—place his livelihood and mayhap even his own freedom in jeopardy— in order to gain yours?"

In those early hours in the cell, she *had* feared he'd forsaken her. Had mayhap even known what would happen to her. But he hadn't forgotten her. Why? "He did so, because...because he'd fallen in love with me."

Smiling, Darby patted her knee. "Very good."

My God, he'd loved her even then, even before she'd come to the realization herself.

"Then what happened?" Darby asked.

Genny gave herself a mental shake. His loving her still didn't change the fact that he was married, hadn't told her, and therefore turned her into an adulterer. "He took me to a friend's

212

hostel to keep me out of the queen's perusal, which was a condition of my release."

Darby grinned. "Where you shared a room?"

"No." When Darby's brow furrowed, Genny said, "He slept in a stall...with his destrier."

Darby blinked like an owl. "You're in love with a handsome and courageous man who saved your life not once but twice, and you made him sleep with his horse?"

"Nay, I didn't make him. He insisted." Tears burned at the back of her throat as she told Darby how she, now realizing she was in love with him and wanting him to ask for her hand, had plotted with Hildy to make him come to the same conclusion.

"And what did he do after he spied you in nature's glory?"

"He told me he loved me, would take me to wife if only he were free to do so. Only I hadn't known then what he truly meant, that he already *had* a wife."

"Oh dear."

"Aye. He then kissed me and turned away."

"Ah, you must have been very hurt."

"I was. To my very core. I'd feared my heart would shatter right then and there."

"So there you are, ignorant of the truth and naked save for a toweling and staring at his back. What did you do?"

Genny, feeling more heat infuse her cheeks, tucked her chin. "I told him I loved him and wanted him to stay."

"Did he?"

"He kept his back to me and said..." The tears she'd been fighting spilled as she choked out, "He said, 'Please, don't... I beg you'."

Darby took Gen's hands in hers and whispered, "But you did, didn't you?"

She closed her eyes and nodded as the painful truth swelled within her breast, played out in her mind. He had tried to leave, had been bent on doing the honorable thing...albeit without telling her why.

Dear God, forgive her for her weakness and pride.

Britt hadn't made her an adulterer. She'd done it to herself.

Chapter Seventeen

"He that won't look before him must look behind."
~ Old Scottish Proverb

Could he have picked a worse day to cross the channel?

The sudden squall had turned the already turbulent waters betwixt the mainland and Skye into a roiling cauldron. A wave, croft-high, tossed their flat-bottomed boat onto its keel, then heaved it headfirst into another dungeon-deep trough. Britt, struggling to keep his balance, stroked Valiant's massive neck as the oarsmen fought their way across yet another fast-ebbing current. "We're almost there, lad. Just a few more heaves and we'll be aground."

His destrier, never a good sailor, wrung his tail like a whip and rolled his white-ringed eyes in response, his huge hooves prancing, thudding, nearly drowning out the roar of the surf and wind. If the MacDonalds didn't make landfall shortly, his wild-eyed mount would pound through the decking, and the Sound of Sleat would be claiming its next victims.

Worse, he had no idea if Genny was safe or not. He could only pray the *Turoe*'s captain had made landfall somewhere along Scotland's coast, hadn't tried to cross the six and twenty miles of open sea to Ireland.

None too soon, the boat surged out of the current and over the breakwater, gliding into the marginally calmer waters below the MacDonald's southernmost watchtower. Not where they'd intended to land when setting out, but the nearest point of terra firma and better than no landing at all.

Hearing the hull scrape gravel, he slipped Valiant's ties and vaulted into the saddle. The moment the men hauled up the gangplank cover, his destrier lunged, and they were through the opening, his destrier stifle-deep in surf. Only when they were above the high watermark did Valiant stop and shake like a wet dog.

Nearly unseated, Britt growled, "Are you quite done?"

Snorting, Valiant shook again, gave his tail a final wring, then squared beneath Britt and arched his neck, coming off the bit, finally the picture of obedient patience.

"Humph!" Apparently his having the upper hand in this relationship was an illusion. His damn horse—like Gen—did as ordered only when it suited.

Britt, hunching against the wind, turned his destrier northeast toward the jagged peaks of the Cuillin Mountains which straddled Skye, separating MacKinnon land from that of the MacLean's to the west and MacDonald's to the north.

He traveled unchallenged through MacDonald territory— something their absent liege would doubtless find alarming— then crested the final black granite ridge that marked the beginning of MacKinnon territory for centuries. Seeing the softer, rounded contours of home which grew ever greener as they sloped toward the sea and the outlines of Pabay and Scalpay Isles, he swallowed the sudden thickness in his throat. His coming home had taken nine years and yet another loss.

On the headland to his right sat his father's granite fortress, Dun Haakon, named for the Norwegian king who, through his daughter, gave the MacKinnons their great height. And there too would be Cassandra, locked in the tower, where by now she should have rotted but had yet had the decency to do so.

Taking a deep breath, readying himself for the inevitable, he nudged Valiant forward. As he drew closer to Dun Haakon, scattering lowing, long-horned cattle hither and yon, clansmen and women, hearing the ruckus, peered out doors and windows. The first to greet him was Hamish, his father's ancient smithy.

"*Mo chreach!* As I live and breathe, if it isn't our prodigal son." The old man, grinning from ear to ear, reached for Valiant's bridle as Britt dismounted.

Britt clapped the old man's thick shoulder. "Good to see you, Hamish. I feared you'd be dead by now."

"Too ugly and bad, lad." Leading the way to the stable, he looked Britt up and down. "I must say you've grown a wee bit."

Britt nodded. Although battle tested, he'd still been more bone than muscle when he'd left. "Is the MacKinnon home?"

"Aye, but strange he didn't tell us you were coming."

"I didn't know myself until just a few days ago."

Mindless of the rain pelting them, Hamish came to an abrupt stop and placed a large, calloused hand on Britt's arm. "Then ye'd best hear this first before going in. 'Tis Cassandra. She's still as insane as ever, but—"

"Britt?"

Startled by the sound of Keith MacKinnon's voice, Britt turned. His father stood on the granite steps before the keep's open door. A smile played at the corners of his father's lips, yet his eyes remained wary, as if Britt might draw his sword. "I've feared I might not live long enough to see you again."

Had it not been for Genny, he would not have.

Britt bid good day to Hamish and strode toward his sire. The years had not been kind to the man who had chosen his daughter-by-marriage over his son. As the old hate welled within his breast, Britt noted his father's hair, once as dark and thick as Britt's, was now the color of ash. The man's handsome countenance had become gaunt, as was his frame, hunched like a weather-beaten pine bent against the sea.

"Father." A simple word, which should have been seeped in decades of love and respect, sounded flat to his ear, carried only feelings of betrayal.

The MacKinnon waved toward the door. "Come. We have much to discuss."

No. They'd said all that needed to be said nine years ago, but tired, hungry and wet to the skin, Britt followed his father into the keep.

The hall, crowded with those waiting out the storm, grew quiet as recognition dawned. A smiling titian took his sodden *breachen feile*. "Welcome home, Britt."

He studied the pretty lass, trying to recall her name.

Apparently sensing his dilemma she laughed. "I'm Wee Trisha, Britt, but not so wee anymore."

"Oh! You've changed so...grown quite lovely."

Blushing, she sketched a quick curtsy. "Why thank you." As others approached to greet him, she spread his wet *breachen feile* before the fire.

After the last of his clansmen had welcomed him home, he looked about and saw that the tapestry depicting the coming of Saint Columba to the Isles that his mother had slaved over for years still hung behind the head table and that the massive whale jaw still arched over the east wall's fireplace, intended as a reminder never to lose faith, that God would provide even when all appeared lost.

He could only pray.

His father motioned toward the high table adorned with the tall Irish candlesticks his mother had adored. "Sit."

Without thinking, Britt pulled out the heavy chair he'd occupied as a youth.

"Nay, here." His father indicated the chair to his immediate right, which had once been Ian's. To a lass Britt again didn't recognize, the MacKinnon said, "Keita, bring the best wine in the cellar."

Britt settled in Ian's chair. When the wine arrived, he took a sip. Italian. "I see you're still trading."

"MacKinnon beef, hides and wool still garner a fair amount of salt and wine."

Britt had long thought it a cruel twist of fate that although they were surrounded by the sea, their salt was useless for curing. For reasons beyond anyone's understanding, isle salt wouldn't break down their lean Highland beef and ruined their fish. They had to buy salt from the continent in order to preserve their meat and catches. And if memory served, his canny father would also garner a bit of grain, green marble and ornate metalwork, which he would later trade for flax, iron and the like along the way.

His father drained his cup, took a deep breath, then said, "Tell me of Alexander's passing."

Britt studied the man who had refused to prosecute Cassandra for killing their firstborn, a son, precious and joyful. At least his sire had not broken the covenant betwixt them...of his agreeing never to be in the same place at the same time with him. Had he, Britt would have been honor-bound to smite the man who had given *him* life.

Britt poured more wine, then related what he knew of their sovereign's passing and the political intrigue already underway.

"So we now await an heir."

"Aye." And if one wasn't forthcoming, they would have to prepare for a bloody and protracted war.

Ever the pragmatist, his father asked, "Who do you think will come to the fore as regent?"

When Britt shrugged, his father asked, "So if not to offer advice on whom to support should war ensue, what finally brings you home?"

"With Alexander dead, I'm at loose ends. I'll take over this year's cattle drive. Not just to Broadford so the MacDonald can take them to market, but as Ian did, taking the drove the entire way south to the Crieth Fair and negotiating the sales."

His father's brow furrowed like a walnut. "We don't need the coins your doing so would garner. If I agree—and I'm not saying I do, having already lost one son to the drove—what shall you do in the meantime?"

"I shan't be underfoot, if that's what you're worried about. I'll be scouring church records in hopes of finding sanguinity betwixt myself and Cassandra."

"Ah, now this makes sense. You're seeking an annulment."

An eerie keen issued from the stairwell, and the fine hairs on Britt's nape bristled. Head snapping around in the direction of the sound, he asked, "What was that?"

His father, also looking toward the stairwell, muttered, "Likely just a shutter torn free in the wind." He motioned to his squire and growled, "Tend to it."

Keeping his gaze on the stairwell as the worried-looking lad dashed off, Britt said, "Aye, I wish to remarry, and the only way that can come to pass is through breaking my tie to Cassandra." When the lad disappeared, Britt turned his attention back to his father and looked him in the eye. "Something I'd have no need of had *you* done what you should have done nine years ago—namely hang the bitch after she killed"—his voice cracked—"Ian."

Just saying his son's name aloud in this place where the precious laddie had lived for only five short months, then died, only served to make Britt's grief rawer, a festering wound that would not heal.

A crash resounded through the stairwell followed by a second, ear-piercing keen. Britt sprang to his feet. "Who the hell is that keening?"

His father rose beside him. "'Tis Cassandra."

"*What?*" Britt had been very specific when he left. The raving bitch was to be kept behind a locked door until such time as she passed into hell.

As he started toward the stairs, his father grasped his arm. "Be reasonable, son. You were gone, and the poor, mad thing would not stop banging her head against the stones. After weeks of it, hoping to distract her, we took her out under guard to the kale yard, where she sat there quiet as you please, talking to herself. We did this for months. When naught went awry, I discussed her release with the clan. In the end, we thought it safe to turn her loose."

Britt jerked his arm free. "She's a murderer, Father! You don't let a frigging murderer loose!"

Discovering what she'd done, mad with grief, Britt had gone after Cassandra, intent on killing her. His father, then younger and stronger, had stopped him. Thwarted, Britt had begged the man to bring her to justice, but his sire had refused, saying hanging Cassandra, mad as she was, wouldn't bring Ian back, that naught but a war betwixt the MacDonalds and the MacKinnons would be accomplished by doing as Britt begged. Furious, swearing never to breathe the same air as either his sire or wife so long as she lived, Britt had extracted his father's promise, then left.

That had been then, and his circumstances had changed, but only by a hair.

Blood thundered in his ears. Intent on recapturing Cassandra and locking her away for good if he had to swallow the damn key, Britt took off at a run, his father's shouts to stop echoing uselessly about the great hall.

He flew up the stairs, running past the hapless squire who was nursing a cut lip and already swelling eye. At the second landing, he caught sight of a blue skirt rounding the landing above.

He had her now. Even if she made it to the solar and barred the door, she was trapped. His father would have to find somewhere else to sleep for the next ten years or however long it took her to die.

Taking the tight, winding stones as fast as humanly possible, he reached the solar. Surprised to find the door open, he raced inside the large chamber. His gaze swept the room. Not seeing her, he whipped aside bed curtains, looked under the bed, inside the massive fireplace, behind the bathing screen and inside his father's many chests. "Where in hell are you?"

The garderobe! Britt ran into the adjacent privy chamber, fully expecting to find her cowering in a corner. Still not finding her, he peered down the hole. No action would be beyond her sick mind. Discovering the channel too narrow even for her, he returned to the solar.

Hands fisted on his hips and panting, he glared at the tall, canopied bed multiple generations of MacKinnons had occupied. "Damn Father for turning her loose."

She couldn't have escaped the solar unless she'd sprouted wings in his absence, which meant she'd somehow tricked him, and he now had to search the five rooms below.

At the second landing, he met up with his winded sire. "Did you find her?"

"Nay, the bitch has apparently grown wily and fleet of foot."

"Son, go down to the hall. I'll have the keep searched. She—and the staff—know this place far better than you after a decade's absence."

"And then what?"

"I'll see her locked away in the tower."

"See that you do. Should I come across her first—"

Without another word, Britt stomped down the stairs and into the hall, where he ignored his clansmen's silent stares and, with hands shaking, grabbed the bumper of wine, filled his goblet, downed the contents in gulps, then filled the goblet again.

When his father, ashen-faced, finally entered the hall, Britt glared at him. "Did you find her?"

"Nay, but we will."

Britt knew he couldn't stay within the keep so long as Cassandra was on the loose. He couldn't trust that he wouldn't do her harm and wasn't about to put his future with Genny at risk. Only his fear of losing Genny forever by imprisonment allowed him to say, "I'll be in the chapel until such time as you lock the bitch away."

Britt snatched his *breachen feile* from before the fire and walked out.

In the dark chapel, a jumble of memories assaulted him. Gazing at the graceful wooden arches supporting the vaulted ceiling, he again recalled his excitement watching their construction, then attending his first mass within, only to fervently wish he could escape after breathing nauseating incense for hours on end.

His footsteps echoed as he made his way down the nave toward the burial alcove as if announcing his loneliness, his feelings of isolation, to the world. Within these hallowed walls, he'd wept for his brother Ian, only to feel the same pain months later at his mother's requiem mass. Not long after followed Marcus's marriage mass, then his requiem mass, he brought down by war. And then his precious wee Ian's.

Since the shutters had been closed against the storm, he found the burial alcove blanketed by deep shadows and strode toward the sconce kept burning for any needing to find solace within the kirk. As his hand grasped the torch, he heard whispers and the sound of tearing coming from behind the altar, a great chunk of granite carved from the Cuillin Mountains to the west. He peered behind it and found a squatting crone shredding pages torn from their family bible.

Astounded anyone would think to do such, he bellowed, "Cease that!"

The MacKinnons had served as abbots of Iona since the coming of St. Columba. Two monks—one gifted in calligraphy and the other in artistic renderings—had slaved over the elaborately decorated and priceless tome for more than a decade.

The crone, issuing a high-pitched squeak, jumped to her feet and spun to face him.

He held out the torch to better view her face. "Oh my God...'tis you."

The woman whom he'd once loved was now barely recognizable. The vibrant hair he'd once so admired was now dull and shot with white. Her once lovely countenance had gone sallow and lined, making her appear two decades older than he knew her to be. Her lush form had also suffered the results of her madness, had shriveled to little more than skin and bone. Only her eyes remained unchanged, were still as dark and defiant as the last time he'd seen her.

Lips curling in derisive fashion over blackened teeth, she pointed to the shredded pages at his feet. "They're gone, so there!"

He looked down and noticed for the first time that the MacKinnon wood-bound and gilt-edged bible lay face-up. She'd not been tearing out random pages but had torn out the last sheets of parchment, those upon which generations of MacKinnons had carefully scribed every birth, christening, marriage and death for centuries.

"You mad bitch! How dare you destroy my family's records?"

"How dare *I*?" She hiked up her tattered skirt, stuck out a muddy foot and stomped on the fragments closest to her, grinding them to little more than dust on stone. "Now try to get your precious annulment!"

Blood roaring in his ears, fearing his chance for annulment—and Gen—might be lost to him forever, he shoved her back and bent to salvage what pieces he could.

"*Nay!*"

His father's voice reverberated like thunder through the nave. Wondering why he had come, Britt looked up and found one of the huge candlesticks from the altar racing toward him, bare inches from his head. Instinct made him duck, but too late. Stars flashed before his eyes as the weighty bronze caught him above his right ear. As he collapsed face-first to the cold granite floor, he was vaguely aware of Cassandra, keening, landing atop him, apparently determined to finish the job. As the world went black, he found himself wishing their roles were reversed. He would gladly see her good and truly dead.

"Son! Please, God..."

The weight pressing on Britt's neck and shoulders lifted, and he was rolled onto his back, his aching head coming to rest on something soft.

"Britt! Son, wake up."

Ah, 'twas his father. He'd recognize that gravel voice—despite its shaky tone—anywhere.

"Open your eyes, damn it."

Britt, confused, did as he was bid, only to find his vision clouded. He swiped at his eyes, wiping away a familiar wetness. Registering the scents of incense, smoke and copper, he looked at his hands. Blood. All came rushing back. He lurched upright, and the world spun. He was in the chapel, had found Cassandra destroying—

"Cassandra?" Had she made good her escape after clouting him? Christ's blood, his head hurt. For this alone, he would see her put in chains.

At his feet, the torch he'd carried had guttered but not before turning centuries of history to ash. How would he ever be able to garner his annulment now?

His father, white-faced, placed a hand at his back to steady him and tipped his head toward the altar. "There."

Britt turned. His wife lay prone on the cold floor in a crimson pool, his father's stag-horn-handled *sgian duhb* protruding from her neck. He knew the answer but still found himself asking, "Is she…?"

"Aye. 'Twas watch her bludgeon you to death or take her life." His father sighed in weary resignation as he came to his feet. "Should have done so long ago, and for that I beg your forgiveness."

His father held out his hand, and Britt took it and came to his feet. "You have it."

His wife was dead. He had no need for church records or an annulment to make Genny his. He was once again free, something he'd so longed to be, so why did he feel no elation? Why did he feel only this immeasurable sorrow looking at the woman who had vowed to love and honor him as he had her, and to bring forth babes and raise them in the one true faith?

He dashed away the tears welling in his eyes. Why this sorrow? For Cassandra, for his father, and aye, even for Genny.

Having no answers, he asked, "How will you explain this to the MacDonald?"

His father, looking older than he had only an hour ago, studied the woman at his feet. "I shan't. None from her sept have even bothered to pay her a visit these past five years. I shall ask Margret to prepare her for burial dressed with wimple and *couvrechef*—to mask the wound—then send word to the MacDonald. Should any from her sept deem to come, we shall tell them she died of dysentery after drinking from the cattle pond." He shook his head. "She was crazy enough to have done so, and all know it."

"And where shall she be buried?" He would not tolerate her being entombed in the kirk next to their son.

Apparently understanding, his father said, "In the cemetery with our clansmen...unless the MacDonald requests her return, which is highly unlikely."

Satisfied, Britt, head still throbbing, bent and scooped the lifeless form of his wife into his arms. How thin she felt, even in a thick woolen kirtle and cloak. "I'll take her inside, then clean up this mess."

His father stooped and picked up the family bible. "A damn shame...all our history lost."

"Surely you and the elders can recall some of what had been written."

His father, eyes glassy, ran a gnarled hand over the smooth, wooden cover. "Mayhap."

The MacKinnon preceded Britt into the crowded great hall. Seeing Britt carried Cassandra's limp body in his arms, his clansmen went quiet. The children who'd been running in play came to abrupt halts. The youngest, with mouths agape, took refuge behind their mothers.

"Listen!" his father ordered. "Cassandra MacKinnon has passed to her final reward, having grown deathly ill after drinking from the cattle pond. We shall hold her wake this eve at gloaming and her funeral at midday on the morrow." He looked about the room, daring any to contradict him. When none did, he said, "I need four volunteers to serve as pallbearers."

Four stout men raised their hands along with an eyebrow or two.

"My thanks. Please go about your business now."

As the hall cleared, Britt muttered, "Da, have you gone daft? They're not blind...can see blood covers her gown."

"True, but they also know what she did and that you're a MacKinnon and she is not."

"Remember the Alpin," Britt muttered. 'Twas the clan's battle cry, a tribute to their famous forbearer.

"Aye, and best you never forget who and what you are, lad, for they shan't. For someday, all this"—he waved a hand—"will be yours with but a nod of acceptance from them."

Britt took a deep breath. "I've given little thought to being liege." He'd not only been the youngest, but he'd been so furious with his father for so long, he never imagined himself returning, much less leading his clan.

"You'd best start, then. I shan't live forever."

True. And lies and half-truths had cost him far too much already. "People, a word, if you please."

Those still in the hall turned to listen. "Our liege tries to protect me and us with his tale. Lady MacKinnon was but a heartbeat from killing me, and the MacKinnon had no choice but to stop her. Say what you wish should you be asked how she died."

Now he must cling to the hope that lies hadn't taken everything.

Chapter Eighteen

"Truth is often harsh to tell." ~ Old Scottish Proverb

Soaked and chilled to the bone, eyes stinging from the assault of salty spray, Genny thanked God that she'd chosen by sheer chance a skilled and sensible captain. Never mind that she was still in Scotland. She was just grateful to be alive.

"Are you sure you don't wish to go on?" Darby shouted as Genny waited for one of the sailors to bring Silver down the gangway. "The repairs to the sail won't take but a day or two at most." Captain O'Neil had miraculously steered the cog through the worst of the storm and brought them into the relative safety of Loch Ryan, where they'd weighed anchor within view of Stranraer until high tide, at which point he raised the torn sail to half-mast and limped into port.

"I'm sure. Buddle is but three days' ride." She'd left much behind when she'd gone with Britt, and now, through an act of God, she'd been given an opportunity to retrieve her possessions and, more importantly, to convert her grain and wool stores to hard coin. Coins she and Greer would need to live, albeit frugally. Provided, of course, the Earl of Ross hadn't learned of her parents' passing and everything hadn't been commandeered by his new trackman.

"All right, but do keep in mind we'll be back in a fortnight. If you're not here, I very much doubt his nibs will wait." She nodded toward her husband, who was busy examining the damage the gale had wrought.

She gave Darby a hug. "I promise. How can I ever thank you for your kindness?"

"No need. 'Twas my pleasure." Darby brushed a loose strand from Genny's face and kissed her cheek. "Take care, and keep that bow and blade handy as you travel."

"I shall." With any luck, the weather would keep the villainous indoors.

Young Mickey, a funny, strapping lad of thirteen, brought her white-eyed palfrey down the gangway and helped her mount. After thanking him, she adjusted the reins and smiled down at them. "I shall see you in this very place in a fortnight. Take care, and thank your dear captain for me."

Waving farewell, Genny turned Silver due east toward home.

Three days later, exhausted and dirty, having slept in the saddle and in shieldings for only an hour here and there, she nearly wept seeing Buddle's rooftops poking up betwixt elm and oak. As she rounded the bend by the kirk, she looked up at the hill that she'd watched Britt charge down, leaping his destrier over tall hedgerows as if they were mere ant mounds. What was he doing now? Did he think about her as often as she thought of him? She hoped so, despite knowing the wish was selfish. Her agonizing over his loss, her acknowledging her vanity and bullheadedness, surely should be penance enough for both of them. But still she wondered.

The moment her cottage came into view, her heart stuttered. "Look, Silver, the roses really are in bloom." Saint Bride, she'd missed the sight but hadn't realized how very much until this moment.

To her right in the far pasture, her sheep grazed in contented fashion, white clouds on a lush field of green. And there on the knoll was her majestic and grumpy ram MacDuff, standing guard. She grinned.

Drawing closer to her cottage, she held her breath, looking for any signs that a new trackman may have already taken up residence. Seeing no smoke puffing from the chimney, no counterpanes being aired over windowsills, no linen flapping on the wash lines next to her kale yard, she turned her attention to the dovecote, shearing shed and stable. "Thank God and Saint Bride, naught stirs."

As tempting as it was to leap to the ground the moment she came abreast of her front door and race into the cottage, she steered Silver toward the stable. Not until she stripped him of tack, wiped down his lathered sides, filled his water bucket and tossed hay to him did she walk back to the cottage. Heart thudding with apprehension, she pressed down on the latch with a shaking hand. The door swung wide, and she crossed the threshold into the cool interior.

"Thank God."

The parlor was just as she'd left it, save for the dust coating the floor and modest furnishing. Taking a shaky breath, she walked through the house and then checked the loft where she found her mother's cedar chest—its contents undisturbed—still tucked under the eaves. In the dovecote, she found her secret stores of grain and wool. Not believing her good fortune, she returned to the cottage and collapsed in the rocking chair and burst into tears.

She'd lost Britt through vain stupidity, but God had granted her a boon by seeing to her and Greer's future. Now she must make every effort to see that His efforts weren't squandered. And all within a fortnight.

Much to Britt's relief, Cassandra's funeral proved a short and simple affair. An aunt and wailing woman from the MacDonald clan had come, much to everyone's surprise, peered into the coffin and then extended their condolences to Britt and his sire. Under a clearing sky, the MacKinnon read a short but appropriate verse from what remained of the family bible, then Britt, as custom dictated, threw the first handful of dirt onto the coffin. When everyone returned to the keep for refreshments, Britt, feeling as if the weight of the world had been lifted from his shoulders, turned toward the chapel.

Inside, he studied his mother's black granite effigy. The stonemason had done a masterful job of not only capturing her beauty but her importance to his clan with the ornamentation of the MacKinnon and Campbell crests lying upon her chest in unyielding stone.

To her right, in the wall vaults next to his brothers, lay his son. Britt ran his fingers over the child's delicate features carved in stone, then down the curve and swell of his gown, feeling small nicks and grooves that shouldn't be there. Frowning, he leaned closer. The stonemason had offered to craft straight wee legs beneath the long gown, but Britt said nay, he wasn't ashamed of his son. He wanted his child to appear as he had in life. But someone had tried to alter the stone.

"Britt, are you all right?"

He straightened at the sound of his father's voice. "Aye." Hand on the marks, he said, "Ian's effigy has been defaced. Why would anyone do such a thing?"

His father drew closer and, looking to where Britt pointed, sighed. "Why did Cassandra do anything?"

Cassandra. Of course.

"What shall you do now, son? Will you remain?"

Britt shook his head. "Now that I'm free, I need to find Genny."

"Damn beasts." Sitting at her kitchen table, chin resting heavy in her hand, Genny counted again the meager coins she'd garnered from what remained of her grain stores after the mice had gotten into the bails. How wee vermin could consume so much in so short a time was beyond kenning. Worse than cleaning what grain she could salvage was the fact that the labor had proved tedious, giving her far too much time to think. Hour upon hour she'd thrashed and fashed over how her sister would take the news of the king's demise, over Greer's birthing, and worse, over her parting with Britt.

Never had she imagined it possible to miss anyone more than she missed Greer, but her longing for Britt went well beyond the ache in heart and mind she felt being separated from her twin. This new pain went bone and soul deep, to the point where she had no desire to eat, only to sleep, yet sleep proved elusive. She only wept. Chores that had to be done to secure her and Greer's future were also proving nearly impossible to do. Her limbs felt heavy, as if lead had replaced their marrow. Had she not breathed without thought, breathing would likely have ceased.

If she were brave, she would write to him. Tell him how sorry she was for running as she had. She should have been woman enough to face him, admit her own complicity in their affair and listened to whatever explanation he might have. Hearing him out wouldn't have made any difference—he was still married—but at least she would have had the satisfaction of knowing she wasn't a coward. But she was a coward, hadn't admitted her own complicity until Darby had made her see the light, so she hadn't written and she wouldn't.

She could only take comfort where she could. The grain was sold, and she and Greer would be safe in Ireland should war break out. That Britt would be in the thick of it should war come she dared not think about, for then her heart would surely stop.

Better she focus on the remaining tasks before her. She had only a week to clean her wool of mouse droppings and find a merchant who'd give her a fair price before making her way back to Stranraer. By sheer force of will she rose, gathered her coins and placed them in her hiding kist. If she missed O'Neil's ship, she'd have to pay another captain for passage to Ireland, something she could ill afford.

Seeing Mittens studying her through narrowed eyes from the windowsill, she growled, "Don't you be lookin' at me like that. 'Tis your fault half my grain was eaten, and I've now wool to nitpick."

The cat, stretching, yawned.

"Damn beasts."

Feet dragging, she crossed the kale yard, her goal the dovecote and what would likely be hours of mindless nitpicking and hours of fashing. She sighed. Reaching for the door handle, she heard a familiar bleating, looked over her shoulder and found auld MacDuff, his huge horns curling about his head, standing on his hind legs, peering over the stone wall at her. "So, you've finally come to say hello."

He bleated again, making her grin. Her wool forgotten, she crossed the kale yard, leaned over the wall and scratched MacDuff behind his ears. "So you missed me. Good to know someone has."

He nuzzled her neck, then gave her shoulder a gentle butt. Taking him by the horns, she pulled his formidable head toward her and kissed his forehead. "I missed you as well, you scraggly auld thing. In fact, I've missed everything here."

Silver nickered in his stall. "Hush, you. I'll not have any jealousy here." God knew she'd suffered enough just thinking about another woman lying in Britt's arms to last her a lifetime. The gray apparently thought not and nickered again, this time shrilly. MacDuff, snorting, jerked away, his attention riveted on something behind her. A deep nickering filled the air. She spun in alarm only to have her heart leap into her throat. A black destrier, his huge hooves flashing in the sunlight, a dust storm rising behind, strode toward her. Atop him, riding straight and proud in the saddle, rode the man she longed for but never thought to see again.

Seeing Genny at the edge of the pasture, Britt, heart soaring, couldn't believe his good fortune. She'd not gone to Ireland after all, but stood, a hand at her breast, not but a few hundred yards from him. Praying she'd not bolt, would hear him out, he put his heels to Valiant's sides.

As he drew closer, Genny, to his monumental relief, grabbed her skirts in hand and started loping toward him. He reined in and leapt to the ground. Closing the distance between them, he saw that she was crying, and held out his arms. She crashed into him much as she had in the wood so many weeks ago, and he scooped her up in his arms. "I was right. You do kiss your beasts."

Her arms flew around his neck. His hand burrowed beneath her hair and brought her lips to his. She tasted of oats and parsley, of salt and honey, of everything that was good in the world.

When they came up for air, her fingers fluttered over his scruffy jaw. As if not believing he was real, she asked, "How...why?"

He pressed her head to his shoulder and squeezed, wishing he could absorb her so she might never leave him again. "I so feared I'd not be able to find you."

In unison, they said, "I'm sorry," then laughed in awkward fashion.

She spoke first, saying, "I'm still angry with you, Britt. You should have told me."

"You've every right." Britt put her down but kept his arms about her. "And you've naught to be sorry about. I should have told you I was married at the very beginning."

"Why hadn't you?"

"I so treasured what little time I had with you that I couldn't bear sullying it with..." He took a deep breath. "I hated her, Genny. Hated her with every ounce of my being. Just thinking about her and what she'd done was so beyond understanding. I just couldn't speak of her. Not then, but she's gone now."

Genny, her winged eyebrows tenting, leaned back to better look at his face. "What did she do, and what do you mean by *gone*?"

Sighing, he took a step back, picked up Valiant's reins, then took her hand. "The telling of Cassandra and me will take some time, so let's first tend to my mount."

Leading Valiant to the stable, he asked, "Why are you here? You told Hildy you were bound for Ireland."

234

"I was." She told him about the O'Neils, the storm and her decision to garner what coins she could before travelling on. "Why are you here?"

"You'd told Hildy only your aunt's first name. I hoped to find her surname in yon kirk records or from one of your tenants. For no other reason than loneliness, I decided to stop here first, and glad I am that I did."

She smiled up at him. "As I am."

He shuddered to think they might have missed each other by only hours.

Once Valiant was fed and watered, he took her into his arms again. "God, you're a
bonnie sight for these poor eyes."

"To mine as well. You've no idea how much I've missed you."

He kissed her again, this time taking them slowly into that lovely place of warm intimacy, his need for her pressing against her belly as their breath and skin heated. Realizing he'd be tossing her into the hay at any moment, he reluctantly pulled away and cleared his throat. "We need to talk before this goes any further."

Inside her parlor, she bid him take a seat and fetched them wine. Having done naught but sit in a saddle for days on end, he paced.

When she returned with clay goblets in hand, he bid her sit in the odd chair with stave rockers and, kneeling before her, took her hand. "You need know I never meant to take advantage of you, that before you ran off I'd already queried the archbishop about an annulment. Wanting to marry you, I'd formulated a plan to make it so." He ran his thumb over her palm. "I never meant to hurt you, Genny. Truly."

"Please tell me about Cassandra."

He released her hand, rose and resumed pacing. "In the isles, we've harsh weather and little arable land. One storm can ravage a year's crops or destroy a fishing fleet, so the wise—ever mindful of starvation—trade, hoard and curry the goodwill of their neighbors through marriage." He knew what he was about to tell Genny would hurt her, but he'd have no more lies betwixt them. "Such was not the case when the lord of the isles and my father brokered my marriage to Cassandra, the MacDonald's niece.

"I was eight and ten years and she a year younger when we were introduced at a gathering. I am not a man of extremes but was immediately smitten. She was as exuberant and gay as a filly. Finding her attractive, I thought myself most fortunate that she returned my favor. During our short courtship, I chalked up her outrageous pouts and tantrums to youth and her being a pampered wench. I thought time and the responsibilities of marriage and family would settle her. But such proved not to be the case.

"Three months into our marriage, she fell ill, her moods swinging from outrageous highs to new dramatic lows as never before, so I, frantic, summoned our *Cailleach*." When Genny frowned, he said, "Our medicine woman."

"Ah. So what did she say?"

"She announced Cassandra with child and then, using her herbs and a string swung in loops above Cassandra's middle, said we would have a strapping laddie. My joy knew no bounds. Nor did Cassandra's. As she grew more ponderous, her frantic activity slowed but not so her babblings or blind rages. Then the day of the blessed event came. I'll not lie. I not only anticipated the birth of our son but the cessation of her constant weeping and throwing of things at my head."

Praying he was doing the right thing by laying bare his soul, he took a gulp of wine, then said, "Cassandra's labor was long and arduous, but finally our laddie came into the world. Hearing his lusty cry from where I paced in circles a floor below, I raced up the stairs and into the solar just as the *Cailleach* held up our son for Cassandra's inspection.

"Upon first sight of our babe's sadly deformed legs and feet, Cassandra screeched in horror, declared wee Ian the devil's spawn and refused to touch him.

"I couldn't understand it." Feeling tears burning at the back of his throat, he turned from Genny and looked out the window. "He was such a bonnie, pudgy lad, with her auburn hair and my dark eyes. A full day went by. All the poor wee lad did was keen for lack of milk. At my wit's end, I finally gave up trying to make Cassandra see reason and summoned a wet nurse."

Genny rose and took hold of his hand. "Oh, Britt, I'm so sorry. You need not speak of this if it's too painful."

"You need hear it all...to understand." He took another drink, readying himself for the worst. "Five months passed. Cassandra's blind rages had turned into sulking silence, then into what appeared to be contented musing.

"Meanwhile, Ian bloomed under the wet nurse's care"—and his love—"growing into a charming bundle of joy, one who could sit on his own and finally creep about."

He let go of her hand and resumed his pacing as she watched from before the window. "Oh, don't mistake me. I had no delusions. I knew life would be hard for a lad unable to walk, but within Ian's dark brown eyes I saw an innate intelligence, mayhap even his grandsire's canniness. With the MacKinnons at his back, I had nay doubt our wee bairn *would* make his own way, mayhap by following his forbearers into the Abbey of Iona to become a scholar or mayhap by taking over our clan's correspondence and complex trading ledgers, but he would succeed.

"Then one day, the wet nurse had to leave the babe for just a moment to fetch clean nappies from the line and left him, fresh from his bath, in Cassandra's care, and Cassandra..."—his voice cracked and he cleared his throat—"drowned our child."

"Oh dear God!" Genny, her bonnie blue eyes wide in alarm, pressed a hand to her heart. "How could a mother...?"

"I happened to be walking by the chamber and found Cassandra drenched to the skin, holding my beautiful laddie beneath the water." Using the heels of his hands, Britt dashed the tears from his eyes. "Ian had apparently struggled, fought to live, and she in her madness had had to work to hold him under water. Blind with rage, I slung her across the room, scooped up my bonnie babe and tried to breathe life back into him, but 'twas too late."

Genny, having apparently heard enough and not wanting to hear more, tugged on his hand. "Come."

He knew without being told that she would lead him to the loft where they would make love until the new moon rose. Knowing a child might come forth from the union, he pulled her close. "Nay, you need to hear it all." He led her to the chair and bid she sit.

"Gen, I tried to kill her that day." He related his finding Cassandra, who'd fled to the hall, and his strangling her, only to be foiled by his father. He told her about his fury when his father refused to bring her to judgment and the conditions he'd asserted for her confinement.

"So she escaped and somehow died?"

Britt told her what transpired upon his return to Skye. "So there you have it. In the end, she still died by my father's hand, and I am free at last."

Genny wiped the tears from her cheeks and shook her head. "I don't know how you've endured such sadness."

He crossed the room and knelt before her. Taking her hands in his, he brought them to his lips. What he now had to tell her would prove the hardest of all to say, for it could mean losing her forever.

"Gen, I did not tell you all this in an effort to garner your sympathy. The truth is that I love you beyond reason, nearly lost my mind when I saw you sail away. I wish to make you mine before God and man, but before I can ask you to bind your life with mine, you need ken one more thing." The smile that had been taking shape on her lovely countenance slowly shifted to one of wariness, her lower lip catching betwixt her teeth. "With me, it could happen again. I could sire another babe with misshapen legs."

There. He'd said it aloud. In a cruel twist of fate, his body, perfect as few were in trunk and limb, had flawed seed. The truth hurt as little had, but she either had to accept the possibility of having a child like his precious Ian, or she needed to send him away and find another more worthy of her. He could not—would not—go through the anguish again.

She studied him for too long a while, then said, "Since you've been honest with me, I too must be honest with you."

His heart sank. Fearing he might be physically ill, he started to rise, but she placed her hands on his shoulders. "Nay. You asked, and so now you must hear." She shifted her hands to either side of his face. "Look at me."

When he did, she said, "Had you posed this question to me the day you crossed yon threshold for the first time, I, having never been in love and never wanting to be, would have said nay, I would not knowingly lie with a man who might give me such a bairn. But I now ken we're all flawed in one way or another...I mayhap more than many. In my ignorance and vanity, I'd initially blamed everyone but myself for becoming the lover of a married man. But no more. I've come to see that I love you beyond measure. Should we have a bairn who is not perfect, I promise he or she"—she grinned—"or *they* will be treasured, for my bairns will be conceived in love with a man I can no longer imagine living without." Fresh tears cascaded down her cheeks. "I thought I'd lost you and found it almost impossible to breathe. I love you, Britt MacKinnon, and so will love any and all bairns we make, whether they be physically perfect or not."

Britt had trouble breathing. "Are you certain?"

She smiled, and her adorable dimple came out of hiding. "Aye, absolutely certain."

Laughing, he stood and pulled her into his arms, then swung her in a huge circle, sending her skirts flying. After kissing her soundly, he said, "Then we must find a priest, for I will make you mine before the cock crows."

"Oh no, we can't."

"Why ever not?"

"Because, dearest, I shan't marry without Greer at my side. We've gone through too much not to share this, the most important day in my life."

"Humph." Britt had given little thought to her twin since Genny had run off. The sisters likely had few secrets betwixt them, and Greer had no love for him. Nor he for her. He trusted her no more than he did Yolande.

His decision on what to do next made, he smiled down at the love of his life. "As you lust. We shall formally wed in Ireland, but first I need ken which man among your sept is the most respected, influential."

"I suppose that would be Smithy. He's the eldest and— *Eeeee!*"

Grabbing her by the waist, Britt caught Genny up as if she were but a bairn of three, gave her hurdies a gentle squeeze, making her squeal again, and strode out the door.

Fists beating his shoulder, Genny shouted, "Have you lost your mind, MacKinnon?"

"Nay, just doing what needs to be done, love."

"What's he doin' to ye, Lady Armstrong?" the tallest of the laddies following them asked. "Should I fetch Da for ye?"

"No!" The last thing she needed was their parents coming to look too. Her face had to be scarlet from all the caresses Britt had administered to her thighs and bottom as he carried her toward the village, not to mention all the delicious things he'd told her he was about to do to her, how he would kiss her—in ways even Hildy had neglected to mention—the moment his mission was done.

Running to keep up with Britt's long strides, another lad said, "Gold spurs! The giant's a knight!"

She heard the clang of steel on steel before catching the pungent scent of sulfur rising off the coals burning in the smithy's forge. Britt finally stopped and lowered her to her feet.

Growling, having no idea what Britt was about, she raked the hair off her face and tried to straighten her gown as Britt slipped an arm about her waist.

"Good day," Britt called to the smithy as he ushered her toward the shade of the stable.

Smithy, a burly man a head shorter than Britt but equal in width, looked from Britt to her, then back to Britt. With hammer in hand, he glowered at Britt. "Are ye all right, m'lady?"

Mortified, she huffed. "Aye, though *he* might not be for much longer."

"And who might *he* be?"

Keeping a firm hold on her waist, Britt bowed. "Sir Britt MacKinnon of the clan MacKinnon of Skye at your service, and I've come to ask a boon for my lady and myself."

"A boon, ye say?"

"I wish you and these gentlemen"—he pointed to two younger men, who, curious, had gathered round—"to bear witness to my handfasting to Lady Geneen."

"Handfasting?" Genny sputtered. "You said we'd *marry*!"

He grinned. "And we shall." To Smithy, he said, "She's yet to select day and place. You ken my situation. She's most fair and fulsome, and I am a mere mortal..."

A look of understanding seemed to pass betwixt the men, and Britt nodded. "So ye see we need be bound by the auld laws."

Smithy looked at Genny. "Is this so, m'lady? Ye've agreed to join with this Canteran?"

Fearing Britt might bristle at the Lowlanders' derogatory term for their northern neighbors, Genny rushed to assure Smithy. "Aye, I've agreed, for he's an honorable knight of girth and sword."

"Humph!" Smithy eyed Britt again, then said to Genny, "All right, then. Hold out yer arms, m'lady."

Having no idea why, she did as he bid. Smithy squeezed the flesh of her upper arms, then grasped her hands and ran his thumbs over her calloused palms. Looking at Britt, he said, "Just making sure ye have the right one. With them ye can never tell who's who lest ye look real hard or one of 'em sings. Yers can't."

As Genny glowered at Smithy, Britt grinned. "So I've noted."

"Then get on with it, sir. I ain't got all day."

Britt took her hands in his and, looking deep into her eyes, said, "Before these witnesses, I, Britt Alexander MacKinnon of Skye, take you, Geneen Armstrong of Buddle, to wife." He repeated it twice more then added, "Not for just a year and a day but for all the days of my life."

Heart swelling, she wrapped her arms about his neck. Into the warmth of their mixed breath, she whispered, "I accept."

"Make way!" a woman shouted, elbowing her way through the crowd that had taken shape around them. "'Tis true, then? One of our ladies is hitched?"

Recognizing the voice, Genny mentally winced. "Mrs. MacFee, how good to see you. Aye, 'tis true and more."

The woman examined Genny from hair to slippers, all of which were in disturbing disarray. "And which Lady Armstrong might ye be?"

Genny sighed. "Lady Geneen."

"Ah, our tax collector."

Since her tone held no malice, Genny said, "Britt, may I present our midwife, Mrs. Maude MacFee."

Britt took the old woman's hand, plump as dough, and bowed deeply. "Britt MacKinnon of Skye at your service, m'lady."

Auld Maude turned crimson, then, collecting herself, flapped her apron at one and all. "Away to me croft, the lot of ye. Can't be having a wedding without buns and mead. 'Twould be unchristian. Hie now, 'fore I change my mind."

A cheer went up. Maude had a knack not only for birthing babes but for making the best mead among the villagers. Someone pulled a whistle from their belt, and to a shrill tune, they all marched to the midwife's croft.

"Saint Columba, I thought they'd never let us go." Britt, stripped of his clothing, collapsed onto the bed, pulled Genny to his chest and draped a thigh over hers. Feeling her breath against his throat, her delightful pink-tipped breasts pressing against his chest, he ran his hands over the sweet velvet of her skin and sighed. *Mine! Every luscious curve, every sunlit tress, all mine.*

Snuggling into his embrace, she patted his cheek. "You've none to blame but yourself. Had you not started the sleight of hand, pulling coins from behind the wee ones' ears, we might have escaped the merriment sooner."

"True, but they were so determined to make our union a joyous occasion, how could I deny them?" Word had already reached the villagers that their king was dead. When pressed for answers, he'd told them an heir was on the way. But the adults knew the ways of nature, that the babe could be stillborn or frail. That even a healthy son might not prevent war. So he'd provided them what little joy he could.

And now 'twas his turn to celebrate the fact that he had the woman he loved in his arms.

Lulled by excellent ale and hearty food, he began their lovemaking in leisurely, luxurious fashion, him taking his time worshiping his hard-won prize, Genny relaxed and giving. As he stroked, she purred. As they kissed, her flesh heated much like a well-tended fire. Her soft breaths became pants. His gentle stroking betwixt her thighs caused her to gasp. Feeling her grow exceedingly slick and arch beneath his fingers, he rolled and settled between her thighs. Looking into her eyes, he smiled and told her, "I've dreamed of this every night since first making love to you."

"Britt."

"Hmm?"

"Shhh." She grasped his neck and pulled his mouth to hers. Her hips arched to meet his, and slick with need, she welcomed him home.

Unlike their first mating, this time there was no anxiety, only wonder. This lovely blonde goddess beneath him—his ladywife—knowing the truth, still loved and wanted him. The knowledge made it all that more difficult to bide his time. None too soon she, panting, went rigid beneath him. *That's the lass.*

Keening his name, she shuddered, her womb throbbing, bidding him come, and so he did.

Chest heaving, glistening with sweat, Britt collapsed onto his forearms above her, then, garnering what strength he had, slowly rolled onto his back, taking her with him.

Genny, heaving an equally contented sigh, rested her head on Britt's chest, deciding this coming together was even better than their first. "Oh my. If this is to be expected with every joining, I might not survive to see my next birthday."

Britt, his eyes closed and breath slowing, stroked her back. "When is it?"

"The first day of June. And unlike last year, I shall celebrate with Greer." At which point she would apologize to her sister. If Greer felt like this—after being loved and held by the king—then she understood how her sister had come to be with child. "Do you think word of the king's death has reached Ireland yet?"

"I'd be surprised if it hasn't, given the amount of trade conducted betwixt our countries."

"Might Greer have already heard?"

"That will depend on how close she is to a port and how politically connected your aunt is."

"I've no idea about either." *Lord, don't let me have to be the bearer of such sad tidings.*

With the crook of his finger, Britt lifted her chin from his chest to better look into her eyes. Sounding aghast, he asked, "Are you saying you had no idea where you were bound when you boarded that cog?"

"Well, I, uhmm...knew the name of her estate."

"Good God almighty."

Hoping to distract, she said, "Kenning we'd be wed in just weeks, why did you handfast with me?" Did he fear she'd renege on her promise?

He huffed and settled back against the pillow. "We ken not what the morrow may bring, *a ghraidh.* War could erupt, taking me from you. The cog could flounder, and I could be lost. I thought it imperative you have my name so if need be, you could seek refuge with my family."

"Stop." She shuddered. "I refuse to give a moment's thought to losing you."

"Thank you, but denial provides no protection. We may have just made a bairn."

A bairn. Not wishing to cause him worry but deciding she had to be prepared for the worst, she asked, "You said Ian would never have walked. What precisely was wrong?"

"He was perfect...except for his lower limbs. They were of normal size but shaped like..." Britt bowed his arms in a circle, flexing his wrist inward at an awkward angle.

"You mean clubbed?"

He shrugged. "We had no word for it, since none within our sept had seen such before."

"Really? Do you recall the lad with the crutch at the party?"

"Aye, the one who walked on tiptoes. I believe his name is Johnnie."

She nodded. "He was born with legs and feet such as you describe."

"But he could walk, albeit awkwardly."

"Aye, thanks to Auld Maude. Having attended his birthing, she took the lad in hand immediately. She showed his mother how to pad his wee legs and feet with fleece, then how to tie them to greenwood strips she had the carpenter make at her direction. The first looked like ladders. As he grew, the wood grew longer and straighter, and so too, slowly but surely did the laddie's legs and feet to what they are now. Not perfect but close. Took years and not a few bruises—the babe was stout and could fling those wood-clad legs like battering rams, but as you saw, he can now get about easily enough."

Britt was now sitting. "You're quite sure his deformity was as I described?"

"Most certain. Maude believes his condition was due to his not having enough room in the womb."

Britt pulled Genny to him and wrapped his arms about her. "Woman, you have no idea how much this eases my mind."

Oh, but she *could*, having imagined all manner of deformities including the possibility of her having a child with flippers like a seal—for anyone who kenned anything kenned many an Isles man had selkie blood in him.

To learn wee Ian simply had clubbed feet was such a relief, she could have wept. Now she just had to learn all she could from Maude about the use of wood bracing in the event she needed the knowledge. Britt, being so huge, was likely to sire another large bairn.

Britt settled back and pulled her down with him. "What do you think your sister will say when she learns that we're handfast and soon to officially marry?"

She ran her fingers through the dark silky hair on his chest. "Why, she'll be most pleased for us."

"I wish I was so certain."

Genny rose onto her elbows and found Britt frowning. "My love, why do you fash? Greer and I may have had our disagreements—particularly over her relationship with the king—but we're twins. We love each other and have always wanted only happiness for the other. You'll see. She'll be most pleased."

Chapter Nineteen

"No hold can be got of water, or of fire." ~ Old Scottish Proverb

Riding through dense wood, Britt couldn't believe Genny had even contemplated traveling through this wilderness alone, much less set out to do so.

Since arriving in Waterford three days past, they'd encountered no fewer than five roving warrior bands. Worse, these Celtic cousins of theirs were well armed and excellent horsemen. No way could Genny have outrun them on her little palfrey. Being fair and fulsome, she'd have found herself caught, enslaved or wed to one of the many warring principals before she'd had chance to scream. Just thinking about it made his skin crawl.

"Are we almost there?" she asked.

They'd been heading north, following the Nore River and a line of tower fortresses in search of Benbirk, the Macintyre's keep, meaning there was something to be said for the Sassenach's obsession with castle building. Made hunting easier. "Aye, the keep should be coming into view shortly."

"I can't wait to see Greer again. By now, she must be glowing, ripe with babe."

He couldn't picture it.

"Look! There it is."

Joy.

He would have cut off his sword arm to avoid this reunion, save for the fact that Genny so wanted it.

They emerged from beneath the shaded canopy, and a bugle sounded. Men, bows at the ready, made their presence known along the parapets. Fearing someone might let loose an arrow, he said, "I'll ride ahead. Stay here."

"But—"

"Genny, for once, please do as I say."

She huffed but reined in, and Britt went on ahead. When he came within hailing distance, he shouted, "Britt MacKinnon and the Lady Geneen Armstrong of Buddle, niece of Lady Margret Macintyre and sister of Lady Greer, seeking entrance."

The men conferred, a moment passed, then a guard shouted, "Enter."

The portcullis ground up, then a massive oak door opened, exposing a small bailey. As Genny came abreast of him, she muttered, "You really need to consider being a bit less suspicious, husband."

He rolled his eyes.

They were greeted at the door by a spritely lass who led them into a modestly furnished but comfortable hall. Genny's Aunt Margaret, a frail, petite blonde of perhaps four score, greeted Genny with great enthusiasm. Upon learning who Britt was and that he and Genny were engaged, she beamed, her eyes filling with tears of joy.

After asking after their comfort and ordering ale, Lady Margaret said, "We've a surprise of our own. Your sister has given birth."

Genny sputtered, "But...but she's not due for months yet."

"Appearances can be deceiving, dear. I'm sure you wish to see her. She's on the third floor."

Genny, her excitement evident, hiked up her skirts and all but flew up the stairs. Over her shoulder, she said, "I can't believe she's already birthed."

Following at a slower pace, Britt mustered a smile as he did some fast calculations. Greer Armstrong had to have already been with child when Alexander took Yolande to wife. Not that her having Alexander's bastard would matter...unless the child was male and the queen gave birth to a weak female...or lost her babe.

At the third floor landing, Genny found her sister's bedchamber door ajar. Peering in, she whispered, "Greetings, sister."

From several steps below, he heard Greer gasp. "Genny! Come in, come in. I've someone to show you."

Genny rushed inside. "Oh, I've missed you so!"

From the doorway, he watched the sisters embrace. Knowing they were twins hadn't really prepared him for seeing them together for the first time. Unease skittered down his spine. Two beautiful women so alike on the surface, yet so different beneath the skin. Was Genny aware of just how different? He doubted she was, having heard her self-deprecating tales of their childhood. Now to learn who, in truth, held sway in this unique relationship.

Greer, propped up in bed and looking a bit tired but happy, pointed to the cradle at her side. "I had a laddie, Genny."

Peering into the cradle, Genny cooed, "Oh, he's darling, and look, he's got red curls."

"Like his father."

Not until Genny bent closer did Greer notice that he stood in the doorway. Turning ashen, she looked at her sister. "Genny, what is the meaning of this?"

Genny scooped up the swaddled babe. "No need to fash, Greer. All's well. I have news of my own. Sir Britt and I are handfast."

Looking incredulous, Greer looked from him to her sister. "You're *what*?"

"Sir Britt asked for my hand, but I insisted we wait to officially wed until you could be at my side, and did the next best thing until such time as we could find you." She held the babe up for Britt's perusal. "Isn't he just the most splendid wee thing you've ever seen, Britt?"

Nodding, Britt mustered a smile and stroked the babe's cheek. For the wee one's ears alone, he whispered, "Long live the king."

"Sir Britt," Greer said, "I lust to be alone with my sister."

Bristling at Greer's imperious tone, Britt, ignoring her, turned to his wife. "What do you lust, Genny?"

Babe in arms, she murmured, "'Twill be all right. She's just been through an arduous ordeal, and now we've taken her by surprise." She then rose on tiptoes and kissed his cheek. "I'll be down in just a few moments."

"I'll be in the hall."

Genny closed the door and frowned at her sister. "Dismissing Britt in such fashion was unaccountably rude."

"What was rude was you bringing him here in the first place, putting my and Alexander's lives in danger."

"Me? You named him after his father, and after all we've gone through."

"Nay, I named him after our beloved dead king."

The comment took the wind out of Gen's ire. She placed the sleeping babe in his cradle and sat on the bed. Taking her sister's hand in hers, she murmured, "My deepest condolences, Greer. How are you faring?"

Greer shrugged. "As well as can be expected having lost Alexander, my home, and having gone through a harrowing birthing among strangers in this godforsaken place."

"Poor dautie." Genny patted her hand. "I can well imagine your pain." She'd keened herself ill just thinking she'd lost Britt.

Greer snatched her hand away. "You've no idea the pain I've been through."

"Not all but some." Not thrilled to relive their time apart but knowing Greer needed to know what transpired, Genny related all she'd endured at the queen's hand in her sister's stead.

By the end, her palms were sweaty and her heart again raced. Greer, apparently unfazed, said, "I still don't understand why you brought him here."

"There's no need for alarm, Greer. Britt has promised to keep your secret."

"How can you be so sure that he will?"

"First, because 'tis best for Scotland. Second, because he knows I couldn't bear the pain if something ill was to befall you or the wee one, and third, because he loves me."

Greer snorted. "Oh, and pray tell how did *that* come to pass?"

"That he loves me?" When her sister nodded, Genny couldn't help but grin. "I know this will sound preposterous, but somewhere betwixt my leaving Buddle with him and my being imprisoned, we simply fell in love."

"Genny, he's married! And what makes you so certain he fell in love with you and not with me? After all, we do look alike, and I often found him watching me whilst I was in Edinburgh."

Since Genny had wondered the same, her sister's question shouldn't have hurt, yet it did. "Greer, he realized I was an imposter almost immediately, and he *was* married, but is now a widower." Genny blew through her teeth, deciding to credit her sister's comment to her being under a dreadful amount of stress. Hoping to alleviate Greer's concerns and her own guilt over their painful parting in Annan, she told Greer about the night she and Britt first made love, how she'd bared her soul to Britt, and then, not a day later, thought she'd lost him forever.

"Greer, I'm so sorry for the accusations I hurled at you before we parted. I'd never been in love, so had no means of understanding what you were going through. Now I do." She took her sister's hand and smiled. "That's why when Britt wanted to marry immediately, I said nay. I wanted to wait until you and I reunited and our troubles were put to rest."

Instead of pulling her into a warm embrace as Genny fully expected, Greer, looking none too pleased, shot out of bed, wrapped a robe about her and started pacing the room.

"All right," she said, "matters could be worse. At least you're only bound for a year and a day. Before you end up with child, we'll make arrangements for you to sleep with me. I'm sure there's a bigger spare chamber somewhere in this keep."

What was her sister going on about? "Greer, I prefer to sleep with my husband, thank you, and besides, I could already be with bairn."

"He's not truly your husband yet, and we won't ken if you are or aren't with bairn until the next full moon, now will we?" She stopped before Genny. "Dearest, I've had naught to do since arriving on these godforsaken shores but think, and have come to the conclusion we must return to Buddle before the fall tithes are due and the earl discovers he needs a new trackman. The howdie-wife said the babe and I should be able to travel after a month. Once home, you can collect the wool and whatnot and send them on as you always do, then resume your gardening and husbandry, which will be enough to keep us from starving."

How presumptuous! "And what shall you be doing whilst I do as all you suggest?"

"Why, I'll be tending my babe, of course, until such time as I get my figure back and can return to Edinburgh."

Genny shook her head, not believing her ears. "And what would you do there?"

"Find a husband, of course."

"How can you even think such when you're in mourning?"

Hands on her hips, Greer shook her head at Genny as if she were the village dolt, too thickheaded to understand even the simplest of things. "Genny, I grieved, but now I must move beyond it. I'm a mother now and need to provide for my child. Besides, only you—and MacKinnon—ken the truth about Alexander."

Lady Campbell knew the truth as well, but Genny wasn't about to inform her sister. Greer was agitated enough and, more alarming, showing a side Genny didn't understand.

Her sister walked to the window and peered out. "My remaining here, in the middle of nowhere, is not the least acceptable. Not only will my staying in Ireland prove a waste of my God-given talents, but truly, this place is so isolated and dull it's beyond bearing."

"Greer, you're not listening. You cannot return to court. To garner my release, Britt promised the queen that she'd never set eyes upon me—meaning *you*—again. If she does, she'll imprison you or worse. More importantly, people will talk the moment you arrive in Edinburgh with your ginger-headed child."

Tipping her head, Greer frowned in apparent confusion. "But I shan't return with him. I'm leaving him with you. And court isn't the only place in Edinburgh where eligible men of means and title gather." Greer sighed. "Genny, we have no choice but to do this. We're one and the same, you and I. We must stick together no matter what."

Genny gaped at her sister. Had her twin always been this self-absorbed and she'd simply been too busy to notice? Or had she been so fearful of being left alone that she chose not to notice? She suspected the latter, but whichever was true, it mattered naught at this point. Greer was what she was, and no amount of wishful thinking would change the painful truth.

Genny stood and, reaching into the cradle, stroked wee Alexander's velvet cheek as he slumbered. She then straightened and squared her shoulders. "Greer, do as you lust as you always have, but I shan't raise your child for you. He needs his mother's love and attention, not his aunt's. Furthermore, I will not sleep apart from my husband and thereby deprive us of the bairns we so dearly want so you might tup your way through a court that has no respect for you. I'm wedding Britt on the morrow and then going with him to Skye."

Greer blinked in apparent surprise before turning scarlet. "How dare you—"

"I'll tell you how I dare. I nearly died protecting you. Were it not for Britt, I surely would have. And you've yet had the decency to offer a word of commiseration, much less say *thank you* upon learning of it. Instead, all you can think about is what you want and what you need." Heading for the door, Genny muttered, "I simply can't believe you. You'd give up your child and expect me to abandon the man I love so you might resume a life that was never meant to be yours in the first place."

"'Twas too! Alexander loved me."

Genny stopped. Ah, there the truth. Not "I loved Alexander," but "Alexander loved me."

Middle roiling with pent-up fury and disappointment, Genny sorely wanted to tell Greer she was greatly mistaken, that she'd never been more than one of Alexander's many mistresses, but instead said, "If you say so."

"What? Why do you say that? What do you ken that you haven't told me?" Her sister, now pale, began twisting her broad silver ring, never a good sign.

The tears that had been burning at the back of Genny's throat took shape as she shook her head. "Good-bye, Greer. I wish you and wee Alexander well."

As Genny reached for the door latch, Greer shouted, "Nay! You can't leave me."

Oh, but she could.

Genny closed the door as her sister stomped a foot like a petulant child, shouting, "Genny, come back here!"

Downstairs in the Lady and Lord Macintyre's hall, she scrubbed her arms as she strode toward the fire before which Britt and her aunt sat in conversation. Apparently sensing her distress, Britt rose and glanced at the stairs. "Is something amiss?"

"Please ready the horses. We've dallied as long as we dare." Without a word, he kissed her forehead and left to do her bidding. Genny, relieved he hadn't asked for an explanation, knelt before her obviously puzzled aunt. Pressing her pouch of hard-earned coins into her aunt's frail hands, Genny said, "Lady Margaret, I cannot thank you enough for taking Greer under your wing in her time of need. Please accept this meager gift of appreciation."

Her aunt shook her head and tried to return the coins. "Oh, you needn't give me anything, dear. I was most happy to be of assistance. Your blessed mother was such a dear friend. Besides, having Greer here has proved a godsend since Lord

John and our sons are forever traipsing off hither and yon, leaving me with naught but the walls to speak to. Greer, bless her heart, is such a good listener. And such a lovely voice that child has. But did I hear correctly? You're taking your leave already?"

"Aye, and I'm truly sorry. We came to be reassured that Greer was all right, and finding that she and the babe are, we must now leave. With our king dead, Britt has many pressing matters he needs to attend." 'Twas the truth, albeit in an around-the-hillock sort of way.

Lady Margaret's pale blue eyes, rheumy with age, grew decidedly glassy. "I imagine he does, and God bless His Majesty's soul, may he rest in peace. Will Greer and the babe be leaving now as well?"

The dear sweet woman was so lonely. "Nay, Auntie. I fear you must put up with them underfoot a wee bit longer. 'Tis too soon for either of them to travel."

Lady Margaret pushed to her feet. Threading her thin arm through Genny's, she smiled up at her as they crossed the hall. "Your handsome husband tells me you'll be making a new home on Skye."

"Aye, with his clan."

She looked about, then whispered, "Now, do be careful, dear. I mean no insult to your husband, for he seems normal enough, but I hear tell that many a Canteran has selkie blood, that they only eat raw fish and oysters, which you ken will make you deathly ill."

Genny managed to keep a straight face. "I shall be very careful, Auntie."

"Very good. Now do be sure to write as soon as you arrive, and I promise to do the same with news of your sister and nephew."

Genny could only hope so. God only kenned what tales Greer would now spin once she was out of hearing. But that was no concern of hers. She and Britt kenned the truth and now had to make a life of their own.

Entering Waterford and spying the wee smithy shop he'd noted upon their earlier arrival, Britt veered left. Beside him, Genny—rousted either by their change in direction or the port's cacophony, pulled out of her silent musings long enough to point a listless hand toward the nest of masts poking up beyond the treetops. "Britt, you're going the wrong way. The harbor is yon."

Their long ride from Benbirk had been punctuated by Genny's heavy sighs, teeth grinding and silent tears, but Britt knew better than to ask why. He had no wish to end up the target of her wrath. Better he just wait her out. Frank to a fault, she'd eventually tell him what had transpired betwixt her and her sister. He was simply grateful Genny was still at his side.

"Aye, but I've something most important to tend to first."

Apparently not caring, reins limp in her hand, Genny murmured, "As you lust."

"This way, then." Thank God her palfrey was content to follow Valiant wherever he went and the land they traveled was flat, or Lord knew what dangers she might have fallen into in her distraction.

Stopping before the thatched shop, he dismounted and handed her Valiant's reins. "I'll be but a wee bit." When she only nodded, her mind apparently again on what had transpired betwixt the sisters, he left her to it.

Inside, the scents of molten metal and coal greeted him, along with a stout redheaded man with a bulbous nose, who asked, "How may I be of service?"

Britt whipped out his prized *sgian duhb*, a gift from Alexander for services rendered, from beneath his chain-mailed arm.

"Whoa now." The man's hands were high in the air. "Take whatever ye like, but leave me throat intact."

Britt blinked at the man, then laughed. "My apologies, sir. Britt MacKinnon of Skye. I've not come to rob you but to ask if you might take the stone and gold from this"—he held out the blade hilt first for the man's inspection—"and make them into a ring."

The smithy, blowing through crooked teeth, took the blade and then eyed Britt from head to toe. "Someone your size should know better than to go about waving blades and frightening honest men."

"My apologies again. I'm in a bit of a hurry."

The smithy snorted, then held the blade to the light to examine the weighty amethyst. "I can."

"Before the next high tide?"

"'Tis doable, but 'twill come dear. And your hand is large. We'll need more gold than ye have here."

"The ring is not for me but a surprise for my ladywife. How much, then?"

"That depends on her size."

Britt shrugged. "She sits on yon gray palfrey before the shop."

The man, muttering to himself, poked his head out the door, then, looking back at Britt, said, "Will ye be trading? If so, I'll take the big black."

Only over my dead body. "Coin." After more haggling, they finally came to an agreement, and the smithy pulled a clay jug from beneath his workbench. After pouring a dram into two wee cups and handing one to Britt, he said, "To your lady, may she remain as lovely to men's eyes in her dotage as she is in youth."

Genny broke into a broad grin seeing Darby issuing orders on the *Turoe's* deck. "Permission to come aboard, mistress?"

Her friend peered over the rail. "Genny! Now aren't you a blessed sight for these sore eyes?"

Genny, grinning in response, jogged up the gangway. "So lovely to see you as well."

Given how distracted she'd been, her spying Captain O'Neil in the chaos that was Waterford's waterfront had been naught short of a miracle. That the *Turoe* was ready to set sail and that

Britt had managed to talk O'Neil into taking them to Skye had been more than she'd dare hope.

Onboard, Darby caught her in a tight embrace. "What a great surprise. When did you make Ireland?"

"A week past."

"So, did you not find your sister?"

She'd found her, all right. "Aye, and found someone else as well." She pointed to the quay where Britt was trying to coax Valiant onto the gangway.

Darby, eyes squinting against the water's reflection, pressed a hand to her breast. "Nay, that can't be who I think 'tis?"

Genny grinned. "Aye, 'tis, and we're now handfast."

"Oh my word. I'm so pleased for you." Giggling with the joy of it, they hugged again, then leaned over the rail. Genny hailed Britt, and he looked up. At her side, Darby gasped. "My, he certainly is handsome, isn't he?"

"Aye, that he is and so much more." With a contented sigh, she turned her attention back to Darby. "I'm so pleased to find you onboard. I feared your husband might have found a new cook by now."

Darby grimaced. "Found and lost one, more's like it."

"I'm sorry."

Watching Britt give up on his reluctant stallion, grab Silver's reins and lead the gray quietly up the ramp, Darby said, "Such is life. At least this way I get to keep a better eye on his nibs."

On the quay, Valiant, apparently thinking he was being left behind by his master, issued a shrill, strident whinny, then reluctantly set a hoof on the ramp. After two tentative steps, the horse bolted up the ramp, coming to a clattering, wild-eyed stop on deck, where he snorted in derisive fashion. As they laughed, Britt, muttering under his breath, grabbed Valiant's reins. After securing their mounts, he came to Genny's side, and she introduced him to Darby.

Britt took her hand and, bowing, brought it to his lips. "'Tis a pleasure to finally make your acquaintance, Mrs. O'Neil. I've heard much about you."

Darby, her hand pressed to her breast, blushed to her hair roots. "All good, I hope?"

Grinning, he assured her, "To be sure." Britt then took Genny's hand. "*A ghraidh,* I've one more thing to do before we set sail."

With that he was gone.

Three hours later, as the sun set and Ireland faded behind them into the mist, Genny hissed, "Britt, I can't read a word he's written. 'Tis all in Gaelic."

He squeezed her to his side as they stood before Captain O'Neil's ledger. "It says that we're marrying, and that since your parents are dead, I do not have to pay the bride price of a cow for you."

"A cow?"

He chuckled. "The Irish have what they call Brehon laws, which dictate every aspect of life from birth to death. A cow is the price every common man pays for a wife. Had I wanted you enslaved, I'd have had to pay two milking cows."

"Do not for a minute think me grateful I'm worth less free than enslaved."

"Never entered my mind. Now hush and sign your name next to mine."

Huffing, Genny took the quill—along with it a leap of faith—and carefully wrote her name. Grinning, O'Neil dusted the ink with sand, blotted, then nodded to Darby, who, singing in lilting fashion, took Genny by the hand and led her on deck. Britt and O'Neil followed.

Once they were situated before the mast, Darby, tears glistening, placed Genny's hands in Britt's and carefully draped a lovely set of green marble rosary beads around them. After kissing her cheek, she murmured to her husband, who began the ceremony. In Gaelic.

As Genny listened to the lyrical cadence of his words, she understood naught but could tell by the look in the eyes of those witnessing the ceremony that O'Neil had a gift to wax poetic, for there wasn't a dry eye to be seen, including Britt's.

Finally he asked Britt a question, and looking at her, Britt said most solemnly, "*Tha fios agam.*"

Wishing to understand, she asked, "What did he ask?"

"If when you fall, if I felt pain? Should your tears take shape, do I taste salt? I told him I have."

Captain O'Neil then turned to her and asked in Scot, "Do you, Mary Geneen Armstrong, feel the same?"

"I do."

"Very good. MacKinnon, do you have the ring?"

Britt reached into his sporran, then, taking her hand, placed a lovely gold ring on her finger. The setting sun's rays caught and bounced off the lovely purple stone, and Genny's throat grew taut. "Oh my." She'd never imagined wearing something so precious and beautiful.

Before them, O'Neil said, "Then as captain of the *Turoe* and before these witnesses and God, I pronounce you man and wife. MacKinnon, you may kiss your bride."

She looked from O'Neil to Britt. "Does this mean we're legally wed?"

"Aye." Britt, laughing, scooped her into his arms and kissed her thoroughly, much to the crew's great delight and Genny's embarrassment.

Three days later, they repeated the process at Dun Haakon on Skye before the Abbott of Iona, who happened to be Britt's uncle, and in the presence of his father and his clan. After responding to similar questions posed by the abbot and then signing the family bible on the front step of the kirk, they took their place within for the celebration mass. While relatives and friends settled behind them, Genny whispered, "Love, I do so appreciate this gesture, but we're already married. Why are we going through this yet again?"

He brought her hand to his lips. "So you might ken how very much I love you, so that that lovely and gracious heart of yours kens beyond any doubt that you are the most married woman in Scotland."

Epilogue

"Nature will withstand the rocks." ~ Old Scottish Proverb

Britt blew through his teeth, studying his account ledger. Genny hadn't been bragging two years ago when she'd told him she knew husbandries as few did. The proof was in the numbers.

Valiant's first colt had fetched a small fortune, and the mare was due to foal again come March. Then Gen insisted the sheep she'd bartered away from the earl *and* the MacKinnon flock remain in pasture all last winter, setting off a battle royal betwixt her and their shepherd, who insisted all cattle be housed with the coming of the first snow. But come shearing time she'd been proved the wiser. The entire flock had produced unexpectedly dense fleece.

And she hadn't stopped there. Oh nay. She spent the spring selecting pullets and goslings and the summer inspecting cattle—bulls and bollocks—from one end of the Isles to the other.

He rolled his eyes. She'd been so busy hieing hither and yon in an effort to build their treasury—so great was her fear of war and losing all she held dear—that they'd barely had time to talk, much less breed themselves. But they finally succeeded. His joy knew no bounds, while Gen's was slightly tempered by the fact that she hadn't heard back from her sister since sharing her good news.

So now they waited for both the birth and for the Privy Council to decide who among the battling chiefs would become regent for the recently summoned Princess Margaret of Norway, since Yolande had sent word that she'd given birth to a stillborn before fleeing to France.

"Love, 'tis time."

Britt looked up and found Genny standing, plump and lovely with child, in their solar doorway, and smiled. "Time for what, *a ghraidh?*"

His wife placed a hand on her bulging middle, a habit he found most endearing. "The babe is coming. Please summon the howdie-wife."

Now? "Holy Columba, are you certain?"

Genny, suddenly grimacing, grabbed the door frame. "Aye, quite."

"Oh Lord!" He raced to her side, scooped her into his arms and gently set her down in the middle of their tall, canopied bed. Placing a pillow beneath her head, he asked, "What can I get you? Need something to drink? Another pillow?"

Curling like a hedgehog, she growled, "The howdie, Britt. Now!"

"Right! Don't move. I'll be right back." Oh God, his son was on the way.

He flew down the stairs, raced into the crowded hall and, grabbing the first lad he spied, shouted, "Go fetch the *Cailleach.* Now!"

Around him, conversation ceased. Raking his hands through his hair, feeling totally useless, he told them, "Lady MacKinnon is birthing."

Three women squealed in delight and, chattering like locusts, fled the hall.

Good, they would know what to do. He hoped. But what if they didn't? What if the babe came before their wise woman arrived? What if, despite Genny's lovely wide hips, the babe had trouble coming into the world? What if Genny started bleeding and the women couldn't stop it? What if she developed childbirth fever? Oh God.

He raced back up the stairs. Inside the solar, he found the three women from the hall undressing Genny and cooing encouragement as they readied for the next MacKinnon's arrival. Spying him, Genny made a shooing motion. Britt, ignoring it, crossed the threshold and kissed her. Tasting salt from fresh tears leaking out from beneath her lashes, he whispered, "I love you more than life itself, *a ghraidh,* would do this for you if I could."

Making a barely perceptible nod, beads of sweat taking shape on her furrowed brow, she squeezed his hand to the point of whiteness. Good God almighty, how could she be in so much pain so soon? This couldn't be normal.

When she finally relaxed and produced a wan smile for him, he reluctantly allowed himself to be ushered out into the stairwell, whereupon he bellowed, "Where's that damn witch!"

Below, his father came into view. Looking up the stairs, the MacKinnon shouted, "Son, calm yourself. She's coming. Now get down here and do what any decent husband with any sense does at a time like this."

"And what the hell might that be?" If the old man suggested he walked crossways to the sun about the keep muttering incantations, he'd commit patricide.

"Drink, son. Whisky."

Whisky. A brilliant idea if ever there was one. "I'm coming."

After three grueling hours of listening to Gen's distant keening, Britt couldn't take anymore and rose from his place before the fire. "Da, I'm going to the chapel."

If he could do naught else for his beloved, he could pray.

In the chapel, he knelt before Ian's marred effigy. "You've a brother on the way, laddie. 'Twould be lovely if you could keep an eye on him. And if you're of a mind, would you be so kind as to say a prayer for Genny? You'd have liked her very much, and she would have loved you."

Resting his forehead on the cold stone, he told his firstborn, "I'm so sorry I failed you, lad." Not once but twice. First, in choosing the wrong mother for him, and then by underestimating the extent of her madness. "I shan't take anything for granted ever again."

As the sun moved across the sky on its journey west and his wife labored hour after hour, he prayed for her safety, for that of their child and for Scotland.

The chapel was dim when he felt a tap on his shoulder. "Son, come."

He shot to his feet. "My lady, is she alive?"

"Very much so, but I expect you'd like to confirm that with your own eyes."

"And the babe? Is it well?"

His father laughed. "Go on. I'll not be answering questions you should be asking your ladywife."

Taking the steps to the solar two and three at a time, he raced to the top, reminding himself with every step that surely his father wouldn't have been smiling if something had gone awry.

At the solar threshold, his heart pounding a frantic tattoo against his ribs, he hesitated in order to drink in the sight of his beautiful wife lying on her side, grinning down at the infant suckling her breast. A more loving and lovely sight he could not imagine. "Hello."

Genny looked up, her grin turning into a radiant smile. "Come meet your daughter."

"A daughter?" That the babe might be a lass had never entered his mind. Heart near exploding, he bent and kissed Genny. "How are you feeling?"

"Amazingly well, truth be told. In fact, I do believe I could go to war at the moment. So, what do you think of her?"

He bent closer. "I can't tell. She's covered head to toe." Genny pushed back the blanket, exposing his daughter's downy head. He laughed, seeing a mass of blonde wisps. "She has your hair."

"Aye, and straight as a mast, but I think she has your dark eyes. She should grow into quite a striking young woman."

Augh. Men who would lust after her, would try—

Mindless of his newfound worry, proud of the bundle in her arms, she asked, "What shall we name her?"

Stroking the soft blonde fuzz atop her head, he suggested, "Mary Geneen, after you."

"Oh, I've been thinking Britney, since she has your appetite. She's taken to breast as if starved. Mhairie says she'd not seen the like."

He hated asking but had to know. "And her limbs?"

Genny, her lower lip caught betwixt her teeth, gently detached the babe from her breast and placed the infant on her back next to her. The babe's cute bow lips grimaced at being so rudely interrupted, but she made no sound, just watched him solemnly from dark blue eyes as if daring him to find fault as Genny carefully opened the swaddling. As the layers peeled away, the old fear for his child and its future skittered up his spine. Seeing perfect arms and hands, he released the breath he'd been holding, his hopes rising. Then the babe's pudgy legs came into view, and he saw that they, although perfect in length, were tucked up and bowed. Tears taking shape, he closed his eyes. Would he and this precious infant now go through the anguish of the past? Would this innocent go through all that poor wee Ian had? Would Gen now go mad too?

Please dear God... He felt Genny's hand on his cheek.

"Britt, look at me." Reluctantly he did and found to his surprise only love radiating from her eyes. "She's perfect, Britt, and beautiful. Absolutely beautiful."

Smiling, he kissed his lassie's velvet brow, then leaned toward Gen. "You are absolutely beautiful." He kissed her then, hoping to impart all the joy, pride and hope he felt for her and their wee bairn.

Their prayers had been answered.

Author's Note

This tale is a work of fiction, but much within the story is based on fact. The ship carrying home three-year-old Margaret, Princess of Norway, new Queen of Scotland, made an as-yet-to-be-explained stop in Orkney. The next morning, infant Margaret was found dead. To this day no one knows the cause of death, but most historians suspect she was murdered to prevent Edward I (you might know him as "Longshanks" from the movie *Braveheart*) from becoming regent.

But Scotland still needed a king, and no fewer than thirteen men stepped forward to claim the crown. When the dust settled, two men were at the fore—Balliol and the Bruce—and neither party would relinquish his claim. In England, Edward I smiled, and the rest, as they say, is history.

As for the queen consort, Yolande, she fled to France. No grave of the stillborn infant she claimed to have birthed has ever been found nor was a stillbirth recorded. The queen eventually remarried in 1292 to Arthur II, Duke of Brittany. Together they had one son and five daughters.

Thank you for taking this journey with me.

Sandy

About the Author

Award-winning author Sandy Blair has slept in castles, dined with peerage, floated down Venetian canals, explored the great pyramids, lost her husband in an Egyptian ruin (she still denies being the one lost), and fallen (gracefully) off a cruise ship.

Winner of Romance Writers of America's © Golden Heart and the National Readers Choice Award for Best Paranormal Romance, the Write Touch Readers Award for Best Historical, the Golden Quill and Barclay awards for Best Novella, nominated for a 2005 RITA and recipient of Romantic Times BOOKReview's 4 ½ star Top Pick rating, Sandy loves writing about Scotland's past.

This is her fifth novel.

When not writing, Sandy, a resident of New Hampshire, teaches international on-line courses on writing and fundraises for Habitat for Humanity.

Life is cheap. So is death.

Maiden Lane
© 2011 Lynne Connolly
Richard and Rose, Book 7

With Rose expecting again, it should be a joyous time for her and Richard. Yet old enemies and new come out of the woodwork, seemingly intent on using whatever means possible to destroy their happiness. Not only is the legitimacy of their marriage called into question, a young man steps forward claiming to be a by-blow of Richard's dark, wild past.

Closer to defeat than he has ever been, Richard musters all his friends and allies to defend against this attack on his own ground. However, no amount of incandescent lovemaking and tender care seems to keep Rose out of harm's way.

Then a mutilated body turns up on their doorstep—and all fingers point at Richard. Rose has no choice but to emerge from his near-smothering concern to do what she must to save the love of her life. Even if she must appear to work against him.

As she lays her heart on the line, Richard fights to keep the violence that marks his past from claiming her life. For if he loses Rose, with her will go his humanity.

Warning: Rose gets her mad on, and Richard gets turned on. Contains married love, married sex and married fooling about. And pink coats with lace ruffles. And swords. And wicked goings-on.

Available now in ebook and print from Samhain Publishing.

She vows to protect her heart…
until love burns away her resistance.

The Courtesan's Bed
© *2010 Sandrine O'Shea*

Régine Laflamme rules as the Queen of Fire, the Paris demimonde's most notorious and accomplished courtesan. Wealthy men shower her with riches and vie to become her next conquest. Respectable women shun her. Other courtesans envy her.

No one knows she was once an innocent young governess, ruined and turned out by a cruel lord. And now, years later, she spies her seducer's son—a man who never answered her frantic pleas for help.

Darius, Earl of Clarridge, has never stopped searching for the woman who haunts him. He doesn't expect her to believe that her letters never reached him. No, he will regain her trust in a way she understands—by promising to give her more pleasure than she's ever known.

In spite of her misgivings, Régine is intrigued and takes Darius up on his boast. To her surprise, he conquers not only her body, but captures her very heart.

Yet beyond the haven of her boudoir, two men scheme to possess her for their own. When one of them kidnaps and enslaves her, she clings desperately to a new hope—that this time Darius will find her before it's too late.

Warning: This novel contains scenes of graphic sex, bondage, S/M, anal pleasuring of the hero, and a two-women-one-man threesome in a brothel.

Available now in ebook and print from Samhain Publishing.

www.samhainpublishing.com

Green for the planet.
Great for your wallet.

PUBLISHING

It's all about the story...

Romance

HORROR

www.samhainpublishing.com

CPSIA information can be obtained at www.ICGtesting.com
Printed in the USA
LVOW041545310512

284114LV00004B/41/P

CPSIA information can be obtained at www.ICGtesting.com
Printed in the USA
LVOW041545310512

284114LV00004B/41/P